MW01127962

SEARCHING
FOR
Sunshine

THE DELANEYS OF CAMBRIA, BOOK 4

LINDA SEED

The author is available for book signings, book club discussions, conferences, and other appearances.

Linda Seed may be contacted via e-mail at lindaseed24@gmail.com or on Facebook at www.facebook.com/LindaSeedAuthor. Visit Linda Seed's website at www.lindaseed.com.

ISBN-13: 978-1722378516
ISBN-10: 1722378514

First Trade Paperback Printing: July 2018

Cover design by Tara Mayberry, Teaberry Creative

SEARCHING
FOR
Sunshine

Chapter One

Breanna Delaney—raised by a no-nonsense mother who believed in hard work—was used to taking orders. But Mrs. Granfield, a tiny, elderly woman with an anxious expression and a pronounced limp, was much less comfortable giving them.

"Breanna, dear, would you mind cleaning the Santa Rosa room before you go to lunch?" The owner of the Whispering Pines Bed & Breakfast, temporarily sidelined by a hip replacement, seemed almost embarrassed to assign the task. She fidgeted with a lace doily on the reception desk, avoiding Breanna's eyes.

"Of course, Mrs. Granfield. I'll do it now." Breanna had been refreshing the coffee service in the B&B's parlor, but she was almost finished. She refilled the sugar bowl, then tidied up the sideboard where it sat and turned to head toward the Santa Rosa room.

"I hate to even ask, but with my hip …" Mrs. Granfield fussed.

Breanna paused to look at the woman with her cap of tidy white hair, her pressed and pleated slacks, and her fussy sweater set. Mrs. Granfield couldn't have been more than five feet tall, and she probably wouldn't have weighed a hundred pounds if she were carrying a sack of cement.

"It's no problem, Mrs. Granfield. It's why I'm here. You don't have to apologize," Breanna reminded her.

"Well, yes, but ..." Mrs. Granfield wrung her small, wrinkled hands.

If the shoe had been on the other foot, Breanna supposed she might be uneasy, as well. Breanna was one of the wealthiest people in Cambria—rivaled only by her own parents and her brothers. It was probably hard to tell someone what to do when that person could buy everything you owned—and everything your family owned—with the interest she earned on her investments over the course of a week.

Breanna went to the woman and rested a hand on her bony shoulder. "I'm here to help. For goodness sake, use me."

Mrs. Granfield, looking relieved, relaxed a little. "Well, it *is* nice not to have to bend over to make beds and pick up wet towels off the floor."

"See?" Breanna said. "I'll have it done in no time."

She headed into the Santa Rosa room—a four-hundred-square-foot space with honey-colored wood floors, walls in a pale buttery shade, and an attached bathroom—and started undoing the damage done by the guests who had checked out that morning.

She could understand being a slob in your own home, but as a guest in someone else's? She shook her head in wonder at the mess one couple could make in a single evening.

She picked up empty food wrappers from the floor in the bedroom, scooped up a pile of wet towels from the bathroom tile, and then went to work stripping the linens from the bed.

Mrs. Granfield might have had a hard time assigning her these kinds of tasks, but Breanna had two boys, so messy bedrooms and wet towels on the floor were a sight as familiar to her as her own face in the mirror.

She was most comfortable when she was busy, when she had a to-do list of tasks a mile long. And she'd always believed in service, in helping others in the community. Mrs. Granfield couldn't afford to hire help to get her through her recovery, so Breanna had stepped in. It gave her something to do now that her kids were growing up and needed her less. And it also helped get her mind off her impatience with a home renovation project that was taking longer than she would have thought possible.

Breanna had bought an old, dilapidated house on Moonstone Beach the previous winter, planning to renovate it as a home for herself and her sons. Since Breanna's husband, a Marine, had been killed during deployment more than nine years before, she and the boys had been living with her parents on the cattle ranch where she'd grown up. It was time that she and her kids moved on and built something that would be just their own.

Almost a year later, the work on the place hadn't started yet. But that was about to change, and Breanna could barely think of anything else. Working for Mrs. Granfield helped her not to obsess over countertops, floor plans, and bathroom finishes.

She remade the bed in the Santa Rosa room with fresh linens, scrubbed the toilet, the shower, and the sink, polished the bathroom mirror, and vacuumed the braided rug next to the bed. Then she put fresh flowers in the vase that sat on the bedside table.

Breanna stood back and surveyed her work. Not bad, she decided. The Amish quilt on the bed gave the room a hint of old-fashioned charm, and the light streaming in through the sheer window curtains gave the whole place a warm glow.

While this wasn't the look she wanted for her place—not exactly—it had the feeling she was after. Warm. Comforting. As though the room's occupants had not only stepped into a pleasing retreat, but had also stepped several decades back through time.

Of course, it might actually be several decades before the job was done.

First there'd been the process of finding an architect and having plans drawn for the remodel, then there'd been the interminable wait for permits. Once that was done, there'd been a false start with a general contractor who had bailed on the project a couple of months after signing on, when he was almost scheduled to start work.

She'd had to find another general contractor, and then—because demand in Cambria for that type of work was high—she'd had to wait months for him to fit her into his schedule.

She was pretty sure she'd found someone good this time—her brother Colin had worked with him on a project in Los Angeles and had recommended him highly—but the wait for him to be available had been so daunting she'd almost wondered if it was worth the trouble.

Now, at last, the renovation was about to begin, and Breanna was so excited she could hardly sleep at night. As she finished up in the Santa Rosa room, she thought about her own house and everything she wanted it to be.

She wanted her place to be a retreat, an escape from the chaos of the world. She wanted to create a feeling of homey luxury, of relaxation, that would have her family eager to return there at the end of each day.

Speaking of luxury, the more time Breanna spent at the Whispering Pines, the more ideas she had for better pampering the guests there.

"Mrs. Granfield?" Breanna pushed the cleaning cart out of the Santa Rosa room and called to the older woman.

"Yes?" Mrs. Granfield was at the front desk flipping through the reservations book.

"Have you ever thought of putting bathrobes and slippers in the rooms? You know, nice and fluffy, Egyptian cotton …"

"The guests stole them," Mrs. Granfield said, a tone of weary regret in her voice.

"They stole them? But couldn't you just charge their credit cards if they—"

"Well, yes. That's what I thought until a couple from Milwaukee sued me, saying the robes had never been in the room in the first place. It's not worth the effort, dear. Believe me."

Breanna was still thinking about Egyptian cotton bathrobes, theft, and the relative risks and benefits of providing such amenities as she left the B&B for the day, driving east on Main Street toward the middle school where her two sons, Michael and Lucas, were waiting for her.

Michael, thirteen, was in eighth grade, and Lucas, eleven, was in sixth. Both boys had always been sweet, loving, and relatively easygoing. Lucas, her baby, was still all of those things, but Michael was beginning to become a handful, and she sometimes worried that she wasn't equipped to be everything he needed.

Their father had been gone a long time now—nine years in June. A teenage boy needed his father, but an IED in Afghanistan had robbed the boys of that, and had robbed Breanna of the only man she'd ever loved.

No sense brooding about that, though—she'd brooded enough, cried enough to last her a lifetime. Now, it was time to move on. Once work began on the Moonstone Beach property, it would be a big step toward that progress forward.

The day was clear and bright, and the sun was warm as she pulled her car into the middle school parking lot. When she saw her boys standing in front of the school waiting for her, she felt a warm surge of love, the way she always did.

Michael, who'd just gone through a growth spurt, was tall and thin, his knees looking knobby beneath the hem of the shorts he insisted on wearing year-round. Lucas, his sandy-colored hair askew, came only to his brother's shoulder. His sweet face was dusted with freckles and was pink from the sun.

She pulled up to the curb and they piled into the car in a mess of backpacks, unruly elbows and smelly shoes.

Lucas, her talker, launched into a point-by-point recounting of his day, from having to run laps in PE to needing a new graph paper notebook to what he'd had for lunch, winding up with a story about how his friend Ethan had gotten in trouble for throwing Doritos.

Breanna listened to it all, thinking how sad she'd be when her son no longer wanted to tell her everything that happened to him—when he no longer thought that an experience wasn't real until he shared it with his mother.

Michael, who sat sullenly in the back seat next to his brother, had entered that dreaded phase already, and his silence worried her.

"Michael? How about you, honey? How was your day?" she prompted him.

But she knew what the answer would be:

"Fine."

He was always fine, even when he wasn't.

She drove onto Highway 1 and headed north toward the Delaney Ranch.

When you were an adult and a mother, going home to live with your parents probably felt like defeat for most people. For

Breanna, it had felt like a warm embrace. Her family had lived and worked on the land since 1865, and the place, with its acres of pasture, its working cattle ranch, its rolling, grassy hills, and the peaceful shade of pine trees and oaks had soothed her when nothing else could.

Sometimes the comfort of home was just what you needed, but sometimes, you had to step out of that comfort in order to challenge yourself to find something more.

When she'd spotted the for-sale sign on the Moonstone Beach property, an abandoned, dilapidated farmhouse in the most desirable spot in Cambria, she'd known that it was what she'd been looking for.

But knowing what she wanted was one thing. Getting her boys on board with the plan was another.

Lucas, as usual, was game for anything. But Michael didn't like the idea of moving, and he'd made that clear since she'd first raised the topic more than a year before.

"I can't wait to get home," Lucas said, rattling off the many varied things he planned to do when he got there.

"It's not our home," Michael said, the sullen tone of his voice becoming more and more familiar to Breanna.

"Of course it is," Breanna told him.

"Not for much longer." Through the rearview mirror, she saw him sink down into his seat, his face dark as he glared out the window at the passing scenery.

Breanna was beginning to think that getting the renovations done would be a breeze compared to dealing with her oldest son.

"Hey, I know what. Do you guys want some ice cream?" They were about to pass Mojo's, which had a good selection of flavors in cones or cups.

"Yeah!" Lucas bounced up and down a little in his seat.

"Whatever," Michael said.

Breanna figured she could use a little sugar right now herself, regardless of what the kids thought.

Chapter Two

By the end of the workday, all Jake wanted was a shower, a hot meal, and a beer. A little mindless TV viewing wouldn't have been unwelcome.

But Sam, his roommate, had other ideas.

Sam, a 150-pound Newfoundland with shaggy black and white fur and a drooling problem, bounded at Jake as soon as he came in the door. Sam's customary greeting was always unsettling—it was all Jake could do not to let himself be hurled to the ground like Fred Flintstone.

"Whoa, whoa, whoa. Sam, get down." Jake ordered Sam to desist, as he did every day.

Sam ignored him, like he did every day.

The dog was standing on his hind legs with his paws on Jake's shoulders, as though they were about to dance. Sam attempted to vigorously lick Jake's face, but a man had to draw the line somewhere. With his hands grasping the dog's armpits—assuming a dog even had armpits—Jake lowered Sam to the ground.

The front door was still open; Jake hadn't even made it past the threshold before the dog had overwhelmed him with a combination of bulk and affection.

Sam, now with all four paws on the ground, was quivering with excitement. Jake wasn't going to get a moment's rest until he walked Sam, who'd been cooped up in the house all day while Jake was at work.

"You could at least let a guy relax a little," Jake grumbled as he went into the house to get Sam's leash.

He grabbed the leash from the hook by the door, then froze in horror.

"Ah, jeez. You've got to be kidding me."

Jake had worried that Sam might have an accident on the floor, but what he'd done had been no accident. It had been deliberate as hell.

While Jake had been at work, the dog had knocked over a side table, ripped a houseplant out of a pot that had been on the table, and dragged the plant around the living room, leaving a trail of potting soil over the carpet and the sofa, and even smearing some on the wall.

The plant in question had been placed inside one of Jake's shoes, as though it were being presented as a gift.

Sam looked at him adoringly, trembling with excitement as Jake surveyed his handiwork.

"Get in the car. I'm taking you to the pound."

Sam's tail thumped against the floor.

"Ah, shit. No, I'm not. But what the hell am I going to do with you?"

Jake had gotten Sam from the animal shelter in Santa Maria a few months before, thinking it would be good to have a friend to keep him company after the implosion of his marriage. Sam had been just a puppy, a big guy as far as puppies went, but not so big as to be unmanageable.

Jake had thought, *How much bigger can he get?*

The folly of that question became clear as Sam doubled his weight over the next month and continued to shoot up in size at a rate Jake would have thought lacked credibility if he hadn't seen it for himself.

Now, when the dog went up on his hind legs, he was only a head or so shorter than Jake.

The thought of finding him a new home had occurred to Jake more than once, but Sam was just so damned glad to see him every day when he came home. It was impossible to reject someone who gave you that kind of unconditional love—especially when you weren't getting it from anyone else.

Jake didn't especially want to go for a walk right now—particularly one that involved him nearly getting his arm pulled out of its socket—but Sam had been inside all day, and the potting soil wasn't the only mess Jake would have to clean up if he didn't get the dog some outdoor time.

Jake grabbed the leash, snapped it onto Sam's collar, and barely had time to close the door before he was yanked down the front walk and toward the street.

He mumbled a few choice words to the dog, grumbling about inconvenience, the dog's impatience, and his own sorry fate. But within a few minutes, both he and Sam started settling into the walk, easing into a comfortable pace that felt good. After a long day of hard work, and getting some fresh air and stretching his legs wasn't nearly as unpleasant as Jake had led the dog to believe.

The neighborhood didn't hurt, either. The streets surrounding Jake's Cambria house were peaceful and tree-lined, with a view of the Santa Lucia Mountains to the east.

Where he'd come from, everything was standard and uniform, a sea of nearly identical stucco houses marching side by side into infinity, the streets tidy and curb-lined and indistinguishable from one another. But here, each house had a kind of rugged individualism, a scruffy determination to defy conformity and forge its own identity.

Jake passed over pavement that disappeared into overgrown green grass and wildflowers, heading up hills and past houses that ranged from the modern to the decrepit, from upscale architecture to 1920s bungalow.

Here and there were large patches of undeveloped earth, green with grass and ferns and pine trees, roamed by deer and quail and wild turkeys.

The air smelled like the ocean, which was less than a mile away. There were plenty of other smells, too, and Sam busied himself investigating them as they made their way along what had become their established route.

Ed, a guy who lived two doors down, waved at Jake as they passed, and Jake waved back. That kind of thing had never happened in the concrete-lined suburbs of Los Angeles, where he'd lived until six months ago. Down there, the only time you talked to the neighbor was when the guy's teenagers got out of hand and left beer cans on your lawn.

Coming up here had been a new start. Setting down roots in an unfamiliar place had its benefits, but it also had its drawbacks. He didn't miss the suburbs, the bland tedium, the pressure to keep your lawn green and mowed and your house looking just like everyone else's. But he got lonely sometimes since his divorce had become final and his ex had gotten the tract house.

He didn't care about the house—not one bit—and he was likely better off without his ex. But he did miss having someone else at home, the sensation of not being alone. The reassurance that if he fell down the stairs and broke his neck, someone would be there to call 911.

Now, if he fell down the stairs and broke his neck, it was likely that Sam would get desperate and eat him before anyone knew he was missing.

As the two of them walked, Jake reflected that he had to find some way to get the dog's behavior under control. Every day when he came home from work, Jake was treated to another display of Sam's pique at having been left alone.

One day, it was a chewed-up pair of shoes—a situation so stereotypical that Jake just considered it the cost of doing business. Then, he'd come home to find that all of the toilet paper in the house had been shredded into a snowstorm of confetti stretching from the living room into the back bedroom.

Today it had been the plant, and Jake had also found a conspicuous set of teeth marks on the leg of one of the dining room chairs.

It was time to do something.

Jake wondered about bringing Sam with him when he started work on the Delaney place on Moonstone Beach. Yeah, that was doable. The lot was fenced, and the house was so much of a mess that if the dog did any damage, people would be hard-pressed to notice.

He kind of liked the idea of it—man and dog together, loyal companions through the hard, manly labor of the workday.

"What do you think, Sam? You want to come to work with me?" he asked as the dog peed on a clump of weeds.

Sam wagged his tail encouragingly.

Jake took that as a good sign.

Jake had not yet met Breanna Delaney, but he knew three things about her: She was filthy rich, she had a shit ton of connections all over the state, and she was attractive as hell.

The first, he knew because it was common knowledge—everyone in Cambria knew. The second was a natural extension of the first; you didn't get to be filthy rich without making connections. And the third, he'd discovered when he'd Googled her and found an array of pictures of her doing all of the things she did: attending local fund-raisers, speaking at a water board meeting, riding on a float in the Pinedorado Parade.

It wasn't that she was beautiful—not exactly. She looked a little too weathered by life, a little too hardened, to be beautiful. But with her dark eyes, her thick dark hair, and her full lips that looked like they were made to be kissed, Jake had found himself looking at her photo much longer than he otherwise might have.

Despite her obvious appeal, he found himself predisposed against her simply because of the money. He'd met a lot of rich people in the course of his professional life, and most of them had been so full of themselves, so convinced of their basic superiority, that he'd wanted to punch them in the face.

But the money and the connections were what had gotten him the job, so he would just have to put his natural prejudices aside for the sake of his livelihood.

Jake had gotten the Moonstone Beach job without an interview and without having met his new client because Breanna's brother Colin, a man with a long history of buying and developing property, had procured Jake's services for his sister. It turned out Colin had been the money behind a project Jake had worked on a couple of years ago down in Los Angeles, and the man had been pleased with the results.

Jake needed this job, not just because of the money but because he was still establishing himself in Cambria, and working for the Delaney family would go a long way toward building his reputation on the Central Coast.

The morning he was to start work, he loaded Sam into his car, drove out to the job site, let himself in the front gate, and unsnapped Sam's leash, letting the dog run with unbridled glee around the fenced property.

Then he waited for Breanna to arrive so they could get the preliminaries out of the way and he could start rebuilding this hulking wreck of a house that, he had to admit, had good bones and could really be turned into something with a generous application of his own genius.

Jake went into the house and started poking around, starting to get his own ideas about what should go where and why. He was upstairs looking out a dormer window when he saw the front gate open and Breanna Delaney step through, her purse slung over her shoulder and a takeout cup of coffee in her hand.

"Jake, are you here? I'm sorry I'm late, I—"

That was all she got out before she spotted the enormous black and white dog coming for her and her eyes widened in shock.

"Oh, God. Sam! Sam! Down, boy!" Jake yelled through the open window. Sam had never responded to *down, boy* before, but Jake was an optimistic person by nature, so he gave it a shot.

Sam, oblivious, barreled toward Breanna with a speed that seemed impossible in a creature so large, his doggy features arranged in bliss inspired by the promise of a new friend.

From his vantage point, Jake couldn't tell whether the takeout coffee went flying because of the impact, or because Breanna had hurled it skyward in fright.

Either way, the beverage, Breanna, and the canine all hit the dirt—Breanna and Sam with a thud, the coffee with a wet smack.

Jake took the stairs two at a time as he rushed down to assess the damage. He dashed out the front door and over to where the woman and the dog lay in a heap on the ground.

"Shit. I'm sorry. Jeez. Down, Sam. Sam! Goddamn it." Jake reached for Sam's collar, planning to haul the dog off of Breanna by sheer brute force.

Sam wagged his tail furiously, his huge body quivering with excitement, his giant, pink tongue all over Breanna's face.

Jake heard some noises coming from where Breanna was pinned beneath the dog. At first, he thought they were cries for help. Then, he wondered if maybe she was gasping for breath.

It was only when he was right on top of them, the dog's collar in his hands, that he realized she was laughing.

Jake yanked the dog off of her, and Breanna sat up, her face alight with amusement. "Well, hello there," she said to Sam. She reached out and rubbed the sides of the dog's face with her hands, her fingers vanishing into the animal's long fur.

Jake had been braced for Breanna to yell at him, so this turn of events was perplexing. She rubbed the dog a little more, then Jake reached out a hand to help her up.

"Sorry about your coffee," he told her. "I can't seem to make him stop doing that to people."

"He gave me a good scare," Breanna said, letting Jake haul her to her feet, then brushing dirt off the seat of her jeans. "He's huge."

She bent over and cooed at Sam the way people did with dogs: in a high, singsongy voice similar to the one they used with babies. "You're a friendly guy, aren't you?" she said. "Aren't you? And you're so pretty. *Sooo* pretty."

Sam's tail swished so vigorously that it created wind.

"I really … jeez. I'm really sorry," Jake tried again.

"No harm done," Breanna said.

"He's been trashing my house, so I thought if I brought him to work …"

"You're going to be bringing him here? Every day? My boys will love him. You mind if I bring them over to meet him?" Breanna bent down to pick up her coffee cup, which had burst on impact with the ground.

"You're really not mad," Jake said, more to himself than to her, as he rubbed the back of his neck.

"I grew up on a ranch. I've been knocked down by animals more times than I can count. I'm not about to let an overly friendly dog rattle me. Even if he is the size of a horse." She gave the dog a companionable scratch behind the ears.

"Huh," Jake said. "I guess I at least owe you a coffee, though."

"Yeah." Breanna looked with regret at the puddle of coffee that was soaking into the ground. "I sprang for a caramel latte today. I'm kind of sorry to see it go."

All of the commotion over the dog had distracted Jake from the fact that he and Breanna had never actually met before this moment. He held out a hand to her. "Jake Travis."

"Breanna Delaney." She shook his hand, amusement about the exuberance of his dog still lingering in her eyes.

Chapter Three

They went inside and talked about the project, about his plans for tackling it, and about her vision for the property. She'd e-mailed him the architect's drawings months ago when she'd first booked him for the job, so he was already familiar with what needed to be done.

He'd dealt with rich clients before, and they usually didn't have much interest in the details of how Jake went about his work. They just wanted it done. More often than not, he didn't even deal with them directly—he dealt with an assistant or some other underling hired to handle the details so the client wouldn't have to dirty his or her designer shoes by stepping onto a work site.

But Breanna didn't have designer shoes—she wore a battered pair of discount sneakers that looked like they were due for retirement.

As they walked through the house together, going over what would be done to what and how, she asked good questions and seemed to listen carefully to his responses.

"Okay, so ..." He gestured toward a wall in the front parlor. "The plans say to take out this wall for a more open floor plan. But it's a load-bearing wall, so that means I'm going to have to install a beam to create the support you're going to need along the line of the ceiling." He pointed with one finger toward the spot on the ceiling where the beam would go. "Unless …"

"Unless what?" she asked.

"Unless you're open to another idea. I could put in an arch from about here"—he pointed—"to here, so you can get a more open feeling without undermining the structural integrity of the wall."

"An arch," she said.

"Yeah. I know open floor plans are the big thing right now"—he put air quotes around *the big thing*—"but I'm thinking you'll want to maintain a feeling for the history of the house. You tear out that wall, and the downstairs is going to look like just another tract house—the kind they put up by the thousands all over Southern California, which, along with the strip malls and the fast-food places and the mattress superstores, have turned the entire southern half of the state into a soul-sucking purgatory."

"A soul-sucking purgatory," she repeated.

"Well … yeah."

He hadn't meant to make a speech, but once it was out, he realized how right he was. This house—mess that it was—had been something beautiful in its glory days, a stalwart but graceful matriarch overlooking her domain on the rugged coastline. Changing her character, forcing her to be something she wasn't, would be so disrespectful to the essence of this place that if Breanna couldn't see it, then she didn't deserve the house in the first place.

Breanna walked to the wall where the arch would be and looked at it for a while. Then she went into the adjoining room where the arch would lead, and looked at that. Jake followed her, becoming more and more determined to convince her of the error of her blasphemous open floor plan.

"*Hmm.*" Breanna came back out into the parlor, where they'd started the discussion.

Sam came into the house, having finished investigating some smells in the yard, and sat down next to Breanna, leaning his heavy body into her left leg. She reached down and scratched his head, still looking intently at the wall.

"Look. If you want something contemporary, there are a thousand beachfront houses that will do the job much better than this one," Jake said. "But this town isn't about *contemporary*. It's about history, and the land, and preserving the sensibilities of the people who came before. It's—"

"You're mansplaining." Breanna shifted her gaze from the wall to Jake.

"I ... What?"

"Jake, my family has lived in Cambria for more than 150 years. But I'd love to hear more about what this town is about." She raised her eyebrows and waited.

Had he been mansplaining? Embarrassed, he realized he had.

"I'm an ass," he said.

"Well ..."

"I'm sorry. I didn't mean to claim that I know more about this area than you do. It's just that this house is a beauty. I mean, it's a disaster at the moment, but ..." *Stop talking, Jake,* he told himself. *Just shut your damned face hole.*

When he looked at her, he expected to see scorn and irritation. Instead, she was smiling.

"You think the house is beautiful," she said.

He rubbed at the stubble on his chin, confused about whether his ass was still in the doghouse or not. Strangely, it seemed not, though he wasn't sure why.

"The house? Oh, hell yeah. Look at these ceilings. Look at the woodwork. The lines—classic but with character. This place was really something back in the day. And it will be again, once I'm done with it."

She looked at him appraisingly, a half grin on her face.

"What?" he asked her.

"When most people see this place, they think I was crazy for buying it and try to convince me to tear it down."

"Tear it down?" Jake was appalled. "Of all the dumbass, short-sighted—"

"That's how I felt." Breanna bent down and rubbed Sam's side with gusto. "Let's go with the arch," she told Jake.

They continued to tour the property, and when they came to the detached two-bedroom cottage toward the back of the lot, Jake asked, "So ... what are you going to do with the guest house? It'd make a nice rental."

"I don't know yet." She couldn't quite see herself as a land-lady, but at the same time, it would be a shame for the cottage to sit empty.

It was something to think about.

Breanna's meeting with Jake had her emotions going in several directions at once. First came the initial terror of being thrown to the ground by the biggest dog she'd ever seen—before she'd realized Sam's harmless intentions. Then came the combination of thrill and discomfort when she'd found that Jake was startlingly attractive, with his deep blue eyes, his unruly dark hair, and the big lumberjack thing he had going on—he was at least six-foot-three and had to be twice Breanna's weight, all of it solid man.

Next, she'd felt irritation when he had tried to explain the spirit of Cambria to her, a lifelong native with roots in the town that went back generations. And finally, there was the warm, dopey, over-the-moon feeling that came with knowing he saw the house the same way she did.

She and the architect had disagreed about the open floor plan, but she'd let herself be talked into it because he'd insisted that the modern approach would be more practical for her family.

Screw the modern approach. The house had history, it had character. Part of her even thought it might have feelings. Jake's rant about tract houses and purgatory had been just what she'd needed to help her trust her original instincts.

She left the house midmorning to help out at the Whispering Pines, feeling good about the place on Moonstone Beach. The house needed so much work—everything from the plumbing to the electrical system was badly out of date, and the roof looked like it was about to fall in. But Jake was going to fix what was wrong, keep what was right, and update everything that needed it.

She drove across town to Mrs. Granfield's place fantasizing about how it would all look when it was done. The property had a surprisingly large lot considering its beachfront location; Breanna pictured herb gardens with winding gravel paths, drought-tolerant plants in bursts of color, Adirondack chairs positioned so she and her boys could watch the sunset over the water.

Until now, it had all seemed like a fantasy that might never come true. But Jake's enthusiasm for the project and for her house made her feel that the ultimate realization of her dream was certain, inevitable.

She found herself humming on the way to Mrs. Granfield's place.

The hum died on her lips as she walked into the Whispering Pines and found Mrs. Granfield wringing her hands anxiously, looking as though she'd aged five years since the day before.

She was about to ask why—but before she could say anything, the reason became clear.

From upstairs, Breanna heard a high, agitated yap—then another, followed by another. The barks at first had an interval between them—*yap … yap … yap*—but then began coming one right on top of the next: *yap yap yap yap yap*.

"The Johnsons' Yorkie," Mrs. Granfield said, sounding stressed and weary. "He's been going like that all night."

"All *night?*" Breanna was appalled. Cambria was a dog-friendly town, and the Whispering Pines was one of many places locally that accepted pets. Usually, the animals presented no problem, other than the occasional area rug that had to be sent out for cleaning. This was the first persistent barker Breanna had encountered since she'd begun helping Mrs. Granfield.

"I'm afraid so," Mrs. Granfield confirmed. "I offered them one of those dog toys with the treats hidden inside, and that got us a quiet half hour. But other than that …"

Yap … yap … yap … yap.

"I offered to find a kennel that would take him overnight," Mrs. Granfield went on, "but they wouldn't have it. Their Little Pookums can't be in a kennel, he'd be too stressed, he's their baby.…" She raised her eyes to the heavens as though seeking strength.

"They call him their little pookums?" Breanna said.

"That's his name. Little Pookums."

They both looked at the spot on the ceiling from where the noise was coming.

"The other guests must be miserable," Breanna observed.

Chapter Four

Mrs. Granfield came back around one p.m., and Breanna took a break for lunch. They had three guests on the books for today, but no one would be checking in for a couple of hours.

Breanna met her sister-in-law, Gen, for lunch, and the two of them sat outside under a shade umbrella at Linn's Easy as Pie Café, a thick sandwich in front of Breanna, a big, leafy salad in front of Gen.

Gen owned an art gallery on Main Street, and she was wearing a skinny black dress and heels, her curly red hair up in a messy bun.

Breanna marveled at how Gen had gotten her figure back just a year after having her baby, remembering how she herself had struggled after her sons were born. *Must be the salads,* she thought, looking at Gen's virtuous lunch, a stark contrast to her own towering meatloaf club sandwich.

"So, work's supposed to start on the Moonstone Beach house today, right?" Gen asked, stabbing a forkful of lettuce.

"Yeah. I met with the contractor this morning. God, I'm so excited. The place is going to be great," Breanna said.

"The contractor," Gen said, drawing out the words in a way that was fraught with meaning.

"Yes …"

"I hear he's a hottie in a burly mountain-man sort of way." Gen wiggled her eyebrows, grinning.

Breanna stopped with her sandwich halfway to her mouth. "Where did you hear that?"

"You mean it's not true?"

"Oh, it's true. I was just wondering where you heard it."

"He comes in for coffee at Jitters, and Lacy told me," Gen said. Lacy Jordan, one of Gen's best friends, was a barista at the coffeehouse on Main Street and had the inside scoop on caffeine lovers all over town.

Breanna wasn't surprised that the women of Cambria were talking about Jake. It wasn't every day that a newcomer to their little village was tall, broad-shouldered, blue-eyed, and rugged, with a body sculpted by hard work and a face that made you think about how much you'd like to have it rubbed against your—

"Hello? Anybody in there?" Gen waved her fork in Breanna's field of vision, interrupting her thoughts.

"What?" Breanna blinked, coming back to the present. "Oh. I'm sorry. I was just thinking about … home renovations."

"Sure you were." Gen gave her a sly, knowing grin. "Listen. I think it's great that your contractor's a delicious beefcake of a man. You should give it some thought."

Give it some thought? Hadn't Breanna just been doing exactly that, before Gen had interrupted her? But if Gen was talking about Breanna actually pursuing anything with him …

"He's probably married," Breanna said.

"He's not." Gen wiggled the eyebrows again.

"How do you know?"

"Lacy scoped it out. He ordered a Guatemalan blend with cream and sugar, and before he'd taken the first sip, she had the basics. It's a gift."

Breanna was torn between wanting to pretend she wasn't interested and wanting to pump Gen for information. If she could manage the pumping without seeming like she was doing it, that would be the best of both worlds.

"He's probably got a girlfriend at least," she said, picking at the crust of her sandwich.

"Nope," Gen said. "At least, not that I know of. He's recently divorced and lives alone with his giant dog."

"Sam," Breanna said. "The dog. His name is Sam."

"I didn't hear anything about a girlfriend, and neither did Lacy." She did the eyebrow wiggle again.

"Is there something wrong with your face?" Breanna demanded. "Do you have some kind of twitch?"

Gen took a bite of salad, chewed, and then took a sip of her iced tea. "I'm just saying, you should think about going there. Or at least visiting there. Seeing some of the local sights."

Breanna shook her head. "No. I mean … no. I couldn't."

"Sure, you could. Why not?" Gen put down her fork and gave Breanna her full attention. "You've been alone a long time, Bree. And you don't have to be. You're beautiful, you're smart, you're warm …"

"I'm a widowed mother with two kids to think about!" Breanna said.

"You are." Gen reached out and put her hand on top of Breanna's on the table. "You are those things. But you're more than that, too. You're more than a widow and a mother. You're a woman. I think it's been a while since you've made time for that part of you."

Breanna wanted to protest, but the fact that she'd immediately rejected Gen's suggestion that she "go there" probably proved the point. She didn't tend to think of herself in those terms anymore. She thought of herself in terms of her roles—daughter, mother, grieving wife.

She'd been so wrapped up in her obligations and her pain—first over the loss of her husband, and then over the sudden death of her uncle Redmond—that it had been hard to think about anything else.

But, of course, she knew there was more to her than that, because the part of Breanna that was just *her* was the part that longed for the house to be finished so she could have something of her own, something wonderful and uncomplicated.

Breanna pulled a corner off of her sandwich and popped it into her mouth. She chewed carefully.

"He would never be interested in me, even if I did have the time for that kind of thing," she said finally. "Which I don't."

"A, of course he would, unless he's completely lacking in taste, in which case, who wants him?" Gen said. "And B, you have time. There's always time for a hot contractor with a really big tool belt." She said *tool belt* as though it were dirty—which was probably how she'd meant it.

"I'm not interested in his … his *tool belt*," Breanna said.

"That's a shame," Gen said. "Because he's going to be hammering somebody sooner or later. Why shouldn't it be you?"

Jake wanted to be hammering something—he felt most comfortable when he was getting his hands dirty on a job—but there was a lot of work to be done before he got to that stage.

Breanna had selected him for her project, and had paid a deposit to secure his services. They'd had their initial meeting. But their business relationship wouldn't truly get underway until he'd come up with a plan, a timeline, and a budget for the project and she'd signed off on it.

That meant calculating the amounts and costs of materials, scheduling subcontractors, estimating labor costs, and writing out a schedule and a targeted completion date—of course, allowing for the inevitable disasters and fuckups that were common to any job site.

He spent some time at the site taking measurements, investigating the current state of the two buildings, examining the architect's drawings to make sure they jibed with the actual site he was looking at, taking notes, and getting the whole scope of the thing clear in his head.

But that last part wasn't easy, because his head was still busy thinking about Breanna.

He told himself he wasn't interested in a personal relationship—well, he was, but not right now. Not so soon after his divorce, and not while he was about to become immersed in a new project. He had work to think about. He had the challenge of settling into a new community.

Add to that the fact that getting involved with his client could potentially introduce an array of complications he needed like he needed a goddamned third eye.

But telling himself all of that was one thing. Believing it was another. He'd found Breanna intriguing from the time he'd first read about her and had seen her picture. Then the actual woman was in front of him, laughing about his dog, smacking him down for his arrogance, and agreeing with his suggestions for the house.

And looking so damned good doing it.

He scolded himself as he stood in the house's ruined kitchen, a measuring tape in his hands.

Get it together, Jake.

Even if he were interested in getting something going with a woman right now, and even if he were open to dating a client, why the hell would Breanna Delaney be interested in him? She was a billionaire, for God's sake. Well, maybe not a billionaire, but she had hundreds of millions, from what he'd read. He was a general contractor, a blue-collar man. He refilled his bottled water out of the tap to save money.

If that meant she thought he wasn't good enough for her, then by God ...

She didn't say that, idiot. You're the one thinking it. Get your head out of your ass.

He was deep inside his troubling and contradictory thoughts when Sam came into the kitchen from outside and dropped a pine cone at Jake's feet.

Jake hadn't thought to bring a ball for Sam to play with, but it seemed that the dog was finding a way to make do.

"Yeah, all right. I guess I've got a minute to throw the pine cone," he told Sam.

He walked outside, waited until Sam was poised, trembling in anticipation, and then hurled the pine cone as far across the fenced yard as he could. Sam tore after it, pounced on it as though the thing posed a danger to the lives of his loved ones, and then plopped down onto the ground to begin the painstaking process of crunching the pine cone to dust in his mouth.

While Sam was very good at chasing the things Jake threw for him, he was crap at bringing them back.

Jake was just about finished for now, so he went back inside to gather his things. He closed his laptop, which was sitting on the kitchen counter, then went upstairs to retrieve some notes and tools he'd left up there.

Standing in the second-floor master bedroom, he gazed out the window toward dark blue water churning with white-tipped waves. The house was going to be a hell of a place when he was done with it, and Cambria was a hell of a place for him to start his new life.

The pine-covered hills, the mountains to the east, the ocean, the ragged bluffs, the wildflowers shifting in the salt-scented breeze.

He could have done worse for himself than choosing this town, he figured. There was a kind of peace here, a kind of quiet you could feel in your soul.

He could use that kind of quiet right now. He wasn't about to ruin it by getting into something with a woman who potentially meant trouble.

Jake had enough trouble just dealing with his damned dog.

Chapter Five

Breanna knew it was going to take time to hear from Jake; the plan for the renovation—complete with budget, timeline, and a contract for her to sign—wasn't something he could put together overnight.

She filled that time doing the things she normally did: working at the Whispering Pines, helping her mother around the house, and attending to the business of raising two rambunctious boys.

The first two were easy enough, even pleasant. It was the third item that required all of her wisdom and patience.

"I don't want to go to school," Michael told her one morning as he lay in bed, refusing to get up.

"Are you sick?" Breanna bent down to put her hand on his forehead.

"Yeah." A hint of a groan in his voice, probably for effect.

She straightened and looked down at him, appraising. "You don't have a fever."

"I have a headache. And my stomach hurts. And I'm dizzy. I think I'm going to throw up."

Ah, the magic triumvirate of symptoms that Michael saw as a foolproof get-out-of-school-free card: headache, upset stomach, dizziness. They were perfect, when you thought about it:

They were not outwardly observable, so they could neither be proved nor disproved.

Whenever Michael claimed this particular collection of complaints, Breanna had the choice to believe him, allowing him to skip school possibly for no reason, or go hard-ass on him, taking the risk that she was forcing a sick child to go to school when she should have been providing motherly TLC.

"You saw Dr. De Luca last month for this same thing. She said there was nothing wrong," Breanna reminded him.

"No, she didn't," Michael insisted. "She said she couldn't *find* anything wrong. That's not the same thing, Mom."

And with that, he'd neatly summarized her dilemma. What if she treated this like a ploy to get out of school, and he really was sick?

"Michael …"

"Mom?" Lucas, still in his pajamas, his bedhead sticking up comically, leaned into the room, one hand on the doorframe. "I need my permission slip today. The one for the field trip."

"It's on the bulletin board in the kitchen," she told him.

"Okay. And, Mom? Can we get pizza tonight? We haven't done it in a really long time, and last week you said—"

"I'll think about it, Lucas. Okay, honey? Now, go get dressed."

"But—"

"Go, please." She turned her younger son around by the shoulders and gave him a gentle push out of the room.

Turning back to Michael, Breanna wondered what to do. Her instincts told her to insist that he get out of bed, get dressed, and have breakfast so he could go to school. But those same instincts also told her that he wasn't doing this to be lazy or difficult. Her boy had a lot of things on his mind, and she didn't want to dismiss that or make him think his feelings were unimportant.

She sat down on the side of his bed and resisted the urge to reach out and run her fingers through his hair the way she had when he was younger, before he began objecting to such small, mother-son intimacies.

"Is there anything going on, honey?" she said. "Besides your stomach, I mean?"

"No." He scowled at her.

"Is this about the move? Because—"

He rolled his eyes at her. He never used to roll his eyes. "It's not about anything, Mom. It's about my stomach hurting, okay?"

"Okay." She kept her tone mild. "But I still think you should go to school."

His face scrunched up in an elaborate show of angst. "But why? School is stupid, and the stuff they teach us is dumb, and it's a big waste of time, especially when I don't need to go to college or get a job or anything."

This last part was a surprise to her, and she found herself rocking back, her eyebrows raised. "Excuse me? What do you mean you don't need to go to college or get a job?"

"Well … Grandma says I can work on the ranch if I want. Maybe even run it someday like Uncle Ryan."

"Your uncle Ryan went to college," she said quietly. "He studied ranch management so he could learn how to do what he does."

"Yeah, but—"

"Get dressed." She stood up and headed toward the door. "I want you to get ready for school, Michael. We'll talk about all of this later."

"But Mom …"

"Please don't argue with me. You'd better hurry. We're leaving in a half hour."

She left the room and closed the door behind her, marveling at the many ways in which kids could make you doubt every choice you'd ever made as a parent.

Breanna got the boys dropped off at school without further incident, but when she got home, it was clear that the undercurrent of conflict hadn't escaped Sandra.

"What kind of bug got into your son's undershorts this morning?" Sandra asked as Breanna came into the kitchen. The older woman, who seemed to find an endless number of tasks to complete in her favorite room in the house, was scrubbing the counter grout with a toothbrush.

"I don't know!" Breanna threw her purse onto the big kitchen table and tossed her hands up in despair. "First he said he was sick, then he said he hates school."

Sandra chuckled as she attacked a particularly dingy patch of grout. "Why, if I had a dollar for every time one of you kids complained about school …"

"That wasn't the thing that bothered me the most." Breanna sank down into one of the hard-back chairs that surrounded the butcher block table. "He said he doesn't need school because he doesn't have to go to college or get a job. Says he can just work here."

"Well, I suppose he can," Sandra said. "But there's a hell of a lot more to it than just fixing fences and shoveling manure."

"I know that!" Breanna slumped down in her chair. "How is it that he doesn't know that? How did I not teach him that?"

"Well …" Sandra paused in her work and propped a fist on her hip. "You've kept them out of the ranching, mostly."

"They're kids!" Breanna gestured with her hands helplessly. "And ranch work is hard, and dangerous, and …"

"Well, I guess I know all that." Sandra came to sit at the table across from Breanna. "But maybe it's time to let Michael give it a go, see what he's getting himself into."

Breanna considered that. "I don't know. Maybe. I've always said I wanted to let them choose their own way, their own interests. Maybe I should let him try it."

"Plus," Sandra said, "that boy of yours has got a lot on his mind. I've always found the best way to quiet your mind is to get your hands and your body busy doing a hard day's work."

She knew what her mother said was true. Breanna herself had always taken solace in hard work, especially during the most difficult times—and after Brian died, times had gotten pretty damned difficult.

"I'll think about it," she said.

"You do that," Sandra told her. "I'm not saying the boy needs to get out there today and start herding cattle and delivering calves"—she cackled at the thought—"but he needs something, some way to show himself he's up to a challenge."

"He needs a man," Breanna said, thinking it over.

"Well, we got more than a few of those around here." Sandra got up from her seat and went back to scrubbing the grout.

Breanna started to head out of the kitchen, but she paused on the way out to look at her mother. "Mom? Do you think I've babied them? Have I made things too easy for them?"

Sandra hesitated before answering, her mouth working. "Those boys lost their daddy. Nothing easy about that. If you babied them a little, kept them close when you maybe should have let them spread their wings a bit, well, I can't say I blame you."

She turned back to the grout, her back to Breanna, the subject closed.

Considering her mother's advice, that weekend Breanna asked her brother Liam to take Michael out on the ranch, put him to work, show him exactly what he was going to be doing if he decided to blow off school for a life of managing cattle.

While Lucas followed his normal Saturday morning routine—sleeping in and then eating cereal in front of the TV—Michael got up before dawn, dressed warmly against the morning chill, and went out with Liam, who'd stopped by the house to pick him up on his way out into the pastures.

The amount of complaining the boy had done suggested that maybe he wasn't really aching for a life tending livestock.

"But, Mom, it's Saturday," Michael moaned as Liam waited for him to finish putting on his coat.

"The cattle need tending on Saturdays, too," she pointed out, not unreasonably.

The plan wasn't to keep him out all day—he wasn't used to that kind of hard physical labor, and he'd likely collapse by midafternoon. Liam had proposed a half day, starting at seven a.m.—a scandalously late beginning to the workday, by Delaney standards—and ending at noon.

By the time Liam brought Michael back home at lunchtime, the boy looked dirty and tired, but much of the teen attitude seemed gone for the moment. Michael washed his hands at the kitchen sink and gratefully sat down to the hot lunch Breanna and Sandra had made for the family.

"So, how did it go?" Breanna asked as she sat down at the table in front of her plate.

Michael shrugged—possibly out of an angsty refusal to communicate with his mother, or possibly because his mouth was too full for him to talk.

"He did fine," Liam said, glancing at the boy. "He's got a lot to learn, but it wasn't bad for a first day."

"Uncle Liam let me bottle-feed a calf," Michael said, when he was done chewing.

"That must have been fun," Breanna said.

"I guess." Michael shrugged, but without the resentment Breanna had been seeing so much of lately.

Later, when lunch was over and Michael had gone upstairs to get cleaned up, Liam took Breanna aside as they both were clearing the lunch dishes from the table.

"He's got a lot going on," Liam told Breanna. He put a stack of plates in the sink.

"You mean he talked to you about it?" This was a surprise—Michael rarely talked about anything these days.

"A little." Liam leaned his butt against the kitchen counter, his arms crossed over his chest. "We got to working and talking, and some stuff came out."

"That's the way it works," Sandra said from where she stood at the kitchen island wrapping up some leftovers. "The boy can't just look at you and tell you what's on his mind. He's got to be distracted by something else before the words start coming. You and Colin were both like that," she told Liam. "Ryan, not so much—he could come right out with it. But he always was more the sensitive sort." She tore a piece of aluminum foil off the roll and covered a bowl of beef stew.

"So, what did he say?" Breanna prompted Liam.

"He's been having some trouble with some kids at school."

"He's being bullied?" Breanna's voice broadcast her alarm.

"Not really." Liam shrugged. "Nobody's picking on him on purpose. It's more kids being assholes just because they can't help it."

Sandra let out a snort at Liam's comment.

"What kids? What happened?" Breanna asked.

"You know Joey Cosentino? That kid he went to the beach with a few weekends ago?"

"Yeah."

Liam shrugged again. "Kid says Michael's not his friend anymore. Joey started hanging around with this new group of friends, and Michael's not in with that group, so …" He left the rest hanging.

"Well … shit," Breanna said.

Sandra grunted. "Typical teenage bull manure. This one's your friend, then he's not. That one's sweet as pie to your face, then bad-mouths you behind your back. Why, I wish I had a dollar for every time one of you kids went through that kind of crap when you were in school."

"You do," Breanna said.

Sandra considered that, said, "*Hmph*," and went back to her work.

"But … why wouldn't he talk to me about any of that?" Breanna said. "If it was bothering him …"

"Because you're his mom," Liam said.

"So? What's that got to do with—"

"A guy wants to look tough in front of his mom," Liam said.

Breanna started to say something, then stopped. She propped on hand on her hip. "Really?"

"Sure. A guy wants the woman in his life to think he can handle things. You're the woman in his life."

That had never occurred to Breanna before, but now that Liam had put it that way, it made a certain amount of sense. "Huh," she said.

Chapter Six

By the time Jake called saying he had a contract ready for Breanna to sign, she was struggling to be patient for the renovations to begin.

"Meet me at Cambria Coffee?" he suggested on the phone as she was running through her morning routine at the Whispering Pines. "I owe you one, anyway."

"You owe me one what?" she said.

"A coffee. To replace the one Sam knocked out of your hand. A caramel latte, right?"

She blinked a couple of times in surprise. "You remembered that."

"I'll see you there at ten," he said.

At ten a.m., Cambria Coffee was moderately busy, with three people waiting in line at the counter and a group of senior citizen bicyclists gathered around the outdoor tables, sipping coffee and reminiscing about the morning's ride.

When Breanna got there, Jake was already sitting at one of the outdoor café tables with two cups of coffee in front of him.

He stood when she approached him, a gesture that struck Breanna as charmingly old-fashioned. He'd recently showered, and his hair was damp.

"Hey," he said. "I'm glad you could make it."

"You ordered already." She looked at the two cups on the table.

"One caramel latte." He pushed one of the covered cups toward her. "Sorry about Sam."

"That's all right. He's a sweetheart." She took a sip of the coffee, which was hot and sweet and satisfying. "Thanks."

The bicyclists were holding a fairly loud and raucous conversation, so Breanna and Jake went upstairs to a small seating area that was, at the moment, empty. They sat down across from each other at a tiny, battered table for two beside a window overlooking Main Street.

Once they were settled in, Jake pulled a sheaf of papers out of a leather messenger bag and placed them in front of Breanna on the table.

"This outlines the timeline for the project, as well as the budget and the payment schedule. The contract outlines what happens if either one of us fails to meet our end of it, what happens if I go over on time or budget, et cetera." He pushed the papers toward her. "I have to tell you, the budget and timeline are my best estimate. It's never exact, especially with an old property like this. Once we start opening up walls and really getting in there, there's no telling what we're going to find. But I've built wiggle room into both, to account for the unexpected."

"The unexpected," she repeated.

"Yeah. There's always something unexpected."

Breanna picked up the papers, looked at them, and set them down again.

"You're going to want to take those home, read them carefully. Maybe even have a lawyer take a look," Jake suggested.

"I'll have my brother Colin look them over," she said. "He's a—"

"A lawyer. Yeah, I know." Jake looked amused. "Everyone knows who Colin Delaney is. Everyone in my business in this state, anyway."

"Ah."

Breanna felt a frisson of nervous energy running through her spine, and she wasn't sure whether it was because of the significant project she was about to take on, or because she was sitting across from Jake, very close to him, with him looking at her the way he was looking at her.

"It's not that I don't know how to read a contract on my own," she said, just to be saying something. "But Colin's the family expert on these things, and I—"

"Sure. I get it," he said mildly. "Take it home. Take your time."

The thing was, she didn't want to take her time. She wanted the house to be finished, wanted her new home to be ready and waiting for her. She wanted the next phase of her life to begin. She was tired of waiting.

She picked up the papers and looked at Jake. "Do you have a pen?"

Once the contract was signed, there still the caramel latte and the comfortable, quiet surroundings of the coffeehouse, and there was still Jake. She knew she should get going—should get to the Whispering Pines and let him do whatever it was he needed to do, especially since he'd be doing it for her.

But she was in a celebratory mood now that she'd taken one more step in the direction of her dream, and she didn't really want to leave.

"Here's to new beginnings," she said, holding up her coffee cup for a toast.

"To new beginnings." He lightly tapped his paper cup against hers.

"You've been in town, what, six or seven months?" Breanna observed. "You must be experiencing some new beginnings of your own."

They talked about that for a while—about his divorce and his subsequent move to Cambria from Southern California.

"Of all the places you could have gone, why come here?" Cambria was unquestionably beautiful with its rugged coastline, its rolling green hills, its peace and quiet, its quaint historic architecture, and its small-town feel. But it would hardly be the first place most people would think about when planning a move.

Jake's mouth curved into a half grin. "My ex and I came through here on our honeymoon, on a drive up the coast through Big Sur. I'd never even heard of Cambria at the time, but … it charmed me. I thought that if I ever decided to get out of LA, I'd want to come here."

Breanna smiled. "That's what Cambria does. It charms people."

"Probably not when you've been here your whole life, though, right?" He sipped his coffee. "I mean, you probably stop appreciating something when you don't know anything else."

She considered that. "No. You'd think so, but … it's still magic. At least, it is for me. I've lived other places, but this? There's nowhere else like this."

"Huh. I thought you'd always lived here. Where else?"

She started ticking locations off on her fingers. "San Diego. Quantico. Washington, D.C. There was even a year in Germany."

He squinted at her with interest. "You were military?"

"Not me. My husband."

•••

The word *husband* was like a quick shot of cold water in Jake's face. She was married? How had he not known that? He'd Googled her and had never seen any reference to a husband. He'd known that he was attracted to her, of course. But he hadn't realized how much until the word *husband* had come flying at him.

"You're married?"

"Widowed," she said, a hint of some ancient sadness showing in her eyes. "He was a Marine. I followed him around from base to base until he was deployed overseas. He didn't come back."

"God, that's … I'm sorry."

"It was a long time ago," she said.

"I didn't know." He fidgeted with his cup, turning it clockwise on the table.

"Why would you?"

"Well … I Googled you. But now that I think of it, I only looked at the most recent entries. I guess I didn't go back far enough."

She looked down at the table, avoiding his gaze. "Brian died nine years ago. Still hurts like it was yesterday."

"You kept your last name," he said.

"I did." She nodded. "It means something to be a Delaney, and I didn't want to let go of that. The boys have his last name—Morgan—but I kept mine. He didn't like that. We argued about it. And then …"

"And then when he died, you felt guilty as hell," Jake finished for her.

She nodded. "Yes."

"It's just a name," he said. "Keeping your name didn't change the way you felt about him. Just like my ex taking my name didn't change how she felt about me. Unfortunately." He gave Breanna a wry grin.

"I want to ask what happened, but it's none of my business, so if you don't want to talk about it …"

"She met someone else." But that wasn't the whole story, was it? It was true, as far as it went—Beth had met someone else. But it never would have happened if Jake had made her happy. He could never seem to do that. They had too many differences, too many gaps between his goals and hers. As easy as it was to blame her, it wasn't honest. She'd gone elsewhere to fill legitimate needs that Jake had ignored.

"Jake?" Breanna was looking at him with concern. "Are you okay? Where did you go just now?"

"Ah, just … divorce sucks, that's all." He shrugged.

"So does widowhood."

Suddenly, he felt embarrassed to have been complaining about his own situation when what she'd gone through was so much worse.

Trying to get back on a happier topic, he grinned. "Hey, we were toasting new beginnings a little while ago. Let's get back to that. Your house is going to be great."

She smiled, and with the smile came a glow of happiness that made him melt a little. "It really is," she said.

He promised himself he'd make it happen for her, exactly the way she was imagining it. Sitting here with her, being charmed by her, he wanted to take away her sorrow.

He couldn't do that, but at least he could give her a kick-ass house.

Chapter Seven

Breanna got to the Whispering Pines later than usual because of her coffee with Jake. Since she was volunteering, she didn't have a set schedule, but she liked to be reliable and consistent. She hurried over to the B&B as soon as she left Jake.

By the time she got there, a couple had just checked out, so she greeted Mrs. Granfield, then went upstairs to start putting their room back in order.

The work was easy and automatic, and it allowed her mind to wander. It seemed to want to go to only one place: her conversation with Jake.

They'd met so she could sign the contract, and she'd done that. So why had they spent so much time talking about his life and hers, his divorce, her grief?

It had started as business, but it had quickly veered into the personal. He'd been so easy to talk to, so easy to listen to. Being with him felt comfortable, and it reminded her how little time she spent being social with someone who wasn't her family or a guest at Mrs. Granfield's B&B.

She used to have more of a social life. She used to spend more time with friends. But the people she'd been closest to just didn't seem to be around anymore. Her sister-in-law Julia was in

Montana. Her other sister-in-law, Gen, was so busy juggling work and motherhood that she had little time for anything else. And, of course, Brian, the best friend she'd ever had, was gone—had been gone so long she sometimes had a hard time remembering what it was like when she'd taken his love and his presence for granted.

Breanna told herself that her conversation with Jake had been nothing more than a lonely woman reaching out to the first available person who showed an interest. But another part of her thought it was more than that. She'd felt a connection. Had he felt it, too?

She carried the laundry from the room she'd just cleaned down to the laundry room and loaded it into the washing machine. As she completed the task, she thought about men—mostly the ones she'd known since Brian had died.

Dating was a tricky thing when you were a widow, and even more so when you were one of the wealthiest widows in the state. When men asked her out, it was usually about the money, about trying to get a piece of the Delaney fortune. When it wasn't about that—when it was just about her—they often had a hard time getting past the shadow of the man she'd loved and lost.

So many men were too insecure to accept the fact that she'd loved Brian, and still did, and always would. That didn't mean she couldn't make room in her life for someone new, but it seemed the male ego had a hard time dealing with competition, even from the dead.

She'd all but given up hope of finding a man who could deal with all of the complications Breanna represented.

Breanna didn't imagine that Jake was that man. Why should she? They barely knew each other, and besides, he was simply doing a job for her—that was all.

Still, she was starting a new life with the Moonstone Beach house. Why shouldn't she also start a new relationship with someone? Why shouldn't she think about dating? Ryan had met the love of his life, then Colin, then Liam. They all had someone. Why shouldn't she?

"Breanna?"

Redmond had died still missing the woman he'd loved, because he'd been too afraid, too stuck in one place, to pursue her. He'd spent so many years alone. She didn't want to end up like that, didn't want to grow old and die pining away for someone who wasn't there.

"Breanna? Dear?"

Breanna was startled to realize that Mrs. Granfield was standing in the doorway of the laundry room, saying something to her.

"What? I'm sorry. I was just … Did you need something?"

"I was just going to ask if you could keep an eye on things while I lie down for a bit to rest this hip. But you were a million miles away." Mrs. Granfield looked at her with concern.

"Oh. That's fine. I don't have to be anywhere until this afternoon. You go on." Breanna felt a slight blush rise to her cheeks, embarrassed to have been caught thinking about something as frivolous as dating.

"Are you sure you're okay?" Mrs. Granfield asked.

"Of course. Yes. Why wouldn't I be?"

"No reason, dear." Mrs. Granfield started to turn away, then stopped. "I ran into that Jake Travis over at the Cookie Crock earlier this morning. Isn't he the contractor for your place at Moonstone Beach?"

"Oh. Yes. He is." There was the blush again.

"What a handsome young man," Mrs. Granfield said. "If only I were thirty years younger."

•••

On demo day at the Moonstone Beach place, Jake gathered his tools and his crew and got ready to dig in. It was always exciting getting started on a new job. The contrast between what was and what would be filled him with enthusiasm and creative energy.

He couldn't wait to get his hands on the place.

He would start in the kitchen, which was going to be a total gut job. He had to take out everything—the cabinetry, the counters, one interior wall—and reconfigure the place to give it more room, more modern convenience. Breanna wanted the room to be inviting, homey, and practical all at once.

He and a couple of guys started by taking the cabinets off the walls, then he got to work with a sledgehammer, pounding through the wall that had to go.

Sam came inside to sniff at things and see what Jake was doing from time to time, but mostly he contented himself out in the yard, either taking a nap in the sun, sniffing at clumps of weeds, or chasing the squirrels that scurried about on the property.

By lunchtime, Jake was hot, dirty, and hungry as hell. He and his guys went to a taco truck on Main Street for lunch. While Jake sat outside at a folding table and ate, he thought about Breanna.

He pulled his phone out of his back pocket, pulled up the texting app, and sent her a message.

You should see your kitchen. Or, on second thought, maybe you shouldn't. We did demo this morning.

A few minutes later, he heard the ping of a response.

Send me a picture.

He grinned, surprised how delighted he was that she'd answered.

I'm at lunch. Will do, as soon as I get back.

He took another bite of his taco and heard the ping of an incoming message.

Is Sam there? He should be good for demo—he's a one-dog wrecking crew.

He laughed, then used his phone to snap a picture of Sam, who was on a leash at Jake's feet. He sent the picture—the frame filled with Sam's furry face—to Breanna.

Her response came in a few moments later: *I wish I could give him a big kiss.*

Jake wouldn't have thought he could be jealous of a dog, and yet here he was, ready to send Sam to doggy day care if it meant getting Breanna's attention for himself.

On the other hand, maybe he could use this to his advantage. He wouldn't be the first guy to use a cute dog to get on a woman's good side. He scowled at his own train of thought.

"Who says I need to get on her good side?" he muttered.

"You say something?" Carl, a young guy with pretty good construction skills and a good, earnest work ethic, was looking at him with curiosity.

"Me? Nah. No." Even as he said it, he realized he was protesting too much.

"Dude, you did," Carl said.

Covering, Jake said, "I was just … talking to the dog."

Sam looked at him with scorn and judgment.

"You just shut up," Jake told him.

Breanna looked at her text messages feeling excited—though she wasn't sure if it was about the progress on her house or her friendly flirtation with Jake.

She hadn't flirted in so long she'd almost forgotten how. And although she knew it would probably be wiser to keep things with Jake strictly business—at least until the house was done—she had to admit that this was fun.

"What's put that smile on your face?" Mrs. Granfield asked. Breanna hadn't heard her come into the kitchen. Breanna was supposed to be arranging tea service and cookies for the B&B's guests, but she'd been caught wasting time playing with her phone.

"Oh … nothing. My contractor has a cute dog, that's all." As proof, she brought up the picture of Sam and held out the screen for Mrs. Granfield to see.

"*Hmm*," Mrs. Granfield said.

"I was just … He started the demo today, so …"

Mrs. Granfield raised her eyebrows, grinning knowingly at Breanna. "He's quite handsome." She reached into a drawer for a handful of cloth napkins. "And I'm not referring to the dog."

Chapter Eight

Jake wasn't sure when he actually made the decision to ask Breanna out on a date. It wasn't one thing that clinched it. It was more that he'd been rolling the idea around under the surface in his mind until it emerged fully formed, already a done deal.

It was a foolhardy endeavor, for sure. She was his client. She was out of his league in terms of wealth and status. And she had kids—a situation fraught with complications and potential heartbreak.

But he wasn't thinking about marriage, he was thinking about—what? Dinner? A movie? Another coffee?

He hadn't worked that part out yet.

He just knew that he liked talking to her. He liked flirting with her, and he wanted to do more of it. Soon.

As he worked at the Moonstone Beach house a couple of days after the texting at the taco truck, he tried to work out how exactly to get her to go out with him, and what they would do if she did.

Jake thought about all of the best dates he'd been on, trying to glean some kind of knowledge, some kind of strategy, from the experiences. But that approach proved to be fruitless. His best date ever, to this day, was the time he and Peggy Carlisle ran out of gas during a drive on the Angeles Crest Highway and ended up having sex in the driver's seat while they waited for a tow truck. He was seventeen.

He didn't think Breanna would appreciate it if he tried to recreate that one.

There was a lot to do around here: the area had countless romantic restaurants, wineries with gorgeous scenery, places to take in the stunning Central Coast views. But she'd seen it all, done it all. Where could he take her that wasn't already old news for her? He was the newcomer here. He was the one who needed to be taken places, shown things.

Of course, that was one approach he could take. He could plead ignorance about the area and ask her to show him around. Who better to do it than someone who'd been here her whole life?

But Jake liked to play the role of the host, the alpha male, when he asked a woman out. He liked to make plans and show her a good time. Giving up that role would be especially problematic when you considered the fact that Breanna was the alpha here in so many other ways. As his client, she was paying his bills. And she had so much money to pay them with.

All of these thoughts about alpha this and that were so much bullshit.

"We're people, not wolves," he muttered as he hauled a load of debris out of the house toward a Dumpster set up in the yard.

"What?" Mark Winslow, one of the guys on the crew, was looking at him with curiosity, and Jake realized he'd said that last part out loud.

Covering, Jake barked, "I said we're people, not a damned pack of wolves. Clean this crap up." He gestured toward the mess that still needed to be cleared away.

He needed to stop thinking about Breanna and start thinking about work—especially since he would be using power tools. Best to keep his head in the game.

He made his move a couple of weeks later when Breanna stopped by the Moonstone Beach site to see how things were coming along.

She was ready for Sam this time—she braced herself, setting one foot firmly behind her for support, as he came rocketing toward her in ecstasy.

"Hey there, big guy." She distracted him with a Milk-Bone she'd pulled out of her pocket. The strategy worked—the dog hesitated slightly before he reached her, which took a little bit of the impact out of his approach. He still landed on her with both front paws on her chest, but she was able to stay on her feet, which she considered a victory.

"How are you today?" she cooed to the dog as she ruffled her hands through the fur around his big face. "Howza boy? Howza good boy?" Sam looked at her with a happy doggy smile, the Milk-Bone already a distant memory.

Jake came out of the house to greet her, grinning with admiration.

"Well, that went a lot better this time," he told her.

He was wearing jeans and a T-shirt, work boots, and a tool belt, with a dusting of some white powder that was probably the remains of her drywall in his hair. Why that was almost unbearably sexy, she could not have said. Must have been something about the very masculine work he was doing. Not that a woman couldn't do this kind of job, Breanna told herself. Though the woman in question probably wouldn't look nearly as scrumptious doing it.

"I just thought I'd drop by to take a look," Breanna told Jake. "I know I should stay away. I don't want to be a pest. But—"

"It's fine," Jake told her. "But you might not like what you see at this point."

"I can take it," she reassured him. "If I can handle Sam, I can handle whatever you've got going on in there."

They went inside to the sounds of hammering and men bantering about various things while they worked—sports and women and good-natured insults about somebody's mother.

"Hey, guys. Ms. Delaney's here," Jake called out as they entered. Probably, Breanna thought, to stave off any off-color language that might have naturally occurred had they not known. Breanna wasn't put off by off-color language. She had three brothers.

Breanna called out greetings to the crew. Most of them were local guys she already knew, and they waved or called back a friendly hello. One or two of the men were strangers to her; she wondered if Jake had brought them in from out of town for the job.

"You ready for the tour?" he asked.

"Absolutely." She steeled herself to see her precious house in complete disarray.

To her surprise, things looked much better than expected.

"Here's the kitchen." Jake ushered her into the room, which was no longer identifiable according to its intended purpose. All of the cabinetry had been taken out—no loss, since it had been old and nearly falling apart—and the room had been stripped down to its bare bones. One wall had been removed to enlarged the space, and a new wall, about three feet back from where the original one had stood, had been framed in, fresh studs forming its skeleton.

"Oh, wow," Breanna said in wonder.

"Is that a bad 'oh, wow' or a good one?" Jake wanted to know.

"A good one." Now that the dark paneling and the oppressively dark cabinetry that had been in this room had been stripped away, the place looked so much lighter, brighter. "There's so much more space. I didn't think three feet would make that much difference, but … wow."

"Wait until we get the new cabinetry and countertops in here," Jake said, clearly pleased. "Once it really starts to take shape, you can see what you've got."

They moved room by room through the rest of the house: the parlor, where the old, freestanding cast iron fireplace would be replaced by a big stone built-in; the dining room, which was losing a little bit of its space to the kitchen; the downstairs bedroom, which was getting an en suite bathroom; and the upstairs bedrooms, each of which would be refreshed with details like new doors, remodeled closets, and restored oak floors.

At this point, many of the changes were still a matter of plans and imagination. But everything had been stripped to the bare drywall, some walls had been removed and others had been framed in, and Breanna could clearly see the outline of what this place would be when Jake was finished.

She looked around in wonder as she went room to room, viewing what had been done so far and discussing what would come next. "This is amazing."

"Really?" Jake sounded surprised. "I kind of thought you'd be underwhelmed. There's not much to see yet."

"Are you kidding? God. It's going to be gorgeous. I can't wait." She bounced a little on her toes.

"You haven't seen the guesthouse yet."

"Oh. I wasn't sure you'd even started that."

He rubbed at the stubble on his chin. "Well, I wanted to get that going, because I figured you might want to rent it out, bring in some extra income. Not that you need it, I guess. Still …"

She was headed out the door and across the yard before he'd even finished his sentence.

The guesthouse was small at just seven hundred square feet. The plan was to increase the size of it, adding an additional bedroom and expanding the galley kitchen into something more workable for a couple or a small family. Breanna didn't know what she was going to do with it yet—maybe she would rent it out, as Jake had said, or maybe Colin and Julia would want to stay here when they were in town. No matter what she did with the cottage, she couldn't go wrong adding a little more space.

This part of the project wasn't very far along. But the concrete foundation for the addition had been poured, so Breanna could clearly see the new footprint the house would occupy when it was done.

"It's not much to see yet," Jake began.

"No, you're wrong. It is." Breanna's heart felt full—full of the life she and her sons would live here in this beautiful place, this place that was theirs alone.

She turned to Jake, thinking to thank him. Instead, she threw her arms around him impulsively. At first, taken by surprise, he didn't return her embrace. Then, he put his arms around her and held her.

"Well. You're welcome," he said, his voice husky.

If this wasn't the opening he was hoping for, he doubted he'd get a better one. It wasn't like she was going to present him with a handwritten invitation to ask her out.

He let go of her and took a step back.

When he was a teenager and painfully awkward with girls, he'd always thought that when he became a man, things like asking women out on dates would get easier. It never did. In fact, it was worse now, because when he was a kid, everyone just assumed he'd be a hopeless mess. Now, the expectations were higher, but the actual asking was still a nightmare of insecurity and vulnerability and a mélange of other things best avoided.

Still, there was no way around it, unless he wanted to stay single into his golden years.

"So …" he began. He rubbed the back of his neck and scrunched up his face slightly as though in pain. "I was thinking. We could maybe … uh … go out some time. If you wanted. But I get that you might not want to, because you're my client and I'm working on your project, and it might be weird, especially if things don't go well and we still have to work together. You know what? That really would be weird. Forget I said anything. Let's just …"

"Jake."

"That's just … It's probably uncomfortable for you that I even asked, right? Shit. I'm sorry. Just forget that I—"

"I'd love to go out with you," Breanna said.

His eyebrows shot up in his surprise. "You would?"

"Sure."

"That's … wow. Okay." He grinned, pleased with himself and the overall situation. "How about Friday night?"

"Perfect," she said. "Should we take a look inside the guesthouse?"

Chapter Nine

Breanna hadn't gone to the Moonstone Beach house expecting to get asked on a date. If she *had* gone over there expecting it, she'd have planned to say no. Yes, she was attracted to Jake. Yes, she'd enjoyed talking to him at the coffeehouse. And yes, their light flirtation had been fun. But he was right—what if things didn't go well between them while they were still working together?

And anyway, she had enough to worry about without a new man in her life. She had her boys, a move to a new home …

It was a lot to think about. And dating Jake would add a new level of stress to something that was already stressful.

Of course, it would also add a new level of excitement to something that was already exciting.

She'd been so pleased and happy about the progress on the property, the *yes* had popped out before she'd even thought about it. And then there had been the hug, which also had been unplanned.

Later that evening, Breanna was making dinner for her family—giving Sandra a rare break from the cooking—and Gen was sitting at the kitchen table feeding homemade macaroni and cheese to her son, James Redmond Delaney, whom they'd all taken to calling J.R.

At thirteen months old, J.R. was chubby, happy, and active. When Gen didn't shovel the food into his mouth fast enough, the boy smacked his hands on the tray of his high chair and made an *uh-uh-uh* noise that suggested a deep and enduring love for food.

"So ... a thing happened today," Breanna said as she stirred a big pot of chili.

"A thing," Gen repeated.

"Well ... not so much a thing as an incident," Breanna clarified.

"What kind of incident?" Breanna spooned pasta into her son's mouth, then scraped the excess sauce off his face with the tiny, baby-sized spoon.

"Nothing, really. Just ... the kind where I hugged my contractor and then he asked me out." She focused on the chili, as though avoiding eye contact with Gen would make the news seem less significant than it was.

"Oh ho!" Gen said.

Breanna set the spoon from the chili on a small plate she'd set aside for that purpose, then turned and looked at Gen. "Let's not make more of it than it is. I probably shouldn't have even said yes."

"But you did say yes?" Gen prompted her.

"Well ..."

"That's great, Bree," Gen said. "Really. You need to be dating. You deserve to have some fun. And he's hot and manly and all ... contractory, with the tools and everything." She looked at Breanna significantly.

"I don't think *contractory* is a word," Breanna pointed out.

"Doesn't make it any less true," Gen said.

Breanna gathered the ingredients for cornbread and started making a batter. "Yeah, but ..."

"But what?"

"But that's part of the problem. He's too ... too *Jake*. How am I going to stay focused on things like the new house, and the boys, and the move, and all of the things I've got going on if my brain is turned to mush over a really hot guy?"

J.R. was banging the tray again to protest the slowed rate at which Gen was feeding him. Gen said, "Okay, okay, do it yourself, then." She gave him the spoon, which he promptly threw to the floor. Gen retrieved the spoon, put it in the sink, and got a clean one out of a drawer.

"So, your brain is turning to mush?" she asked Breanna. "That's intriguing."

Breanna faced Gen, both hands on her hips. "I didn't say my brain was turning to mush. I said my brain *might* turn to mush if I were dating him. And that would just be really..."

"Awesome?" Gen suggested.

"Distracting," Breanna corrected her.

"God, Bree," Gen said, frustration in her voice. "Just have some fun. I mean, why not? Look at what your life has been these past God-knows-how-many years. You take care of the boys. You help your mother with the housework. You cook and clean and do laundry, you volunteer at the school, you work at Mrs. Granfield's place for free ..."

Breanna was starting to feel the sting of tears in her eyes. "What are you saying, Gen? Are you saying none of that is worth anything? That what I do doesn't have value?"

"No!" Gen looked alarmed. "God, no. You and Sandra are the heart of this house, and you know it. You make things better for all of us. And the kids—you've busted your ass to be both parents at once. You've given all of yourself to them. You give all of yourself to anyone who needs it. I'm just saying, it's time to give something to yourself."

J.R. had started to spit out the food Gen was giving him—a sure sign that he was full. Gen wiped his mouth with a damp washcloth and lifted him out of the highchair and into her arms.

"Well … that's what the Moonstone Beach house is about. It's for me. Doesn't that count?" Breanna heard a hint of a whine in her own voice, and she silently chided herself for it.

"Of course it counts," Gen said in a soothing voice as she held J.R. to her shoulder and rubbed his back. "It's a huge, terrific first step. I'm just saying … maybe take the second step." She raised her eyebrows significantly.

There was one good thing about having a date lined up with Jake for Friday night: obsessing about the date meant that Breanna wasn't obsessing about the progress at her house.

On Thursday morning, she did a visual inventory of the clothes in her closet and realized that, somewhere along the line, she'd stopped dressing like a woman and had started dressing like a mom.

"When did I get so frumpy?" she asked herself as she sorted through the jeans, the cardigan sweaters, the practical fabrics, the permanent press slacks.

Cambria was a casual town—there was nowhere locally where you'd put on a cocktail dress to go out to dinner—but that didn't mean she wanted to look like she'd come to her date straight from a water board meeting.

Since Gen was the one who'd insisted she had to go through with the date, Breanna figured Gen should be the one to help her with her wardrobe problems. Breanna drove to Main Street, where Gen's art gallery was located, and popped her head in to find Gen alone at the reception desk, tapping at the keys of her laptop.

The Porter Gallery was all blond wood floors and clean white walls punctuated by colorful canvases. Here and there, pedestals held small sculptures or pieces of blown glass done by local artists. One wall was dedicated to the more tourist-friendly items: watercolor seascapes, locally made jewelry, and reasonably priced ceramics made by Central Coast artisans.

The early February day was cool and crisp, and only a handful of tourists were scattered on the Main Street sidewalks.

"Hey, Bree," Gen greeted her as she came into the gallery. Gen was wearing a sleek black dress and pointy high heels—her usual gallery attire—and Breanna reflected that at least one of them knew how to dress like a girl.

"I have a problem," Breanna said, plunking down into a chair across from Gen's desk.

She laid out the issue: a date with a sexy man on the horizon, and not a single outfit that said *I'm an attractive, vibrant woman who has a life outside of housework and child-rearing.*

"Oh," Gen said thoughtfully. "I hadn't considered that."

It wasn't like Cambria was full of stylish boutiques where a youngish woman could find a kick-ass date outfit. The town had a number of shops with beautiful clothing, but the styles tended more toward *upscale artistic woman nearing retirement* rather than *I'm under forty and I'm trying to lure a delicious hunk of man into my bed.*

Was she trying to lure him into her bed? She pushed that thought aside, preferring to deal with one problem at a time.

"I'd loan you something, but . . ."

There was no need for Gen to finish the sentence, as her meaning was clear. Gen was six inches shorter and her figure was curvy and womanly, while Breanna had a more athletic build.

"We could drive down to Santa Barbara," Gen suggested. "Alex is coming in to work at eleven, and I have the sitter for the whole day, so—"

"I can't," Breanna moaned. "I told Mrs. Granfield I'd put in a couple of hours at the Whispering Pines, and the boys get out of school at three."

"Sandra could pick up the boys."

"But I can't skip out on the Whispering Pines. Mrs. Granfield has a doctor's appointment, and I said I'd be there."

"Crap," Gen said. She appraised Breanna for a moment, a thoughtful look on her face. "I have an idea. Hang on, let me make a call."

Breanna's figure wasn't at all like Gen's, but she was very similar in build to one of Gen's best friends—Kate Bennet, who owned the Swept Away bookstore a few doors down on Main Street.

Kate closed the bookstore for an hour at lunch—which she'd been planning to do anyway—and Breanna and Gen met her at her Marine Terrace house a little after noon.

"I'm not exactly fashion-forward," Kate told Breanna as she sifted through the things hanging in her closet. "But we're about the same size, so that should be okay, at least."

Kate, a slim brunette with short, spiky hair and a sense of style that skewed toward the funky side of traditional, pulled a silky, hot pink blouse out of her closet and held it up to Breanna.

"Nope. Not right for your coloring," she said, putting the hanger back on the rod.

"Thank you for doing this," Breanna said. "But I don't want to put you out. If you'd rather not—"

"She's looking for excuses to cancel the date," Gen told Kate.

"Ah. Nerves," Kate said knowingly.

"No, I'm not," Breanna protested.

"Of course you're not," Kate said in the kind of soothing voice that said she knew it was bullshit but was trying to be compassionate. She pulled another top out of her closet, this one in a rich shade of magenta. She held it up to Breanna and nodded. "Okay, now we're getting somewhere."

Chapter Ten

Breanna wasn't used to wearing makeup—she usually didn't see the point. She liked to look presentable, of course, but that usually meant that she was tidy, her clothes clean, wrinkle-free and appropriate, and her hair brushed.

The idea of getting dolled up for a date seemed foreign to her, as though she were making an awkward but not entirely unpleasant visit to someone else's life.

Also, there was the fact that Jake hadn't said where they would be going. In selecting her overall look for the occasion, she had to factor in that the destination was unknown.

Was all of this worth it, just for the possibility of a little romance? When Jake showed up at the front door of the Delaney house to pick her up, she decided that it was.

She'd only ever seen him in his work clothes—jeans and a T-shirt, sometimes liberally dusted with various kinds of dirt and debris. It turned out, he cleaned up well. He was wearing a pair of khaki chinos and a dark blue button-down shirt open at the throat, and his short, dark hair was combed back from his face. He was freshly shaven, and he smelled lightly of some kind of manly cologne.

He smiled when he saw her, and the smile undid her. When was the last time a man had given her that kind of smile? His eyes were deep blue, and the lines around them hinted of a life well lived.

"Wow," she said when she opened the door.

"Wow yourself," he told her. "You look great." He didn't say it like someone who was trying to be polite. He said it like he meant it.

As she began to walk out the door, he asked, "Is your family home?"

They were. The inside of the house was a veritable clown car of Delaneys, including her parents, Sandra and Orin; her brother Ryan, Gen, and J.R.; her brother Liam, who was over for dinner with his fiancée, Aria; and of course, Michael and Lucas.

"You don't want to go in there," she told him.

"Why not?"

"Because if we go in there, you'll have to meet everyone, and they'll make small talk that will seem like it's friendly, but it'll really be them grilling you about your intentions."

He laughed. "I'd like to meet your family. I think I can take the grilling."

"It's just easier this way," she said, coming out onto the porch and closing the door behind her. "Trust me."

Jake had asked around, and it seemed that pretty much everybody took a first date to Neptune, which was considered to be the best restaurant in town. Jake bucked that trend, taking Breanna to a restaurant at a winery in Paso Robles instead.

The restaurant looked romantic and inviting, with a lot of dark wood and candlelight. Soft jazz was playing on the sound system. Breanna thought she'd been here once before, years ago, but she wasn't sure if this was the same place.

It was nice to be somewhere new, since she'd eaten at every restaurant in Cambria so many times she could recite the menu selections.

"This is pretty," she said as the hostess showed them to their table.

"I don't even know if you like wine," Jake said.

"I like wine."

They ordered a local Chardonnay and drank some of it with hot bread the waitress had brought them. They ordered their entrees—sea bass for her, seafood pasta for him—and started the standard getting-to-know-you chat while they waited for their food.

Naturally, she asked him how he was settling into Cambria, and how he was adjusting to the change from the bustling metropolis of Los Angeles.

That brought them to the subject of Jake's divorce.

"There were too many memories in LA," he told her. "I needed a new environment. A new start. A new ... everything."

"So you're here hiding out from your past?" she asked, only partly teasing.

"No, actually. I don't feel like I'm hiding from the past. More like I'm moving toward the future."

"Well, that sounds positive." Breanna sipped some wine, then broke a piece of bread off and popped it into her mouth.

"I think so."

"Was the divorce amicable?" she asked. This might be territory best unexplored for now, but the question was right there waiting to be asked.

"More or less," he said, without going into any further detail about the *more* or the *less*. "I'm not trying to be evasive, but if we get into a discussion about my divorce, then our first date is about my ex-wife. I don't really want that, do you?"

"No. I don't." She considered that. "In that case, we won't talk about my husband, either. At least, not yet."

"Deal."

With that agreement in place, they avoided talk of former relationships and focused on each other: his work and the challenge of getting settled in a new town; her plans for the move to the new house and what it was like being a Delaney.

"It's not what people think," she told him on the subject of her family and her status. "I mean, people around here get it, but other places ... You tell someone you're a Delaney, and they think it's all butlers and boarding schools and chauffeured limousines."

"I can't really see you in a chauffeured limousine," Jake commented.

"I've been in one once, when my brother got married. I was crammed in there with six other people." She shook her head and grinned. "It's not all that it's cracked up to be."

He laughed. "All that money, though—it's got to be great in some ways. And hard in others."

She considered that. "For me, it's all I've ever known. But it's hard for the people in my life sometimes. They tend to feel ... inadequate. Or overshadowed."

Breanna wondered if Jake understood she was talking about her husband. But they'd agreed not to bring spouses into this, so she left it vague.

If they made it past the first date, or the second or the third, there would be time to talk about that. But this evening wasn't about the past. It was about right now, tonight. She wouldn't allow herself to think about whether it would ever amount to more.

•••

The thing Breanna had said about people feeling over-shadowed and inadequate made Jake think—specifically, about whether he could be with a very rich woman without having those feelings himself.

He liked to think he was confident enough in his manhood that he didn't need to prove his worth as a provider. But, hell. He was subject to the same male bullshit as any other guy.

How would it feel to be in a relationship with a woman who probably made more money in a week—just from the interest on her investments—than he did in a year?

Jake had never wasted time wishing he were rich. He liked his lifestyle, simple as it was. He enjoyed his work, and he made enough to pay his bills and take an occasional vacation. He'd rarely found himself wanting or needing more than that.

But the women he'd dated—and the one he'd married—had all been on a more or less equal level with him in terms of money. He'd never experienced a situation as lopsided as this one.

How would he feel if this really went somewhere?

He knew a lot of guys would jump at the chance to get in-volved with a woman like Breanna just for the money, regardless of whether they had feelings for her.

But Jake wasn't a lot of guys. He was simple at heart, and he rarely longed for anything he hadn't earned. If he chose to pur-sue things with Breanna, the situation would be anything but simple.

"Jake?" Breanna was looking at him curiously, probably wondering where he'd gone when he'd been musing about the potential complications of a life as Mr. Breanna Delaney. "Is everything okay?"

"Yeah, of course." He gave her a reassuring smile. "How's the sea bass?"

•••

They ate and talked and lingered over coffee, and by the time they got up from the table, neither one of them realized that more than two hours had passed. Talking to Jake was easy, Breanna thought. So easy it was as though she'd known him much longer than she had.

As they walked out of the restaurant, Jake's hand resting lightly on the small of her back, she thought she might be in trouble. When he took her home and kissed her on the front porch of her family's farmhouse, she knew it for sure.

It wasn't the kiss of someone intent on getting her into bed and then forgetting her. She'd had kisses like that before, and this one was different. This one was soft at first, gentle, a feather's touch, and then more insistent as he put his hands on her face and leaned in to taste, to caress her mouth with his.

It was the kiss of someone who liked kissing and knew how to do it.

At the first touch of his lips to hers, she felt a surge of adrenaline, a little electric jolt of excitement. Then, as the kiss progressed, she felt her insides go soft and hot, as though her body had been waiting for him and recognized him as the thing it had always needed.

Her mind was in a white, blank state of bliss when he pulled away, leaving her with her eyes still closed, her lips still slightly parted.

"I guess I'd better say goodnight," he said, his voice a little ragged.

"Oh … right." Breanna slowly came back to the present and to the fact that she was a responsible adult—a mother, for God's sake—with her family just inside. "That was—"

"Thank you for coming with me tonight," he said. "I'd like to do it again."

At first she thought he meant that he would like to kiss her again, and she was acutely disappointed when she realized he'd been talking about another date. Though that, too, would be welcome.

"I'd like that."

When she went inside, her mother was standing in the front room, making a production of dusting a side table that didn't need dusting.

"Have a good time, did you?" she asked without looking up.

"Were you waiting for me?" Breanna asked.

"What? Hell, no. You're an adult, I figure. It's not like I need to wait around for you to come home like I did when you were a teenager." She let out an irritable grunt to indicate the absurdity of the idea.

"You dusted that same table yesterday," Breanna pointed out.

Sandra scowled. "It's not like the dust stops accumulating just because you think it should!" She scrubbed at the table with her rag one last time for emphasis.

"I did have a good time," Breanna said with a hint of a smile.

"*Hmph.* I figure I've got a right to dust my own damned table."

Breanna went to her mother, pressed a kiss to her cheek, and gave her shoulders a squeeze. "Thanks for waiting up for me," she said. "I'm going to go up to bed."

"*Hmph,*" Sandra said again.

Chapter Eleven

The next morning when Gen asked how it went, Breanna tried to act nonchalant.

"It was fine," she said. The two had run into each other at Jitters, and they were chatting at the counter as Gen sipped her coffee and Breanna waited for her latte.

"'Fine'?" Gen asked, wrinkling her nose in distaste. "What does 'fine' even mean? A good dental checkup is 'fine.' Having my taxes done is 'fine.'"

"It wasn't like having my taxes done," Breanna said.

"I would hope not," Gen quipped. "My tax guy is fifty-three and bald."

In truth, Breanna was aching to tell somebody about the date, and about the kiss in particular. But she wanted to act like the mature woman she was and not like a lovesick seventeen-year-old.

"It might have been better than fine," she allowed.

"Ooh," Gen said. "Well, I know it ended before eleven p.m.—Sandra told me that—so there couldn't have been sex. Or, there could have been, but—"

"There was no sex!" Breanna said, appalled. "It was our first date!"

"But it was good, or at least better than fine," Gen prompted her. "So …?"

Breanna's latte came, and she and Gen took a small table toward the front of the coffeehouse. The place was moderately busy, with several locals and a smattering of tourists at the tables or waiting to order at the counter. A bulletin board on the wall held advertisements for local bands, pet sitters, and handymen, and the room smelled of French roast and espresso.

"We went to a winery restaurant in Paso," Breanna said. "The food was good. We talked a lot, about a lot of things. And then he brought me home."

Gen closed her eyes, tipped her head to the side, and made a loud snoring noise.

"Gen!"

"I'm sorry, but you're holding back the part that was better than fine."

Breanna sighed and slumped down into her seat, figuring she might as well come out with it.

"The whole thing was better than fine," she said, looking at her coffee cup to avoid Gen's gaze. "We talked so easily. I mean, it was like we'd known each other a really long time. Before I even knew what happened, we'd been sitting there for hours. And the kiss—"

"There was a kiss?" Gen perked up. "Ooh."

"There was a kiss," Breanna confirmed. "On the front porch when he brought me home. Which is really old-fashioned when you think about it. And really sweet."

"Oh. So it was a sweet kiss." Gen looked disappointed.

"No. Definitely not. I said it was sweet that it happened on the front porch when he brought me home. The kiss itself was … not sweet. I *melted,* Gen. I mean, you hear about that kind of thing and you think it's just a thing people say. But there I was, all … melty."

Gen sighed happily. "I love melty kisses." She looked at Breanna with a mixture of curiosity and concern. "So, I'm guessing it wasn't like that with Brian?"

"It was nice with Brian. Really nice. We loved each other, and we had a lot of the same core beliefs." Breanna made a face. "And now that I'm saying that, it sounds really boring."

"No. It sounds good," Gen said.

"It was. It really was. But the kiss last night with Jake … There was this *chemistry* …" She could have explained how her body had responded and how her panties had nearly gone up in flames. But that seemed indelicate, so she just left it there. "I feel guilty saying that. Comparing Jake with Brian that way."

Gen reached out and put her hand over Breanna's on the table. "You have nothing to feel guilty for. You loved Brian, but you've been alone a long time now. Why shouldn't you have someone? Why shouldn't you melt?"

The problem, Breanna thought, wasn't that she'd had that moment of intense chemistry with Jake. The problem was that now she wanted to have it again, and soon. And that stirred up a lot of feelings she didn't know what to do with.

"I just … all I wanted was to hire somebody to fix up my house. I wasn't looking for all of this." She toyed with her coffee cup, turning it in her hands.

"You weren't looking for it, but it found you anyway," Gen said. "Maybe that's because you're ready."

Was she? She was ready for something. Some new adventure, some exciting change.

But she didn't know whether she was ready for Jake Travis.

•••

Breanna stayed away from the Moonstone Beach house that day. She told herself it was because she had to let Jake do his work, and she didn't want to get in the way. But it actually had more to do with the awkwardness of seeing him after the melty kiss.

How was she supposed to act? What was she supposed to say? She couldn't just see him and pretend it hadn't happened, but she didn't want to appear needy or clingy, as though she'd shown up at the work site just to stare at him with loving puppy eyes.

So she stayed home when she otherwise might have gone over there. There was plenty to do—the boys' sheets needed to be washed, and the front flower beds needed weeding.

And the very fact that she was hiding out washing sheets and weeding flower beds was almost comically pathetic.

"I thought you'd be over at that house of yours, seeing how things are coming along," Sandra observed around midmorning. Breanna was on her knees scrubbing the inside of the oven, her hands encased in bright yellow rubber gloves.

"I had a lot to do here," she said.

"Well, I don't suppose this oven would turn to dust if you put it off a day," Sandra said, her hands on her hips.

"I didn't need to put it off a day," Breanna said, her head most of the way inside the oven. "I was here, and I had time, so I'm doing it."

"Uh huh," Sandra said doubtfully. "Well, I hope he calls before you scrub a hole in the damned thing."

"I am not waiting for him to call!" Breanna protested.

"Uh huh," her mother said again.

He did call, around midafternoon. It was good that he did, because Breanna had already washed the sheets, weeded the flower bed, cleaned the oven, scrubbed the top of the refrigerator, and mopped the kitchen floor. If he'd waited any longer, she might have started resurfacing the driveway.

"Hey," he said when she answered her cell phone. "I didn't see you at the site today."

"Well … I had a lot to do," she told him.

"It's coming along," he said.

When she was starting to wonder whether he'd called just to give her a construction update, he said, "I had a really good time last night."

"Me too." Her cheeks were starting to feel hot, and it had nothing to do with the room temperature.

"And that kiss …"

"It was nice. Really nice," Breanna said.

"So … I was thinking we could do it again."

"The kiss?"

"Well, that too. But I was talking about the date."

"I'd like to do it again," Breanna said.

"The kiss or the date?" There was a gentle tease in Jake's voice.

"Both."

She definitely wanted to do both.

Breanna was smiling too much. Normally, that sort of thing would not have been a problem. But the smile was starting to arouse suspicion among her family members, and that was just awkward.

"God. What is *wrong* with you, Mom?" Michael groused at her over breakfast the next morning.

"What do you mean? There's nothing wrong." She'd made pancakes and bacon for the boys during the second wave of breakfast; the first wave had been before dawn for the men who'd be working on the ranch, and the second was for everyone who had the luxury of taking it easy on a Sunday morning.

Michael was picking at his pancakes, a sour look on his face. "You're just all … *happy*." He shuddered theatrically.

"Is it so wrong for me to be happy?" she asked.

"No. It's just weird."

"I like it when you're happy," Lucas, her sunny, cheerful child, piped in.

"Thank you, sweet pea." Breanna leaned down and kissed him on top of the head.

Breanna knew not to make too much of Michael's comments. He was turning into an angsty teen, after all, and to him, everything that wasn't utterly familiar was weird.

But that was the point, wasn't it? Breanna being happy wasn't utterly familiar to Michael. And it should have been. Was it really that unusual for him to see her smiling and cheerful in the morning? And if so, how had she let it get that way? How had she let herself become someone who just went through the motions? Why hadn't she demanded more for herself and for her boys?

"You should get used to it," she told Michael. "You're going to see more of it."

She'd been in mourning too long—mourning not just for Brian, but for the life she should have had. Too much sadness, and then, when the sadness had faded, too much of just existing day to day, just getting through.

She wanted more.

The Moonstone Beach house was part of that, but it was just one part. It was too soon to know if Jake would be another part. But he was certainly a good start.

•••

Jake was looking forward to his date with Breanna. He was looking forward to it so much, in fact, that he was distracted on the job. Considering the fact that he worked with a table saw and a nail gun—among other highly dangerous tools—he figured he'd better get his head in the game before someone got hurt.

"You okay, boss?" one of his guys asked him after he'd sawed a two-by-four to the wrong length—twice.

"Yeah, yeah," Jake said. "Mind your own business."

Even Sam knew something was up. He was sitting a few feet away from Jake, his head cocked to the side, eyeing Jake with curiosity and not a little concern.

"And what exactly is your problem?" he asked the dog. "Go chase some squirrels or something."

The irritability was just a cover, and not a very good one. He actually found himself whistling while he worked—an alarming state of affairs, as he was a man and not one of the Seven Dwarfs.

He felt good. Buoyant, in fact.

And that was alarming, because if Breanna Delaney made him feel this way after just one date and the promise of another, then he was in real trouble.

He didn't seem to mind, though, and that was probably another bad sign.

Jake saw one of Sam's tennis balls on the floor, picked it up, went to the front door of the house, and hurled the ball across the yard. Sam shot after it in a blur of black fur and drool.

The dog brought the ball back and dropped it at Jake's feet, giving him a big, doggy smile.

"I've got work to do, you know," Jake told him. "I can't spend all day playing with you."

Nonetheless, he scooped up the ball, which was damp with dog saliva, and threw it again.

Jake could do with a little more play, now that he thought about it.

"You sure you're okay?" the same guy asked him again.

"Shut up," Jake said.

Chapter Twelve

Their next date was lunch on a Tuesday. A Tuesday lunch wasn't the most romantic of all possible dates, Jake figured, but he hadn't wanted to wait until the following weekend, and they'd already done dinner. Throwing a little variety into the mix seemed like a good idea.

They met at the Sandpiper, a restaurant on Moonstone Beach with a good view of the surf, and sat outside on the patio with the gulls cawing and the cool breeze smelling like saltwater.

He ordered a steak sandwich and she ordered a Caesar salad, and it was all feeling very good and exciting, yet familiar, when Breanna got a call on her cell phone.

She checked the screen, then looked at him apologetically. "I have to take this. It's the boys' school."

"No problem," he told her.

She answered, and Jake could tell by the tone of her voice that something had happened—something you didn't want to hear about from your kid's principal in the middle of the school day.

"Yes. I understand," Breanna said into the phone. "I'm so sorry. I don't know why he—" Silence as she listened. Then: "Okay. I'll be right there."

She tapped the phone to end the call and looked at Jake, clearly upset. "I'm so sorry. I have to go."

"What happened?"

"Michael got into a fight." She shook her head, the space between her brows furrowed in concern. "He's never done this before. They want me to come and get him."

"All right. Let's go," he said.

"You ... That's ..." Breanna rubbed at her face with her hands. "You don't have to come. Stay here and enjoy your lunch. I don't want to ruin your afternoon."

"Nothing ruined about it." He called the waitress over and asked for their food to be packaged to go.

The principal, a trim, tidy, pants-suit-clad brunette named Mrs. Woodley, told Breanna that Michael was being suspended for hitting another boy.

"Why did he hit him?" Breanna asked. Michael was sitting outside in the hallway while they talked.

"The reason doesn't matter," Mrs. Woodley said. "We have a zero tolerance policy for violence."

"Of course the reason matters," Jake said.

Mrs. Woodley, seated behind the kind of large, fake wood grain desk most commonly seen inside cubicles, folded her hands on the desktop and looked at Breanna.

"If we were to attempt to determine the reasons for every dispute between the kids at this school, we'd have time for nothing else. And it's often impossible to determine the real story."

"Because kids lie," Jake supplied.

"Often they do, yes. That's why we have a policy of suspending anyone who participates in a fight, with no exceptions."

"I see," Breanna said.

When she, Michael, and Jake got out to Breanna's car, they all got in and headed back toward the Delaney Ranch.

"Mom," Michael started.

"We'll talk about it at home," she said.

"But—"

"I said we'll talk about it at home."

Breanna was angry, and she didn't want to talk to her son when she was angry. She wanted to be calm and clear-headed. Her hands were so tight on the wheel that her knuckles had turned white.

After they'd been driving for a few minutes, Michael said, "Why is *he* here?"

Breanna opened her mouth to answer, but before she could say anything, Jake answered, "I'm here because I'm your mother's friend, and sometimes it's nice to have a friend when your kid gets busted for fighting."

It *was* nice to have a friend, Breanna thought. But now Michael had one more thing to give her attitude about.

They rode the rest of the way in silence.

Breanna dropped Michael off at home and sent him to his room, with instructions to Sandra to keep an eye on him to make sure he complied. Then she drove Jake back to the work site, where he'd left his truck.

"You know, the reason does matter," Jake said when they were sitting in her car outside the Moonstone Beach house.

"He's suspended either way," she said, her voice weary.

"Yeah, but it's one thing if he was bullying someone. It's another if he was defending himself. This one-size-fits-all discipline is bullshit. The reason matters."

"I know." But she also knew that Mrs. Woodley was right: She might never get to the bottom of what really happened. She was certain that both of the boys involved would tell a story that skewed reality to their own benefit. In the end, you had to listen, but you also had to assume your child wasn't an angel. You had to resist the urge to treat your kid like a special unicorn who had only goodness and purity in his heart.

"I hope I wasn't out of line coming with you," Jake said. "I know it wasn't my place, but—"

"It was nice to have the support," she told him. "But I'm sorry about our date."

"There will be other dates."

"Will there?" Right now she felt as though she'd ruined things simply by being herself, a person with kids and issues and obligations.

"I certainly hope so." He leaned toward her and kissed her softly. Then he opened the car door and stepped out. "Now go home and give him hell," Jake said, leaning in through the passenger side door and giving her a wink.

By the time Breanna got home, some of her anger had burned off and she just felt weary.

Michael was going through a rough time, and she doubted her own ability to handle the increasing challenges of dealing with his turbulent feelings. Her date had been ruined, and while she was trying not to prioritize that—her son mattered more, after all—she was, nonetheless, feeling somewhat bitter about it. And Michael had made it clear in the car that he was not on board with her seeing someone.

It was a lot to deal with, and Breanna was feeling the strain of it.

Still, she gathered her motherly resources as she climbed the stairs to his room, and she was admirably calm as she came in and sat on his bed to talk.

"Michael."

He was lying on his bed with a book open in front of his face, studiously concentrating on not looking at her.

"Michael, put down the book, please."

When he didn't, she gently took it out of his hands and set it on his bedside table.

"Would you like to tell me what happened?"

"No." He was scowling and looking at the ceiling, his arms crossed over his chest.

"Who were you fighting with?" she tried again.

"Why was that guy with you when you came to the school?" Michael asked.

Breanna knew that if she let him get her off track, she'd never get the answers she needed. "We're not talking about that right now."

"I am. I'm talking about it right now."

"Well, I'm not." Breanna's voice was growing louder and more shrill, and she took a deep breath, forcing herself to bring it back under control. "Michael, please tell me what happened at school today."

His eyes narrowed. "I'll tell you that when you tell me why that guy came with you to the school."

Breanna stood. "I think you should stay in your room for a while. We'll talk some more about this later."

She made it all the way out of the room before her vision grew blurry with tears.

Liam had gotten through to Michael before, so Breanna thought of him when she couldn't get her son to open up about what had happened.

She hadn't had lunch yet and her stomach was growling, so she ate her takeout Caesar salad in the kitchen. Then she called Liam on his cell phone.

Liam agreed to take Michael out to work on the ranch again. Breanna didn't tell Michael that the purpose was to see if he would be more forthcoming with his uncle than he was with his mother. Instead, she told him there was no way she was going to allow his suspension from school to become a vacation. If he wasn't in class, he was at least going to be working.

The strategy worked. When Liam brought Michael home at the end of the day, he took Breanna aside to give her the rundown.

"I'm kinda proud of him, really, if his story isn't bullshit," Liam said, scratching his head thoughtfully as he and Breanna stood out on the front porch. "He was sticking up for this kid in his fourth period class who was getting picked on. Bunch of assholes were giving the kid a hard time because he takes dance lessons. Michael punched the ringleader."

"Dance lessons."

"Yeah." Liam shrugged. "Not manly enough for the in crowd, I guess."

"But … why didn't he tell *me* that?" Breanna said.

Liam shrugged again. "He was embarrassed."

"Embarrassed? But why? If he was helping a boy who was being bullied …"

"Hell, he's thirteen," Liam said. "That age, everything you do is embarrassing, especially when it comes to your mother."

Breanna knew better than to take Michael's word for it without any kind of independent verification. So she called a woman she knew who also had a kid in Michael's fourth period class. The woman put her son on the phone, and the boy gave pretty much the same story Liam had recounted.

As soon as the bell rang ending class, the boy told her, a kid named Mason Thomas had been surrounded outside the classroom door. A group of four bullies had been calling him names—the usual ones when someone's manhood was being called into question, words Breanna didn't want to think about.

Michael had asked them to stop, and when they hadn't, he'd punched the most aggressive, most vocal one of the bunch.

Breanna had never heard Michael talk about Mason Thomas; she hadn't realized they were friends.

They weren't, the kid told her over the phone. They barely knew each other.

Somehow, that made what Michael had done even more noble.

After dinner that night, Breanna went into Michael's room, where he was lying on his stomach on his bed, pretending to do homework. She knew he was pretending from the look on his face—intense, as though he were working hard not to acknowledge Breanna's presence.

"Michael?" She gently took his pen and his notebook from his hands and set them on the bedside table.

"What?" That one word—one syllable—was loaded with all of the defiance, angst, and anger the boy was feeling.

"I called around, talked to some people from the school," she said. "Why didn't you tell me you were protecting a boy who was being picked on? I would have talked to the principal. I would have—"

"They don't care," Michael said, sulking. "You heard what Mrs. Woodley said. The reasons don't matter."

"They matter to me."

He didn't respond, so she tried another angle. "From what I heard, you and Mason aren't even friends."

"We're not."

"But you stuck up for him anyway."

Michael shrugged, then sat up. "People should be able to take dance lessons if they want to, even guys. It's not like he was hurting anybody."

She reached out and pulled him into a hug. He resisted at first, then put his arms around her and squeezed.

"I won't do it again, Mom." His voice was muffled within her embrace.

"Don't say that."

He pulled back a little and looked at her. "What do you mean?"

"I mean, I don't want you to promise that. You did fine, Michael. I'm proud of you. Don't change a thing." Her voice was rough with emotion.

He pulled away from her, avoiding her gaze, embarrassed.

"But I don't understand why you didn't tell me what happened," she said.

He scowled. "That guy was there."

That was all he said: *that guy.*

If Breanna was going to continue seeing Jake—something she very much wanted to do—Michael wasn't going to make it easy.

Then again, a lot of things weren't easy. That didn't mean they weren't worth doing.

Chapter Thirteen

Breanna and Jake redid their date on Friday—same time, same restaurant. Over the entrees, Breanna told him about what had happened with Michael.

"Damn," Jake said, admiration in his voice. "That took guts. Especially if there were four of them."

"It did," she agreed. "But I wish he'd told me instead of making me play detective to find out for myself."

"A man doesn't make excuses," Jake said. "A man just accepts the consequences."

"But it's not an excuse if it's the truth."

"I didn't say it was rational," Jake said, pointing his fork at her for emphasis. "I just said that's how men are. And Michael wants to be seen as a man."

Breanna poked at her salad, considering what Jake had said.

The restaurant was less than half-full—not uncommon for a weekday in winter. The air was cool and crisp, and the sound of the surf added a gentle, thrumming undercurrent to their conversation.

"That's probably what he needs," Jake went on. "To be thought of as a man. I mean, when you're thirteen, you're right in the middle: you're not an adult, but you're not really a kid, either. You end up not knowing who the hell you are."

"He's unhappy about the move," she said. "The way he sees it, I'm taking him away from his home."

"You're trying to create a new home," he said.

"That's not how it feels to Michael."

It felt good to be talking to Jake about this, good to get his insight and pour out her worries. She didn't expect answers from him, she didn't expect easy solutions. But he was listening to her—really listening—and that went a long way toward comforting her.

When lunch was over, he walked her to her car and kissed her.

She relaxed into him, and he held her with the ease of someone who felt right at home doing something he was born to do.

"This feels good," he said, and they both knew he wasn't just talking about the kiss.

With the second date finally completed after two attempts, Breanna started fretting about sex: when they would have it, how she would feel about it, and how it would affect her life.

There was no question about *whether* they would have it; barring some bizarre accident or Jake's sudden need to escape from the law, that part seemed pretty much certain.

Breanna told herself to slow things down in her mind—this wasn't the time to mentally play out sex, marriage, a lifetime of togetherness, and eventual death in each other's arms. They'd had two dates. It was hardly time to start writing *Breanna Travis* on her notebook with glitter pens.

Still, after two good dates and some great kisses, the issue of sex was certainly on the table. She would get to know him better, and once she had, the only thing stopping them would be her fear—or possibly a no-holds-barred move by Jake's ex-wife to get him back.

There's an ex-wife, she reminded herself. And her own children. In fact, this budding relationship contained quite a few people beyond just Jake and herself.

I need to be careful.

While she was thinking about that, there was something else she wasn't being careful about. Distracted, she nearly burned the crap out of her hand while she was making eggs and toast for the boys on Saturday morning.

"For God's sake, girl," Sandra told her scornfully, an apron around her waist and her fists planted on her hips. "I'd think you'd know by now that when a pan's been sitting on a fire, it's bound to get hot."

"I know, I know." She slipped an oven mitt over her hand and tried once more to pick up the pan. It went much better this time.

"Something on your mind? Because it sure isn't kitchen safety." Sandra cackled at her own humor.

"No. Not a thing. I'm fine."

When the boys finished up, Breanna shooed them out of the kitchen and started gathering up plates sticky with strawberry jam and dribbles of melted butter.

On his way out, Lucas ran up to Breanna, threw his arms around her waist, and squeezed. Then he dashed out to do whatever it was he planned to spend his school-free morning on: Minecraft, maybe, or those mindless cartoons he loved so much.

"That boy's a sweet one," Sandra remarked approvingly.

"He is. I'm not looking forward to the stage when he grows horns and starts breathing fire." She sighed and carried the dishes to the sink.

"*Hmph*. Might never happen," Sandra commented. "That boy's essential nature is sweeter than sugar. You might just escape the worst of it with him."

"Unlike Michael," Breanna said, sulking.

Sandra shrugged as she wiped the big kitchen table with a damp cloth. "A boy who'd step in to help somebody who needs it? I'd say he's doing all right."

"I guess," Breanna said. "But he's sullen all the time. And he's mad about the move. And he doesn't like Jake."

"Well, I don't guess a woman's kids get to choose who she goes out with. You're the one who has to date the man, not Michael." She attacked an invisible spot on the table, her muscles working as she rubbed at it.

"Sure, but … what if this thing with Jake goes somewhere? Not that I think it will …" She *did* think it would—at the very least, she thought it certainly *could*—but that wasn't something she was ready to admit at this stage.

"If it does, it does," Sandra said. "That's your business, not Michael's. The boy will have to adjust."

"But it's his life, too."

"Not yet it isn't, unless you're planning to elope with the man over the weekend."

The nice thing about talking to Sandra was that she put things into perspective bluntly and with an effectiveness that was rare in most people.

"You're right. I'm being silly." Breanna loaded the dishes into the dishwasher, avoiding her mother's scrutiny.

"Well, now, I didn't say that," Sandra commented thoughtfully. "I figure, if you're already thinking about what that contractor of yours is going to mean to your kids, it's not because you're desperate for things to worry about." She let out a grunt. "Must be some chemistry there."

Breanna didn't answer, but that didn't stop Sandra from going on about it.

"Been a long time since you've dated and had a good time doing it," Sandra said. "Don't you let your son's attitude ruin this for you. Why, he'd just as soon have you all to himself until he's on Social Security. But the best thing you can do for him is to give him a happy mama."

Having delivered her speech, Sandra gave the table one last buff, said, "Well, I guess that ought to do," then threw the cloth onto the counter and walked out of the kitchen.

Breanna and Jake's lunch date—the second one—had been Friday. Today was Saturday. She hadn't heard from him, and she was trying hard not to be pathetic about it.

She refused to wait around for him to call her regarding some imaginary plans that hadn't yet been made. Instead, Breanna called Gen, who called Liam's fiancée, Aria, and the three of them made plans to do a girls' night out.

They went to Ted's, a bar about a block off Main Street, and settled in at a scarred wooden table with mugs of beer for Breanna and Aria and sparkling water for Gen, who was eternally health-conscious.

A collection of '80s rock was playing on the sound system over the usual array of bar noises: people playing pool or darts, people loudly bantering with each other from across the room, people hollering to the bartender for another round.

Ted's was a dive by most standards, with its sticky floors and its aroma of spilled beer and old sweat, but the fact that this was Cambria—along with the fact that Breanna had known almost everyone here for so long that she couldn't remember a time when she hadn't—gave the place a harmless, friendly feel.

"I thought you might be out with Jake tonight," Gen remarked, giving Breanna a significant look.

Breanna didn't mention the fact that she had thought the same thing. Instead, she feigned surprise. "Really? Why? We went out yesterday."

"Yes, but when the chemistry's there, things can move fast. Once Ryan and I started seeing each other, we barely did anything else."

Breanna fidgeted with her beer mug. "Jake and I have had two dates."

"I knew Liam was the one after two dates," Aria put in. "I didn't want to admit it to myself, but I knew."

"Could we talk about something else?" Breanna asked irritably.

"Why?" Aria asked.

"Because it's Saturday night and he didn't call," Gen said, divining the source of Breanna's mood as surely as if she'd had a GPS map pointing to the spot.

"He doesn't have to call," Breanna insisted. "We saw each other yesterday, for God's sake."

"And how did that go?" Aria asked. Her thick, dark hair was pulled back into a ponytail, and her clingy T-shirt and skinny jeans showed off a figure that was lush and curvy. A number of the guys in the bar kept shooting looks at her, but Aria took no notice. There was no need for her to, since everyone knew she was with Liam, and nobody wanted to get their teeth extracted with Liam's fist if he found out they'd made a move.

"It was fine," Breanna said. Then she told herself to drop the pretense. She was among friends, and if she couldn't tell her sister-in-law and her future sister-in-law what was really going on in her love life, then who could she tell? Her shoulders dropped and she slumped a little in her chair. "It was great, actually. I mean, really great. He's warm and smart and easy to talk to."

"And hot," Gen added.

"Yes. And he's hot," Breanna agreed. "And he kissed me— more than once—which made me realize how long it's been since I've had sex. It's been a really long time."

"You could call him," Aria suggested.

"No, I couldn't."

"Why not?" she said. "Why should antiquated gender roles prevent you from—"

"It's not that," Breanna said, a hint of misery in her voice. She took a long drink from her beer to drown it.

"Then …" Aria began.

"She's trying to play it cool," Gen said. "She's trying not to be needy."

"I'm *not* needy," Breanna said. "I've been living without a man in my life for a long time now, and I've been doing all right."

"You have," Gen said soothingly. "But … maybe it's time for you to do better than all right."

Breanna had been thinking just that for a while now. She'd been all right, but she was starting to want more. Jake hadn't awakened those feelings in her—they'd been stirring for some time. But his arrival in her life had made the longing seem so much more real, so much more urgent.

"Call him," Aria said. "Go to his place. Strip naked and climb all over him. Simple." She shrugged, as though the whole thing were as easy as that.

"I can't do that. I have kids."

"Well, I assume they wouldn't be there," Aria said dryly.

"Just because you're a mother doesn't mean you stop being a woman," Gen said.

"I know that," Breanna shot back. "Don't you think I know that? But I can't just jump in with both feet. I have the boys to think about. I want to give this thing with Jake a chance, but I have to be careful. Whatever moves I make, I have to think about them. I have to know I'm doing the right thing. Because it's not just my life I'm dealing with."

And that, she thought, neatly summed up the last nine years of her life. Since Brian had been gone, all of Breanna's decisions had been not just about herself, but about the boys as well. It wasn't that she denied herself pleasure for their sakes. She wasn't a martyr, wasn't Saint Breanna. But the pleasures she did choose to indulge in had to be carefully chosen. She was no longer a kid who could blithely follow her heart. She was an adult woman with adult responsibilities.

"Kids do change everything," Gen reflected. She'd been a mother for just over a year, but Breanna knew that was enough for her to know. One day was enough.

"So. Taking it slow, then," Aria said. "If you're not going to call him, then you should probably try to stop thinking about him—for tonight, anyway. Who wants to play pool?"

The thing about Breanna, Jake thought over frozen pizza at his house on Saturday night, wasn't that she was beautiful—though she was—or that she was smart and thoughtful—though she was those things, too. The thing, when you got down to it, was that she seemed utterly familiar, as though he'd known her his whole life, had been separated from her so long he'd almost forgotten she existed, and now was finally reuniting with her after a long period of hard and painful deprivation.

He wasn't ready to feel those things after just two dates. He wanted to feel mild and intriguing interest, some attraction, while still being able to focus on other things.

He wanted thoughts of Breanna to be there at the outskirts of his life, ready to be brought forward at appropriate times but easily put back in their place when he needed to apply himself elsewhere.

Was that so much to ask for?

As it was, he'd had to actively force himself not to call her. He'd gone out with her yesterday, and when you went out with someone two days in a row, that was making a statement—a declaration that you were moving full steam ahead with whatever it was the two of you were doing.

Jake wasn't ready to make that kind of statement—not yet.

The fact that he was thinking of making that statement at all, and was having to actively restrain himself from doing it, was alarming.

Jake wasn't a guy who had trouble committing—he wasn't one of those clichéd males who used women for sex and then kept them otherwise at a safe distance. He could do emotional intimacy just fine.

The problem was that he was less than a year out from his divorce. Anybody with half a brain knew you didn't get into something serious with someone new that soon after having your ass handed to you.

There was a reason rebound relationships rarely worked. You were lonely and desperate for validation; you needed to prove that you could still be attractive to someone after your life had been thrown into a wood chipper. You made bad decisions in the interests of not feeling like shit for a change.

He normally trusted his instincts, but he couldn't trust them now, not when he hadn't fully regained his equilibrium.

He thought he recognized something in Breanna, yes. But maybe what he was really seeing was his own desperate longing to heal.

Still, frozen pizza sucked.

Feeling sorry for himself for being stuck at home eating DiGiorno on a Saturday night, he thought *screw self-pity* and called Mark Winslow. Mark had been bitching about his lack of a girlfriend for some time, so Jake figured it was a good bet that he'd be free.

He was.

A beer and some hot wings—or whatever kind of bar food they had at that dive just off Main Street—seemed like a better bet than a night of *Law and Order* reruns.

Chapter Fourteen

Jake had thought that an evening at a bar would take his mind off Breanna. So he froze in surprise when he walked into Ted's, scanned the crowd, and saw her at the pool tables talking to a curvy brunette.

"Shit," he muttered under his breath.

"What?" Mark squinted as he looked around, trying to divine the source of the problem.

"Breanna Delaney," Jake said, pointing to where she was bent over the table about to take a shot.

Mark, a big guy with a scruffy three-day beard, a receding hairline, and a weight issue, incorrectly interpreted the issue. "I don't think she's going to care that you're here drinking. I mean, you're not on the clock."

Jake let him think what he wanted to think. "Still …" he said.

Mark was a local, and he'd known Breanna casually for some time. "She's cool," he assured Jake. "She doesn't have a stick up her ass." He clapped Jake on the back companionably. "Let's get a table."

Breanna was about to hit the nine ball into the side pocket when she saw Jake heading toward a table in the center of the room. She noticed him midstroke, and her stick glanced off the edge of the cue ball, sending it skittering in a direction nowhere near where she'd intended.

"Good thing you're not playing for money," Aria remarked. Then her gaze followed Breanna's and landed on Jake. "Well, well."

"Take your turn," Breanna said.

"Aren't you going to—"

"Just take your turn."

Gen came back from the ladies' room and looked from Aria to Breanna and back again. "What happened? Something happened."

"He happened," Aria said, pointing at Jake.

"Ooh," Gen said.

"Would you please just take your turn?" Breanna asked Aria, desperate for them to change the subject.

"Aren't you going to go over and talk to him?" Gen said.

"No."

"Why not?"

"Because she's playing it cool," Aria said. "She's not going over there because she doesn't want him to know that she really wants to go over there."

"Right." Gen propped a hand on her hip and considered the situation. "He didn't call her, and she wants him to think that she wasn't waiting for him to call her because she has better things to do."

"I wasn't waiting," Breanna said. "I do have better things to do." She kept her back turned to Jake so they could avoid the dreaded moment of eye contact, when they would both have to decide how to play it.

"You have to go over there, though," Aria said, leaning on her pool cue. "If you don't, it's going to be weird."

"You could always go out the bathroom window," Gen suggested. "It's a pretty small window, though."

"I'm not going out the window," Breanna said. Then, to Aria: "Would you just take your turn?"

"Fine." Aria bent down, lined up her shot, and sank the three into a corner pocket.

Breanna knew that as a mature, adult woman, there was no reason she should feel awkward about seeing Jake here at Ted's. They'd dated a couple of times, and they liked each other, and they were on good terms. There was no reason either of them should not be here. So, what was the problem?

The problem, she thought in answer to her own question, was that he hadn't wanted to see her tonight. Otherwise, he would have called. So now she was in the position of having to go up and talk to him knowing that he'd planned—and even wanted—an evening without her in it.

But the alternative—ignoring him or taking the window option Gen had suggested—didn't seem viable.

So, she had to talk to him. What would she say? What should her tone of voice be when she said it?

She was still planning her approach, studiously looking at the wall rather than at Jake, when he decided the issue for her.

"Mind if I have the next game?"

His voice washed over her like warm water, and she became aroused just hearing it. Which wasn't a good sign when it came to her own sense of self-possession.

"You go ahead," Aria said, sounding perky. "We just finished. Here, you can use my cue." She handed it to him, and she and Gen hustled off to the bar, leaving him and Breanna alone.

They hadn't just finished—they were still in the middle of a game—but Breanna guessed that hardly mattered now. Jake gathered balls and began loading them into the rack.

"I didn't mean to interrupt your girls' night," he said, though he'd done just that.

Breanna looked over at Gen and Aria, who were huddled at a table whispering together and shooting covert looks this way. "They don't seem too put out about it," she said.

The guy Jake had come in with was busy chatting up a blonde at the bar. The woman was speaking to him animatedly, gesturing with hands adorned with multiple rings and brightly colored acrylic fingernails.

"Mark seems to be doing okay," Jake observed.

Jake took the break, but he didn't sink anything. Breanna lined up for her shot and put the six ball in the corner pocket.

"I was going to call you," Jake said.

Breanna straightened, put up a hand, and said, "Don't."

"Don't what?" Jake looked at her in surprise, his eyebrows raised.

"There's absolutely no reason you were obligated to call me. So, don't make excuses. There's no point, when we've only been out twice, and—"

"I wasn't going to make an excuse. I was going to tell you about a thing that happened. Are you going to shoot, or what?"

Flustered, Breanna looked at the table, then tried to put the five ball in the side pocket. It bounced off the bumper and careened helplessly across green felt.

"Okay," she said. "What's the thing that happened?"

"I was going to call you," he started again. "But then I thought, I can't call her for a date so soon after a date. That's going to seem desperate and pathetic. I need to play it cool. So I didn't call, even though I really wanted to. And then, in a futile attempt not to seem desperate and pathetic, I called Mark, a guy I barely know, to come to the bar with me so I wouldn't be sitting at home eating frozen pizza and watching *Wheel of Fortune*."

Charmed by his speech, she grinned. "Are you going to shoot, or what?"

"Right." Jake bent down, positioned his cue, and hit the eleven into the side on a nice rebound shot.

Deciding it was only fair to meet sincerity with more of the same, she said, "I wanted you to call. Then I decided that was desperate and pathetic, so I called Gen and Aria and made them come out with me so it would seem like I had something better to do than wait to hear from you."

Jake glanced at her from where he was bent over the table, a half grin on his face that made Breanna a little bit weak-kneed. "I guess we're both desperate and pathetic, then."

"I guess."

"Or," he said, "we just really like each other, and we don't have the patience for bullshit like playing it cool."

"Maybe that's it," she agreed.

Though she would never admit it outright—mostly because she didn't want to seem giddy and lovestruck—she was unreasonably pleased by the fact that he'd wanted to call her, and that he'd said he really liked her. She tried not to smile in a way that would give her away, but she couldn't seem to help it. She could feel the smile on her face, and there didn't seem to be much she could do about it.

The pool game was forgotten. They stood there with their cues in their hands, giving each other the goofy smiles of people who were about to fall hard, and who didn't much care about how they might land.

"Will you go out with me, Breanna? Right now? Playing it cool can go screw itself." The way he was looking at her made her stomach flutter not with butterflies, but with raw desire.

"Yes," she said.

•••

Jake guessed it might have been rude to leave Mark at the bar alone after they'd come here together. But Mark was making progress with the blonde, so when Jake approached him with his apology planned and ready to go, he didn't even have to use it.

"Mark," Jake began. "I know it's not cool of me, but—"

Mark pushed off his barstool, took Jake aside, and said, "You mind if I kind of, you know, do my own thing?" He put a hand on Jake's shoulder in a just-us-bros kind of way. "I think I can get Krista here to let me take her home."

Jake looked over at Krista, who did, indeed, seem amenable to whatever Mark might have in mind. That was a stroke of luck for both of them, it turned out.

Still, Jake had to give him a little bit of shit just for sport.

"Well, I don't know ..."

"Come on, man," Mark pleaded. "I haven't been laid in eight months. Eight fuckin' months."

"Aw, I guess," Jake said, looking profoundly put out.

"Thanks. I owe you. Here, have a round on me." Mark reached for his wallet.

"Save it," Jake said.

When Mark and Krista were gone, Jake looked around and saw Breanna talking to the two women she'd come with. She said something to them, and they laughed and looked at Jake. Then Breanna grabbed her purse and her coat and came over to where Jake was standing.

"All set," she said.

"Your friends okay with it?" he asked.

"They're my sisters-in-law. And yes, they're fine."

The women were wiggling their fingers at them in the kind of wave that said they knew what Jake and Breanna wanted to do to each other, and they very much approved.

"Let's go, then."

Chapter Fifteen

Since neither of them had anything planned, they grabbed some takeout Mexican from Medusa's on Main Street and took it to Jake's place, which was much more private than the always teeming Delaney Ranch.

Sam met them at the door in ecstasy, thrilled both that Jake hadn't abandoned him forever and that the scent of enchiladas and tacos was wafting from the bag in Jake's hand.

"Whoa, now," Jake said to the dog, holding the bag of food over his head as Sam planted his paws on Jake's shoulders and licked his face.

Breanna peered around Jake and into the living room, where a flurry of something white blanketed the sofa, the armchair, and the floor.

"Looks like he's been busy," she said.

Jake disentangled himself from Sam and looked into the room with trepidation. He walked over to the sofa, picked up a handful of white fluff, and exhaled. "Just a roll of paper towels," he said with some relief. "I was afraid he'd pulled the stuffing out of my favorite chair."

Breanna ran a hand through Sam's fur, the dog trembling happily. "Some training might not be a bad idea."

"I know, I know." Jake set the bag on the kitchen counter and started scooping bits of paper towel up with his hands. "I've been busy."

Breanna helped him clean up the paper towels while Sam watched innocently, his tongue lolling out and his tail wagging.

"Hang on. He's gonna eat our food if I don't put him away." Jake rummaged around in a kitchen cupboard for a chew toy—a piece of beef-flavored rawhide as big as Breanna's forearm—then put the dog and the toy into the bedroom and closed the door.

"You've got your hands full with him," Breanna said, amused.

"Yeah, well."

He told her the story of how he'd gotten Sam as a puppy without realizing the realities of the dog's breed.

"So, you had no idea he was going to be the size of a small ox," she summarized when he was finished.

"Live and learn," Jake said.

With Sam comfortably ensconced in the bedroom, Jake set out the food on the kitchen table and grabbed a couple of beers from the refrigerator. They ate and drank and talked, and when they were done with that and the trash was thrown away, they made out on Jake's sofa like a couple of teenagers.

The kissing was nice. Breanna sat wrapped around Jake, her mouth on his, their bodies pressed together. She liked the feel of Jake's strong arms around her and the sensation of his hands tangled in her hair.

When he slid his hands down to her ass, she liked having them there. She hadn't had a man put his hands on her with this kind of confidence, this kind of mastery, in so long. But when those hands started to move under her shirt, she backed up a little and gave him an apologetic smile.

"Let's maybe ... take a minute," she said.

"Okay." He ran his fingers through his hair, his breathing a little ragged. "Sorry if I overstepped."

"You didn't." She straightened her clothes a little. Her skin felt hot, and her heart was pounding. "I wanted to do that. I just think we should maybe slow it down a little."

"Yeah. Okay." She could see him mentally changing gears, adjusting to the fact that sex wasn't imminent. "You want to maybe watch some TV?"

"That would be nice."

They found a movie on Netflix—a comedy with just enough raunch to make Jake guffaw, but not enough to make Breanna wince—and they watched it on the sofa, his arm around her, Breanna leaning into the warm and comforting presence of his body.

Since they were done with dinner, they let Sam out of the bedroom, and he jumped up next to Breanna, taking up fully half of the sofa.

Breanna thought it was a nearly perfect date.

The next day, both Gen and Aria showed up at the house early, wanting to know what happened.

"So? Did you do the deed?" Aria asked as the three of them gathered around the kitchen table with thick white mugs of coffee. In the center of the table was a basket of banana muffins Sandra had baked that morning.

"No, we did not do the deed," Breanna said, a hint of scorn in her voice.

"But why not?" Gen asked.

"Because it was our third date." Breanna spent a lot of time getting the cream and sugar ratio in her coffee just right, partly because it allowed her to avoid looking at the other women.

"I read somewhere that a new couple starts having sex on the fourth date, on average," Gen said thoughtfully. "Though I have to think the one-nighters and the wait-until-marriage crowd skew the statistics."

"Well, then we have one more date before we should even be thinking about it," Breanna said, as though having empirical evidence on her side decided the matter.

"She didn't say that," Aria put in. "If they were to study when people start *thinking* about it …"

"It's probably in the first five minutes," Gen concluded.

"I'm thinking about it," Breanna admitted. "A lot."

Aria picked a muffin out of the basket, broke off a piece, and popped it into her mouth. "So what did you two do last night, if you weren't getting busy?"

Breanna told them about how she and Jake had eaten take-out Mexican at his house and then had watched a movie.

"You were at his house," Gen said. "And nothing happened?"

"Well …" Breanna fidgeted with a muffin. "I didn't say *nothing* happened."

She filled them in about how things had started getting intense on the sofa before she'd stopped.

"I just don't want to make a mistake," Breanna said.

"That kind of mistake is the best kind," Aria said.

Gen nodded wordlessly.

"I'm not nineteen anymore," Breanna told them, feeling a little sorry for herself because of the burden of responsibility. "I have kids. I have obligations. I have to think ahead, and I have to act like a mature adult."

"I get that," Gen said thoughtfully. "I mean, I haven't been a mother for long, but it changes you. Everything I do now, everything I think, is all viewed through the lens of J.R. How's it going to affect him? Is it good for him, or is it going to ruin his emotional development forever?"

"Exactly," Breanna said. "And your kid has two parents to worry about his emotional development. Mine only have me."

"You know, the whole making out on the sofa thing, only going to first base? That's kind of sweet." Gen's muffin, only half-eaten, sat on a plate in front of her. She broke off a small piece and held it between two fingers. "There's something to be said for taking it slow."

"Yeah, now that you mention it," Aria agreed. "By the time you two get around to doing it, the anticipation is going to be intense." She raised her eyebrows significantly.

If and when Breanna and Jake got together—and she was certain it would be *when* rather than *if*—she suspected it would make the wait worthwhile.

Jake woke up the next morning feeling perkier than he had any right to be, given the fact that his sexual tension had gone unreleased.

Well, mostly unreleased. Once Breanna went home, what he might have done in private was nobody's business.

The general wisdom among men was that getting all amped up for sex and then not getting it was a torture on par with having your fingernails ripped out one by one. But Jake was finding that he didn't much mind the pain. The flirtatious dance that led up to sex was nice, and the idea of prolonging it was surprisingly appealing.

And why shouldn't she take some time to decide whether she really liked him? Why shouldn't he take the same time to decide about her? That kind of thing tended to get lost these days. Why not ease into things and enjoy the process?

He thought about all of that as he sipped his morning coffee on the back porch of his house in the Happy Hill neighborhood overlooking downtown and Moonstone Beach.

The sun was bright, but there was a hint of nip in the February air. A group of three deer had wandered past a few minutes ago, and now the golden grass and the pine trees swishing in the breeze were the only movement.

He had a big, free Sunday stretching out in front of him, and he considered what to do with it.

He wouldn't have minded working—he liked working—but his guys had families and lives to attend to, and most of them wouldn't have looked as favorably on a weekend spent swinging a hammer as he did.

He had a few guys he could call to go see a movie or take a hike up at Big Sur, so that was a possibility. He could do some work around the house—the front porch had a floorboard that looked to have some wood rot.

Yeah, he could do any of those things. But whenever he considered a scenario for his day, his thoughts went back to Breanna.

At first, the thoughts were about sex. Would they do it? When would they do it? Would it be as good as he expected? What would happen between them afterward?

But soon, he started to think about the bigger picture. Where would things go between them if they kept seeing each other? She had kids, and he wasn't sure if that was good or bad. He liked kids, but he'd never had any of his own, so he figured he was about as qualified to parent one as he was to build a jumbo jet out of spare parts.

Thinking about kids, and about the fact that he'd never had any, made him start to think about his ex-wife.

Usually, thinking about his ex was an unpleasant experience, one he tried to avoid whenever possible. But now, it seemed like thinking about her might be helpful, even necessary.

The split had not been especially acrimonious, as far as these things went. Even so, it was about as much fun as an unmedicated root canal—one that lasted eighteen months.

Beth had been the one who'd decided to leave. Jake never would have done it on his own. In retrospect, that was only because he was too much of a pussy to take care of business, the way Beth had.

She'd always been the kind to just dig in and do what had to be done, and the divorce had been no different.

There had been a lot of arguing—there had always been a lot of arguing—and then, suddenly, there wasn't. That should have been his first red flag. Once she'd made her decision to go, she hadn't even cared enough to get into it with him anymore.

The leaving part hadn't been a big, emotional scene. He'd come home from work one day and she'd had some boxes packed and stacked up in the front hallway. She'd been businesslike. She'd given him the phone number and address where she'd be staying, and said she'd send someone to pick up the boxes. Then she'd simply walked out the door.

He wasn't really surprised—that was the thing. Even a day earlier, if someone had asked him, he'd have said they were fine. But when it actually came to her packing up her things and leaving their apartment, he'd thought, *there it is,* as though he'd been expecting just this for some time.

The issues between them didn't look like much on paper. He didn't like LA, but she loved the busy vibe of the city. She wanted to go to graduate school, but he didn't think they could afford it. He wanted kids, but she wanted to focus on her education and the career that would result.

Yes, they were substantial issues, but nothing that couldn't be worked out, surely. They were the kinds of things couples negotiated every day. Except Jake and Beth didn't negotiate. They argued, and then they didn't. And then she left.

He'd learned to cope with the fact of the breakup, and he'd made peace with the idea that if things had blown up the way they had, then they weren't right together in the first place.

But the thing that still nagged at him was the question of what he'd done wrong and whether he would do it again if he got into another serious relationship. He wasn't enough of an asshole to think everything had been Beth's fault. But if it wasn't hers, then it had to be at least partly his. And he still didn't have a handle on what he should have done differently, if anything.

Maybe they just weren't a match.

If that was the case, then at the very least, it meant he was crap at choosing a mate for himself. What made him think he'd do any better the next time around?

Sam, apparently sensing a certain amount of angst, came over to where Jake was sitting and rested his big head on Jake's leg.

Jake scratched him behind his ears as the sun rose higher in the sky, glinting through a copse of pine trees.

Jake didn't have any answers, but he knew he wanted to see Breanna again, soon and as often as possible.

As he sat there petting his dog, Jake thought about Breanna, and about her sons, and about how he could see her again, and often, without being obvious about it.

A tiny kernel of an idea came to him, and he rolled it around in his head a little, looking at it from different angles to see if it would hold up.

He remembered what Breanna had told him about her oldest boy and how he was developing an attitude about school, about hard work, and about the impending move.

Jake wanted something. Michael needed something. Breanna was caught in the middle.

Maybe there was a way to help everybody.

Chapter Sixteen

Breanna was thinking about Jake while trying not to think about him. That was working about as well as could be expected—you could go your whole life without thinking about purple pigs, but as soon as you told yourself not to think about them, they started dancing through your imagination in shades of lavender, plum, and lilac.

The only thing to do was dig into her usual routine, focusing on her day-to-day tasks instead of on the question of when she might be able to kiss him again.

Midday Sunday, she helped her mother make lunch for the family, which included Orin, Ryan and Gen, Liam and Aria, and both of the boys. Afterward, there was the cleanup to attend to.

Then she put in a load of laundry for herself and the boys; instructed Michael and Lucas to clean their rooms, and scolded them when they didn't do it the first time she asked; weeded the vegetable garden and harvested some leeks and kale; and, with that done, went over to the Whispering Pines to put in a couple of hours helping Mrs. Granfield.

The idea, she supposed, was that tiring herself out would make her forget about Jake, and about the possibility of sex.

But that goal got shot utterly to hell around four p.m., when Jake sent her a text message.

I've got an idea I want to run by you. Can we get together?

Breanna stood behind the reception desk at the Whispering Pines and stared at her phone. What kind of idea was he talking about? White cabinetry in the kitchen at the Moonstone Beach house instead of cherry? Another date? A naked sex romp at his place?

The sheer number of possible directions this could go had her mind spinning.

She wrote back: *What kind of idea?*

The answer came just seconds later, but it did nothing to satisfy her curiosity.

I'll tell you when we talk, he wrote. *Pizza at JJ's? 6:00?*

That would, in fact, be another date. But the idea he'd spoken of couldn't have been the date itself, because he wanted to spend the date talking about the idea.

Thinking about it was beginning to make her head hurt, so she typed back: *I'll meet you there.*

This was doing nothing to get her mind off possible sex.

And that thought reminded her that she needed to take a bottle of champagne and a vase of roses up to one of the guest rooms. At least someone was going to get their frustrations relieved.

J.J.'s Pizza was popular with the locals but it wasn't much of a tourist draw, tucked off to one end of Main Street away from the boutiques and the more upscale restaurants that attracted the weekend crowds.

Breanna slid into a booth across from Jake at five after six. The extra five minutes had been spent greeting several people she knew who were out on the patio with sandwiches and beer.

"Sorry," she said as she settled in. "It's hard to do anything around here without stopping to chat with people along the way."

"I can see that," he said. "LA was the opposite. I could go days at a time without talking to anyone but my Starbucks barista. And even she got my name wrong."

Breanna laughed. "How did she mess up *Jake*?"

"She wrote it as *Jack* so many times that I considered changing my name just to make things easier."

They consulted on their food and drink options, then Jake got up to order for both of them at the counter. Breanna couldn't help noticing how good he looked from the rear in a pair of jeans.

When Jake turned back toward her and noticed her looking, she blushed and then scolded herself. She was an adult woman acting like a giddy, lovesick girl, for God's sake.

Have a little dignity, she told herself.

Then again, where did it say that a dignified, adult woman couldn't appreciate a nicely formed male behind? She had eyes, after all. Was she not supposed to use them?

The little grin on Jake's face when he came back to the table suggested that he hadn't minded being ogled, and had possibly enjoyed it. He slid into the booth across from Breanna and folded his arms on the table.

"So, what did you want to talk about?" Breanna fervently hoped that getting down to business would restore some of her equilibrium. If it didn't work, it might still get both of their minds off of his ass.

"How are your kids doing?" he asked.

She waved a hand airily. "Oh, the same. Lucas is fun and happy and talkative, and Michael is sullen and withdrawn. Whenever I bring up the move, he makes some kind of remark about how I'm tearing him away from his home. He asked if he could keep living at the ranch. Without me! He's my son. Of course he's going to live with me."

The subject was making her feel upset and agitated, and she didn't want to feel those things. So she took a deep breath to calm her mind, then gave him a bright smile. "You didn't invite me here to talk about that," she said.

He leaned in and looked at her thoughtfully. "Actually, I did."

"You did?"

A tattooed guy with an apron around his waist showed up with their pizza, and Breanna waited until he'd set it down and left.

"What do you mean?" she asked.

"I had an idea," he said.

He'd mentioned an idea in his text message, but she'd forgotten that in the haze of lust she'd felt after watching his ass. Now, she was intrigued.

"Okay, shoot. What's the idea?"

Jake wasn't sure what Breanna would think of his plan. He wasn't sure if he was stepping into something that was none of his business, or if his concept would even work. But it seemed like a way to kill two or more birds with one proverbial stone. He could see Breanna more often. He could get to know her family. He could maybe even help her out with a problem that was bothering her.

It was a win-win.

Or a lose-lose, depending on how it went.

"I wondered if maybe Michael could help work on the house," he told her.

She sat back, eyebrows raised. "You did?"

"Sure."

"But—"

"Just listen for a second." He explained his thoughts. If Michael could spend some time working on the Moonstone Beach house, it would accomplish several things: He could learn some new skills. He could work out some of his aggressions by hammering nails. He could get to know Jake a little, which would help if he and Breanna continued dating. And, most importantly, he could develop a sense of personal investment in the house that would soon become his home.

Having laid out all of his arguments, Jake sat back and crossed his arms over his chest. "So, what do you think?"

Breanna didn't answer right away. She looked at him for a moment, then picked up a slice of pizza and took a bite.

"Isn't that going to make your job harder?" she asked after a while.

"Maybe a little," Jake allowed. "I mean, yeah, I'm going to have to take the time to supervise him, teach him a few things, keep him safe on the job site. But he's not a little kid. He should manage fine."

Jake had no idea if that last part was true. Michael was old enough to do the work, but the question of how he would manage remained to be seen. Though it seemed like it was worth a shot, at least.

"*Hmm*," Breanna said. "It's an interesting idea." She took another bite of her pizza and chewed thoughtfully. "A very interesting idea."

Later, at home, Breanna reflected that her pizza meeting with Jake hadn't exactly been a date, but it had been both enjoyable and intriguing.

What if she let Michael work on the house? Jake was right—if Michael put some of his own time and effort into the renovations, it might make him feel that the house was really his. Plus, Breanna had been babying Michael. He needed more hard work in his life in the Delaney tradition.

Michael had been rude and unpleasant whenever the subject of Jake arose. She'd tried to reassure him that there was nothing serious going on—at least, not yet—but he was hostile toward the very idea of his mother having a man in her life. If he got a chance to know Jake, it would be a lot harder to hate him.

Of course, there was another side to that part of it. What if Michael got to know Jake and started to really like him? Then, what if things didn't work out? Would she be introducing a strong male role model into her son's life only to yank him away?

The boys were in their rooms, each of them flopped on their beds looking at their cell phones. Breanna went into her own room and took out her own phone.

"You'd have to keep our relationship out of it," she said, without introduction, as soon as Jake picked up the phone. "Not that we have a *relationship*, exactly. Yet. I mean, we *might*. But …"

"Go on," he prompted her.

"You'd have to keep it about the house, the work, that kind of thing. Chatting about school. Keep it light."

"You don't want me presenting myself as his new future stepdad," Jake put in.

She let out a little gasp. Stepdad? Did he think she wanted marriage? Was he worried that she was taking things too far too fast? "Wait, wait …"

Jake laughed. "Don't worry. I was joking. I just meant that I get it. We don't know what this is yet—this thing with you and me. So there's no need to bring him into it."

She let out a breath and relaxed a little. "Right. That's exactly right. But if you're willing to give it a try, I'm open to it."

"Ask him what he thinks," Jake said. "Put the balloon out there and see if it floats."

Chapter Seventeen

The balloon didn't float at first—it sank like it was made of bricks and fruitcake. So Breanna decided to get it up in the air by any means necessary—even if she had to use a catapult.

"I'd like you to give it a try," she said mildly as Michael sulked at the breakfast table. "You might even enjoy it."

"Sure. Right. I'm going to enjoy hammering things and carrying boards and stuff around so we can move out of our *home*." He said the last word with so much pathos that Breanna almost faltered. Almost, but not quite.

"You said you don't want to go to school," she reminded him. "If that's the case, then you're going to have to learn a trade. Maybe construction will be an option if ranching isn't to your taste."

She delivered the lines straight, with no hint of sarcasm or irony. She could tell from the look on Michael's face that he was trying to figure out whether she was playing him.

"It's not like you're going to let me stop going to school anyway," he said, wary.

"Probably not," she admitted. "But there's the question of college. If you decide not to go, you're going to need a backup plan."

He seemed to consider that. After a while, he looked at her hopefully. "Do you think I'd get to use a nail gun?"

"Anything's possible," Breanna said.

Michael started work on a Tuesday after school. His last class let out at three p.m., and Breanna had him over at the Moonstone Beach work site by three thirty.

That schedule worked, Jake thought, because they usually knocked off at around five, and an hour and a half of hard labor was probably all he could expect out of a thirteen-year-old with an attitude.

And anyway, if the kid held him back, it would only be for a small part of the workday.

The boy had his mother's dark hair and deep brown eyes. But unlike his mother, Michael wore a pissed-off scowl that made Jake begin to reevaluate whether he really wanted to work with him.

"Hey, there, Mike," Jake said in his best friendly adult voice.

"It's Michael." Fair enough, but the kid said it like he meant *go fuck yourself.*

"Michael it is, then." Jake put a companionable hand on Michael's shoulder, and the boy shook it off.

"You're being rude," Breanna told her son.

"Whatever," the kid said.

Jake pretty much figured the boy would do nothing but sulk. But to his surprise, Michael did what he was told, even if his attitude didn't improve much. Jake was in the middle of framing a wall for the addition to the guesthouse, so he gave Michael a hammer and some nails and showed him where to use them.

As Michael moved, he gave the impression that his body was too long and skinny to fit him—a sure sign that he'd just been through a major growth spurt. Jake remembered that awkward period from his own adolescence, when his pants were perpetually too short and his facial features looked like they'd been cobbled together from spare parts.

"You're choking up too much on the hammer," Jake told him. "You need to hold it closer to the end of the handle, like this."

"I thought there was gonna be a nail gun," Michael groused.

"There is," Jake said. "But not for you."

"Why not?"

"I'm afraid you'd shoot me with it."

Jake thought he caught a hint of a smile—not that Michael would ever have admitted it.

At the end of the workday, Jake drove Michael home to the ranch, Sam whining in the back seat because he usually rode shotgun and had been displaced. Jake could have just dropped Michael off, but he walked him to the front door instead, in hopes of seeing Breanna.

As it happened, she was the one who answered the door, and Jake felt himself flush with pleasure at the sight of her. Which was probably a bad sign in terms of the potential anguish and heartbreak in his future.

Right now, none of that seemed to matter.

"I told you I'd bring him back in one piece," Jake said, pleased with himself.

"So, how did it go?" Breanna asked her son.

"Fine." Michael pushed past her and into the house.

"He actually did pretty well for his first day," Jake told her. He was standing on the front porch, sunlight slanting onto him through the trees. Breanna looked fresh and young, her face bare of makeup, her hair pulled back into a loose ponytail. He wanted nothing more than to pull her to him and kiss her, though he managed, just barely, to keep the urge in check.

"Did he behave himself?" she asked, coming out onto the porch and closing the front door behind her.

"He did okay."

And he had, Jake figured. He could deal with a pissy attitude as long as the kid followed directions and stayed safe—which he'd done. And anyway, Jake knew better than to criticize a mother bear's cub, even when the mother bear was as appealing as Breanna.

"Do you think he liked it?" she asked.

Jake let out a laugh. "Well, I wouldn't go that far. But this was just the first day. I'll bring him around."

He had no idea whether he would, in fact, be able to bring Michael around. But it sounded good when he said it, so he just went with that.

"I don't know if I should laugh at your naïveté or be grateful," Breanna said.

"Laugh now, then be grateful if I actually manage it," he suggested.

They'd begun drifting closer to each other as they talked, and now they were just inches apart. Jake imagined that he could feel the warmth of her body from here, though that probably was wishful thinking.

"How was your day?" he asked. His voice was low, a kind of sexual purr that he hadn't intended but couldn't seem to prevent.

"Challenging." She said the word with a whisper of a smile that he imagined she might have on her face during sex. Not that he should be thinking of sex—though right now, with her standing so close to him, the thoughts flew into his head unbidden.

"Yeah?"

"I couldn't keep my mind on anything I was doing. I seem to be easily distracted these days." She touched the neckline of his T-shirt with her finger, then drew the fingertip slowly down his chest.

Breanna hadn't meant to touch him, but here she was, doing it. She hadn't meant to flirt, but she'd thrown out that line about being distracted, a distinct sensual caress in her voice when she'd said it.

Why didn't she just strip down and throw her naked body at him, for God's sake? And now *that* thought was in her head, making it even less likely that she'd start acting like the responsible grown-up she wanted to be.

"I ... uh ..." He cleared his throat. "I might be a little distracted myself."

They were supposed to be talking about Michael, weren't they? Her son? The reason Jake was here?

But the way Jake was looking at her, mussed from work, his T-shirt clinging to his hard, muscled body, his mouth ...

Oh, God, his mouth ...

Later, she would not be able to say which one of them had kissed the other first. She only knew that the kiss was happening, warm and urgent, his arms wrapped around her, her body pressed tightly against his.

She forgot everything, all thoughts of responsibility and parenthood, everything but the feel of being held in his arms and being completely, thoroughly kissed.

•••

"We're on your parents' front porch," Jake murmured against Breanna's neck. His heart was pounding and his body was reacting to her in ways both intense and predictable. But somewhere in the middle of the kiss, some dim, distant part of his mind was calling for caution.

"*Hmm?*" Breanna seemed to have barely heard him.

He nuzzled her ear with his lips. "Your family ..." he tried again.

"Oh."

The response indicated that she'd heard him, and yet neither of them seemed to be pulling back.

"Breanna."

"*Hmm?*"

His lips were on her neck, and he felt the vibration through her skin. "It's just ... I think ... someone's watching."

That got her attention. Her eyes, which had been at half-mast moments ago, flew open, and her head snapped around as she looked back at the house.

A curtain at the window next to the door had been pulled aside, and Gen was grinning, flashing Breanna a double thumbs-up.

"Is that general approval of the two of us, or a commentary on our technique?" Jake wondered.

Jake seemed amused by the situation, but Breanna wasn't. It didn't matter what Gen saw; Gen knew everything anyway and had been urging Breanna to throw off her inhibitions and go for it. But what if that had been Michael at the window? What if it had been Lucas?

She didn't imagine either of them would be scarred by the sight of someone kissing. But Breanna hadn't yet told them that Jake was more than a friend. She wanted to introduce them to the idea in her own time, in the right way. She didn't want them to find out like this.

Breanna waved Gen away, then turned to Jake, feeling the flush of embarrassment on her cheeks.

"I ... kind of forgot where we were," she said.

"Yeah. Me too."

They stood a couple of feet away from each other, him with his hands stuffed into his pockets, her with her arms crossed over her chest as if to ward off any further uncontrolled passion.

"If one of the boys had seen us ..."

"You've told them we're dating, right?" Jake asked.

"Well ... not exactly."

The look on his face—was that just surprise, or was he hurt, too?

"Jake—"

"Yeah. All right." He rubbed at the stubble on his chin with his hand. "I get it."

"We should talk about this."

"That's all right. Hey, I guess I'd better go." He turned and walked down the steps and off of the porch, then got into his car and left without another word.

Chapter Eighteen

Jake felt like an idiot.

She didn't owe him anything. They'd only been out a few times; it wasn't like they had some kind of commitment. So why was he bent out of shape that she hadn't told her kids she was seeing him?

He was acting like they were sixteen and she'd refused to wear his letterman's jacket.

Don't be an asshole, he told himself. *Grow the hell up.*

But as much as he didn't want to feel hurt, it didn't change the fact that he did. Because it all came back to the question of *why* she hadn't told them, and he didn't like any of the potential answers.

One: Maybe she didn't think they'd last. If she didn't tell her kids and things didn't work out for them, she could pretend it had never happened. And, hell, it was true that maybe they wouldn't last. But it sure as hell was happening, and he didn't like the idea of it being erased from her reality—a fact so insignificant it was like it didn't exist.

Two: Maybe she thought her family wouldn't approve. And why the hell should they, now that he thought about it? They were, collectively, billionaires—or so he'd read on the financial websites he'd found when he'd Googled her. He was just a contractor, a blue-collar guy with modest credit card debt and furniture that was either secondhand or from Ikea.

Or three: She was embarrassed by him, and she didn't want to be seen with a working-class stiff like himself.

Rationally, he didn't believe either of the last two options. He knew enough about the Delaneys to know that they lived simply, like regular people who didn't have a net worth equal to the GDP of a small country. They didn't seem like rich people, and they didn't seem like snobs.

Still, the idea nagged at him that he wasn't good enough—or that Breanna thought he wasn't.

He drove away from the ranch cursing himself for being such an imbecile, his truck bumping over the rough unpaved road that led off of the property.

What did he expect? They'd had a few dates, they'd made out a couple of times. Did he expect her to present him to her family as her significant other?

Which led him back to the idea that he *wasn't* significant—not to her.

"Man, I'm losing it," he said to Sam, who sat happily in the front seat now that it was once again available. "I'd better get a fuckin' grip."

Sam didn't disagree.

Breanna wasn't sure what had gone wrong with Jake, but she knew something had. He'd left so abruptly, with his entire demeanor transformed from just moments before.

Surely it wasn't because she hadn't told the kids about him.

Was it?

She went back into the house, where Gen was waiting for her.

"He left in a hurry," Gen commented. "It seemed like things were going well. What happened?"

"You were spying on us," Breanna said.

"Maybe a little," Gen admitted. "So, what was that about?"

Breanna's shoulders slumped. "I told him that the kids don't know we're dating."

"Sure they do," Gen said. "They've got eyes. They've got ears. They're not dumb."

"Right. But I haven't *told* them," she said.

They stood together in the front room, near the window where Gen had been looking out. Gen looked thoughtful, while Breanna's face was creased with worry.

"He's getting serious," Gen said.

"What? No, he isn't."

"He is," Gen insisted. "There's only one reason a guy gets upset because his girlfriend hasn't told her kids about him. And that's because he's getting serious and he's afraid she's not."

"I'm not his girlfriend," Breanna said. "We've only dated a few times. I'm not his ... anything!"

"Well, he wants to be your something," Gen said. "So you'd better start thinking about whether you want that, too."

The idea that Jake wanted to be Breanna's *something* weighed on her as she went to work at the B&B the next day.

She knew she was attracted to Jake—*strongly* attracted—but she didn't know where she wanted this to go. Did she want to have a fling with him? Date him? Marry him?

The first option just wasn't her style. And the last was such a foreign and frightening prospect that she might as well be juggling chainsaws.

That left the second option.

Okay, so they were dating.

That was fine—dating was a normal thing that normal people did. Just because she hadn't done it in a few years didn't mean it was over for her, gold watch on her wrist, her jersey number retired.

She could do this.

But Jake had to understand that she couldn't jump into something impulsively. She had to take her time, for her children's sake. She had to be careful.

Breanna considered all of that as she stashed her purse behind the front desk at the Whispering Pines and went about her tasks—checking the coffee urn in the kitchen to make sure it was full and the sugar and cream were refreshed; looking in on the vacant rooms and freshening them up for the arrival of new guests; tidying up the common rooms; and checking in with Mrs. Granfield to see whether anything else needed her attention.

Mrs. Granfield had an appointment with her physical therapist, and she'd been waiting for Breanna so she could get going.

"The Jordans are checking in at four, so please have some fresh cookies in their room. Oh, and Mr. Jordan requested roses for his wife. Isn't that sweet?" Mrs. Granfield was gathering her purse and her sweater.

"The Jordans? Any relation to Lacy Jordan over at Jitters?"

Mrs. Granfield looked thoughtful. "You know, I believe they might be. They said something about their niece recommending the place."

"We'll have to impress them, then," Breanna said. "Don't worry, I'll have everything ready."

"I'm sure you will, dear. You know, I feel terrible putting you to so much work. I should be able to walk up the stairs again soon. In the meantime, if I could just pay you a little something ..."

"We've talked about this," Breanna said. "I'm here to help. You'd better get going or you're going to be late for your therapy."

"But there's no reason I couldn't—"

"Bye! You're ride's here! You'd better hurry!" Breanna gently turned Mrs. Granfield around by the shoulders and nudged her toward the door.

When she was gone, Breanna checked the clock, saw that she had a good bit of time before the Jordans' arrival, and spent a few minutes reviewing the reservation book to see what was coming up over the next few days.

After that came the laundry—there was a load of clean sheets in the dryer that had to be folded.

The problem with folding sheets was that it was busy work that didn't require any thought. Which meant she had time to brood some more about Jake and about the way he'd left the ranch angry—or at least irritated.

What right did he have to be angry? So she hadn't told her children they were dating. So what? Who said that was a requirement at this stage? Where was that in the rule book?

But what if he hadn't been angry? What if he'd just been hurt?

You'd know that if you'd talked to him, she reminded herself. *But you're a coward.*

She hadn't called or texted him since yesterday, though she'd picked up her phone to do just that at least a dozen times.

Each of those times, she'd had another excuse not to call him:

If he's angry, I should give him time to cool off.

If he's angry, then he's being a jerk, and I don't want to encourage that kind of behavior.

I don't know what to say. I'll call him when I've thought more about it.

I don't even know what he's upset about. How can I start a conversation if I don't know what's going on?

And then, working up a head of self-righteous steam:

The way I handle my boys is my business, and he's just going to have to get used to that.

He's the one who should apologize. If he wants to talk to me, he'll call.

By the time the Jordans had checked in at four, he still hadn't called. She hadn't taken Michael to the work site today—much to Michael's relief—because she hadn't wanted to face Jake until she knew what was going on with him.

Finally, telling herself that she'd had enough of immaturity—both his and hers—she grabbed her phone and tapped in a text message before she could talk herself out of it.

What the hell's your problem?

She hit SEND before it even occurred to her that her wording wasn't exactly an example of mature discourse.

Now that it was out there, she couldn't call it back. Why in the world hadn't someone invented a way to recall a faulty text message?

She was just about to write another message—some desperate story about how her phone had become sentient and had begun sending messages on its own, maybe—when his reply came in.

I don't have a problem. I don't have secret relationships, either.

Breanna blinked. Was that what they had? A relationship?

We should talk, she wrote after a while.

There was a long pause. Just when she was sure he wasn't going to answer, her phone pinged with his response.

Sure. When?

Chapter Nineteen

The thing was, Jake didn't think the sentence *we should talk* ever led to anything good.

It led to many significant things: breakups, divorce, cancer diagnoses, firings. Probably more than one criminal investigation. But it rarely led to anything a person could actually look forward to.

We should talk. You've won the lottery. Yeah, that wasn't going to happen.

He wasn't going to be devastated if he got dumped so early into this thing with Breanna. He wasn't so naïve as to believe a few dates meant anything. Except they had kind of meant something to him. Otherwise, why had it bothered him so much that she hadn't told her kids?

In any case, he resolved to man up and act mature and reasonable when Breanna gave him the news that she was done. He wasn't about to act like a wounded, kicked puppy. If he felt like that once it was all over, well, that was his own business.

They'd agreed to meet upstairs at Cambria Coffee before work the next morning. They got a table upstairs, away from the crowd down on the sidewalk of Main Street. Jake had a black coffee—its stark severity seemed appropriate for a dumping— and Breanna had tea, the tag hanging outside the lid of her cup.

He'd decided to be preemptive, so he launched right into it as soon as they sat down.

"Look. There's no reason this has to affect our working relationship. I'm going to be completely professional about your renovation, so you don't have to worry about that. If you still want Michael to come over and help out, I can do that, too, though if you've changed your mind about that ..."

"What are you talking about?" She was looking at him as though he were speaking some unknowable foreign language.

"I want you to know that just because we're not seeing each other anymore—"

"We're not? Oh .... You don't want to see me anymore?"

The hurt and surprise on her face shot straight into his gut.

"I thought that was what you wanted to talk about," he told her. "You said, 'We should talk.' "

"I meant we should talk about when to tell the boys about us. But ... you want to break up? Not that this is a relationship, exactly. Yet. But—"

"Hell, no." Jake had to quickly recalibrate his mental state. Relief and confusion flooded him in equal measure. "No, no, no. It's just that when you said 'We should talk,' I thought—"

"You thought it was *that* talk."

"Yeah." He scrubbed at his face with his hands. "Shit. Can we just ... you know ... start over? Hit the reset button?"

"Please."

So they did, starting with each of them clarifying their intentions. He wanted to keep seeing her, and she wanted to keep seeing him—thank God. With that out of the way, they were finally able to get to the actual purpose of the talk.

"I wanted to explain why I didn't tell the boys," she said, fidgeting with the tag of her tea bag, which was dangling outside the cup. "Jake, it's not about you. I haven't dated much since

Brian died, but when I have, I've tried to keep the boys out of it. They don't need to get attached to someone and then deal with that loss if it doesn't work out. When I tell my boys that I'm seeing someone, it'll be because it's serious. Because I anticipate the person staying around."

"Don't you think they already know something's going on?"

"I'm sure they do," she said. "But it's one thing for them to *think* something's going on, and it's another for me to bring somebody home for dinner and announce that I have a boyfriend."

He nodded. "Yeah, okay. I can see that."

"I lost my right to act impulsively when I lost Brian. I'm the only parent those boys have."

"I get it." He reached out and put a hand on her arm, and was grateful when she didn't pull it away. "I thought …"

"What? Tell me."

He didn't want to tell her that he'd thought he wasn't good enough for her, that maybe he didn't meet up to the Delaney standards. It seemed a little silly now, in comparison to her concerns as a widowed mother. Still …

"I thought maybe your family wouldn't approve of me." Better to get his cards on the table.

She looked surprised, and the surprise seemed genuine.

"What? Why not?"

He shrugged. "I'm a contractor. I make a decent living, I guess, but nothing like what you must be used to."

Something in her eyes hardened, and he knew he'd made a mistake.

"I married a Marine. Do you think they get paid in piles of gold bars?"

"No. Shit. I just …"

"I don't know what you think of me or my family, but you don't know us if you think we're going to look down on you because you work for a living. Do you know what my brothers do? What my father does? They're up every day before dawn, out there with the cattle, working their asses off."

"Breanna—"

"I have to get going. I have *work* to do." She got up and walked out, leaving him sitting there with his coffee and his regret.

"God, I made a mess of that." Breanna was standing in Gen's gallery later that morning, needing to talk to someone. "Why did I do that? Why did I walk out like that?"

"It's not like his insecurity about the money was completely out of left field. Guys are like that. They want to be the bread-winner."

"I know!" Breanna threw her hands skyward in exasperation. "But that's just it. Brian was always so insecure about the money. We fought about it I don't know how many times. He could never get past it. Sometimes I wondered why he even married me."

"He married you because he loved you," Gen said gently.

"Yeah. Yeah, he did." Tears shimmered in her eyes. "And I loved him. But I don't want to set myself up for that again. For the fighting, the constant ego-stroking ..."

"Then you shouldn't," Gen said. "You're only a few dates into this. And that's what dating is for. To see if the other person's baggage is something you're willing to haul around. If it's not"—she shrugged—"you put it down."

"Right." Breanna nodded firmly. "You're right. I just ... haven't felt like this about anyone in a really long time."

Gen rubbed Breanna's upper arm with gentle, circular strokes. "Give it a little time. Slow things down. Give him a chance to put down the baggage himself."

She hoped he would. Because despite her feelings, despite her lust, despite the fact that he made her feel wants and needs and *life* that she hadn't felt in so very long, she was too smart to repeat old mistakes.

She valued herself and her boys too much.

Breanna vowed to take a step back. But that didn't mean work on the Moonstone Beach house had to stop. And it also didn't mean Michael couldn't continue to help with it.

She dropped Michael off at the work site after school, telling herself that there was no need for a big, dramatic scene with Jake. He'd said some things, and she'd overreacted to those things. Now, they could just move forward in a mature, sensible fashion.

Michael was complaining about having to do the work when the two of them got out of the car.

"Why can't I just go home?" he moaned. "I was at school all day. I just want to chill."

"You can chill tonight after dinner," she told him.

"No, I can't, because I have homework." He scowled at her, and she recognized that look—she saw it every day on her own mother's face. Genetics were a powerful influence.

"Well, you'll figure it out." Breanna kept her voice airy and light, as though they were sharing pithy observations about something they both found interesting and pleasing.

Michael was about to launch into another argument when Sam came bounding out of the house to greet them.

The transformation on Michael's face was immediate. In an instant, his expression went from sullen defiance to delight.

"Sammy! Sammy boy!" Michael opened his arms for the dog, who threw himself into them. Breanna was amazed that Michael managed to stay upright. The dog licked Michael's face—a sight Breanna observed with a mix of amusement and mild revulsion—as Michael petted and scratched and ruffled the dog's fur with enthusiasm.

"Well, he's sure got a new friend," Jake said with approval as he came out of the house to greet them, his hands on his narrow hips.

Breanna wasn't sure whether he was talking about Sam or Michael.

"I expect you to give Jake your best effort," she told her son. Then she turned to Jake. "I'll be back around five to get him, if that's okay." Then she turned and started back toward her car.

"Wait, wait." Jake went after Breanna, unsure about what he was going to say. He'd just figure it out as he went, he decided.

Breanna turned toward him, her face carefully arranged in a mask of pleasant neutrality. "Is it all right that I brought Michael again today? Because if it's not, I could—"

"Yeah, yeah. Yes." He ran a hand through his hair, making it spike up in odd places. "It's fine, you know he's welcome. Look. The way we left things …"

"There's no need to hash it out," Breanna said. "You expressed an honest feeling you were having about my family, and I had no right to invalidate that. We don't have to agree on everything. It's not like we're in a relationship."

A couple of thoughts went through Jake's head. One was that it sounded like a rehearsed speech. And the other was that he was through hearing that bullshit about them not being in a relationship. Yes, they'd only been out a few times. But wasn't that where relationships started?

As he pondered all of that, a third thought came to him: He really wanted to kiss her. He couldn't act on the impulse—not now, not with Michael a few feet away—but it was there, all the same.

"I kind of do think we should hash it out," he said.

She shot a significant look in Michael's direction. "Right now isn't the best time."

"I'm sorry I acted like an asshole," he said. "That's pretty much all I wanted to say. The rest can wait." The kissing part, that could wait. As long as it didn't have to wait too long.

"Oh."

From the look on her face, she hadn't expected an apology—she'd expected a confrontation. Well, he could be full of surprises. He took her gently by the arm and drew her a little bit away from the boy so they could speak in private.

"I really want to see you again," he said under his breath.

"Oh," she said again.

"Not tonight, though. You want to slow things down, I get that. So, let's draw it out a little. How's Monday night?"

She looked at Michael, then looked at Jake. Then she blinked a few times in apparent bewilderment.

"Is that a yes?" he prompted her.

"Uh … yes."

"Okay, then." He gave her a crisp nod and then turned back toward the house. "Come on, Michael. Let's get to work."

Chapter Twenty

Breanna hadn't gone over to the house expecting to agree to a date. Her entire goal had been to get away without an ugly confrontation.

But then he'd apologized, and that had disarmed her defensiveness to such an extent that when he'd asked her out, she'd agreed before she'd even known what she was doing.

So, now she had a Monday night date, a basket full of misgivings, and no idea at all where this thing with Jake might be going.

"You don't have to know," Gen said when they talked about it later that night after dinner. "Just go along for the ride. Wherever it goes, it goes."

They were sitting in Gen's kitchen, Breanna perched on a barstool at the kitchen island, Gen holding J.R. on her hip as the baby grabbed at a hank of her curly red hair. Ryan was padding around the kitchen in his socks, looking for something in the refrigerator.

"But I need to know where this is headed," Breanna protested. "I can't just stumble around blindly, hoping for the best."

"That's what we all do, Bree," Gen said. "That's dating and, hell, even marriage in a nutshell."

"Do we have any of that good cheese left?" Ryan asked, his head in the refrigerator and his backside pointing toward them.

"Upper left corner, top shelf," Gen told him.

"That can't be how it works," Breanna said. "There's got to be some sense to it all. Some ... order."

Gen looked at her thoughtfully. "Have you ever thought that you're a little bit controlling?"

"I am not." She turned to her brother to defend her. "Ry? Tell her I'm not controlling."

"I just came for cheese," he said, holding up the item he'd just located in the depths of the refrigerator. "Now I'm getting the hell out of here."

As Monday night approached, Breanna had to admit that Gen might have a point about her. If she weren't controlling, would she be obsessing like this about where they might go, what they might do, what they might say to each other?

Or, she had to admit, whether he might kiss her or even do quite a bit more than that?

She needed to find her sense of inner calm. She needed to learn to let go of her anxieties and just let things be.

Though she probably wasn't going to learn all of that today.

She hadn't wanted Jake to pick her up at the ranch because she still didn't want to bring her dating life to her sons' attention. So they'd agreed to meet at Neptune.

Breanna wore a dress—something she didn't do all that often, living on a cattle ranch—and Jake looked almost impossibly handsome in dress slacks and a jacket, his button-down shirt open at the throat.

As she followed him to their table, she caught a whiff of some spicy, musky cologne.

"You look beautiful," he told her, his hand resting on the small of her back as he pulled out her chair for her.

Those words being murmured into her ear and the feel of his hand on her back electrified her, as though a current of desire were running through her veins where her blood should have been.

She already knew she was in trouble.

Take it slow, Jake told himself as he walked Breanna to the table behind their hostess. *That's what she wants. Just take it one step at a time, slow and easy.*

But the way she looked in that dress caused all rational thought to dash from his mind like small woodland creatures fleeing a forest fire.

The dress: black, short but not too short, body-skimming but tasteful, its neckline showing just enough creamy cleavage to make him forget where he was, what he was doing, even his own name. Her hair fell around her shoulders in dark, silky waves. Her eyes, deep and unfathomable, inviting a man to dive in and never emerge.

Get hold of yourself, Travis.

He willed himself to be a gentleman even while all of his instincts were screaming otherwise. They sat together like civilized people did, and he offered her the wine menu.

"It's been a while since I've been to Neptune," she told him. Candlelight danced on her skin, making it look warm and flawless.

The dinner was interminable.

The food was good, he supposed, but he barely noticed it. The wine, which he did notice, relaxed him just enough that he didn't crawl out of his skin wanting her.

He'd told himself to play it cool, but he knew he was going to have trouble with that before they'd even finished their dessert, before the check even arrived.

You're a civilized man with advanced brain function, he reminded himself. *You are not going to fall on her like a lion on a gazelle.*

He would control himself if he had to; he knew he would. If she didn't want him, he would say goodnight with grace and courtesy and admirable self-control. But if she *did* want him …

Well, he couldn't promise it wouldn't be the lion and the gazelle.

"Come back to my place?" he asked as they stood outside the restaurant, on the sidewalk on Main Street. "Please?"

"Jake. I don't know …"

And here was the part where he had to be a better man than he wanted to be.

"All right." He nodded. "I had a lovely time. I'll just walk you to your car."

But when they got to her car, she was the one who turned and, in one swift motion, threw herself into his arms and kissed him. She was the one on fire with need.

She was the lion.

He damn sure didn't mind being the gazelle.

Breanna could not have said what flipped the switch, what happened between *I don't know* and the moment she launched herself at him. She just wanted him, that was all. She wanted him in a way she'd rarely wanted anything. So many years now, she'd set aside her wants in favor of her children's needs. She'd set aside her wants until they'd built up into a mountain so high she could barely see the top of it from where she stood.

There were a thousand reasons to wait, to say no—or at least not yet. A thousand *shoulds* and *shouldn'ts,* a thousand fears.

But her rational brain couldn't do everything. It couldn't control everything.

It just wasn't powerful enough to control this.

If they'd been all over each other in a heat of unbridled need, she could have used that as an excuse, a reason she'd ignored her more rational nature. It might have been good to have an excuse. But they arrived at his house knowing exactly what they were doing, and exactly why.

"Are you sure?" Jake asked as he led her through the front door, turning on lights and taking off his coat.

"No," she said. "And, yes."

"Look, I can take you home. This doesn't have to happen today. I can just …"

His words trailed off because she was sliding his jacket off his shoulders. It fell to the floor with a muffled *whump*.

Her fingers were on his shirt, unhurried, sliding buttons through buttonholes slowly, one at a time.

"Breanna." The word was a plea and a promise.

She took her time. Because she wanted to remember, she wanted every moment to be clear and vivid. Because she didn't want, later, to blame anything on the heat of the moment. Because she wanted to be fully present and fully responsible for this, for everything.

She was still as he turned her around, gently, and unzipped her dress. He matched her pace, slow and leisurely, easy and deliberate. But she knew it was anything but easy for him; she could hear the catch in his breath.

The dress slipped down off of her shoulders, past her hips, and the fabric pooled at her feet.

She turned to him, and he took in the beauty of her, the simple fact of her.

She wasn't perfect, she wasn't some unattainable dream. Her face carried the marks of too much experience, too much life, for that. Her body showed the evidence of childbirth, of maturity and hard work.

But looking at her like this, seeing her near bare and vulnerable in her bra and panties, he knew her. This wasn't about perfection; it was about what was real. He wanted nothing more than to hold her and touch her and learn everything, all of the secrets of her heart.

He put his hand on her cheek, then ran it slowly, slowly, down to her neck, her shoulder, her arm.

She didn't speak, but a sigh escaped her lips, a gentle breath of longing.

They undressed each other the rest of the way with care and deliberation, then their bodies came together tentatively, that first touch of skin on skin like a whispered prayer.

On the bed, they lay together with his body covering hers, and the feel of him, the way he looked at her, was everything. It was the past and the future, it was hope and ruin. It was a look back and the way forward.

It would have been impossible not to think of Brian for just an instant, just a flash. Grief and pleasure, mixed as one. Because nothing real was ever one thing. It was everything at once, everything good weighted with all that had happened before.

Moments, impressions: a condom. A scar on his bicep from some long-ago wound. The rumple of sheets, the smell of him. The thrum of a car passing outside his window.

And then he eased into her, and her body sighed.

"Are you okay?" His voice a low murmur.

A tear fell from her eye, and he brushed it away with his fingers.

"Yes," she said.

Chapter Twenty-One

Afterward, Jake lay with Breanna in his arms, sated and warm.

He had the sense that she'd gone somewhere, though. Somewhere unknowable, where he couldn't follow.

"Breanna? What are you thinking?" He ran a hand down her side, over the curve of her hip.

She didn't answer. Maybe she didn't know. Or maybe she didn't want *him* to know.

"You're not sorry we did this, are you?" he asked. "Because I really don't want you to be sorry."

"I'm not." She turned in his arms and looked at him, her face so open—the softness of her skin and the gentle curve of her lips. "It's just complicated."

"It doesn't have to be."

She pulled away from him, drawing the sheet up around her to cover her breasts.

This moment, right here, was going to be important, he sensed. This was where it could go wrong.

She swung her legs over the side of the bed and got up, slipping out of the sheet and gathering up her clothes from the floor.

"Don't go," he said.

"I have to."

"Okay, then … not yet."

She didn't turn around. "If I don't go home, the boys …" She left the thought unfinished. Carrying her clothes in a bundle clutched to her chest, she walked into the bathroom and shut the door.

He recognized what he'd heard in her voice, what he'd seen in her body language. It was shame.

There was no way in hell he could let that stand. She would not be ashamed of what they'd done. Of him.

Breanna stood behind the bathroom door with her clothes in her arms, her eyes closed, trying to quiet her mind.

A jumble of feelings was roiling around inside her, and they were coming at her so fast she didn't know what to do with all of them.

Jake had made her feel things—good and powerful things she'd thought were lost to her. But an irrational, undeniable part of her felt like an unfaithful wife. Because she'd never stopped being a wife, had she? Not when Brian had died. Not ever.

She'd had sex since he'd died, of course. But that was just sex, and it could be dismissed as the very occasional release of a physical need.

This was different. This hadn't been just sex. She and Jake had made love, and *that* was something she hadn't done since Brian.

She needed time to process it, that was all.

She got dressed, put herself back together the best she could, took a few deep breaths, and then came back out into the bedroom. Jake was standing there in a pair of jeans, his chest bare, his hair tousled.

The hurt on his face shot straight to her heart.

"So, you're going, then."

"I have to be home for the boys."

"That's not all this is." His eyes were on her so intently that she had to look away.

"No," she admitted. "It's not. I just have to think."

He nodded, his jaw tight. "All right. Think. Take your time. I'll be here when you're done."

Breanna was a mature woman, but she felt like a naïve girl. She felt like a fool.

She'd considered what would happen if she slept with Jake. She just hadn't considered what would happen if it meant so much.

Sex was one thing. If she wanted to give her body to someone for a bit of mutual pleasure, what was wrong with that? But this hadn't been just her body. This had been her heart.

She'd succumbed to the bane of every sixteen-year-old girl who lost her virginity on prom night: She'd become too emotionally involved.

She drove home to the ranch berating herself for her stupidity.

Was it wrong to have sex with someone you had feelings for? No. Of course not. The problem was, the sex could make you feel things you weren't ready to feel.

Breanna was definitely not ready to have these feelings that were swirling around inside her.

Stupid. Stupid, stupid, stupid.

She parked in front of the house and got ready to do the walk of shame. Was it still the walk of shame when you were home at a reasonable hour with your hair tidied up and all of your undergarments accounted for? It didn't matter. It *felt* like the walk of shame, and she willed her family to take no notice of her as she slipped into the house and headed toward the stairs.

Breanna's father, Orin, was just coming out of the kitchen, his slippers on his feet and a mug of tea in his hand.

"Oh. Hey there, hun." He seemed surprised to see her—though Orin seemed surprised by any number of things that someone else might take for granted: rain, running out of toothpaste, meatloaf for dinner.

"Hi, Dad. I'm just gonna …" She pointed up the stairs to indicate her intentions.

"Have a good time?" In the overhead light, his scalp shone through a layer of hair so thin it was mostly symbolic.

"Yeah. I did. I'd better get upstairs."

"You okay?" He squinted at her.

"Yes. Fine. Why?"

"You look kinda … flushed." He gestured vaguely toward her with the mug, the tag from the teabag swinging.

If even her father, the least observant of her family members, could see that something was up, she had no hope at all if she ran into her mother.

"It's just … hot, that's all."

He looked at her in puzzlement. "It's about, what, fifty degrees outside? And it can't be more than sixty-eight in here. Why, with your mother and the power bill …"

"In the car," she said, scrambling. "I meant, it was hot in the car. I had the heater on high. I'm just going to … go now." She turned and hurried up the stairs and into the safety of her room.

The next day, she made the decision to play it as though the date were no big thing. She should have predicted that Gen would see through that as though Breanna were wearing a sign that said, CONFUSED AND TROUBLED AFTER GREAT SEX. Now that she thought about it, a sign would have eliminated a great deal of bothersome talking.

Breanna went through her usual Tuesday morning routine—helping to make breakfast, getting the boys ready for school, putting a load of laundry into the washing machine—feeling hopeful that maybe she could avoid the topic altogether.

But those hopes were dashed when Gen stopped by the house on her way to work, clicking across the kitchen floor on her high heels, one of her black gallery dresses on, her curly red hair piled on top of her head.

"So? How was it? Spill!" Gen demanded, scooting up onto a barstool at the kitchen island.

"Where's J.R.?" Breanna attempted to change the subject. "I thought Sandra was watching him today."

"Ryan's taking the morning off to have a little father-son bonding time. Speaking of people spending time together ..." She batted her eyelashes at Breanna meaningfully.

"That's sweet," Breanna said. "Ryan and J.R., I mean. What are they going to do together? I'll bet J.R. would like the park down in Morro Bay. Even though he's too little to do anything, he could watch the other kids, and maybe—"

"You're stalling," Gen said.

Exasperated, Breanna tossed her hands into the air. "It was fine. The date was fine. It was ... a date!"

"Uh oh," Gen said.

"Why? What is the 'uh oh' for? I said it was fine, and it was."

"Ah, jeez. What happened?" Gen looked at her in sympathy.

"You know what? I kind of don't want to talk about it."

"Oh, Bree. I really had hopes for you and Jake. Was it awful? Did he—I don't know—talk about his ex the entire time? Or pick his teeth at the table?"

"No."

"No to which one?"

"Either. Both."

"Then what—"

Breanna could feel herself on the verge of tears, and she turned to Gen with a pleading look. "Thank you for caring. Really. I mean it. But … I'm not ready to talk about it. About any of it."

Gen plunked down off of the barstool, then went over to Breanna and pulled her into a hug. "Okay. But I'm here if you want to talk. All right?"

Breanna nodded.

"I have to go to work," Gen said. "Are you sure you're okay?"

"I'm fine. Go on, you'll be late."

Gen left, shooting a concerned look at Breanna as she went.

Breanna was sure this wasn't going to be the end of it.

Chapter Twenty-Two

Jake slept in a little that morning—he'd told the crew not to show up at the work site until ten—then took Sam out for a stroll around the neighborhood, showered, and headed into town for coffee. Of course, he could have made some himself, but he was feeling out of sorts, and he needed to be around people and activity.

He was at Jitters on Main Street, waiting in line to place his order, when he saw Gen Porter walking past on the sidewalk outside the big front window, heading in the direction of her gallery.

Gen glanced into the coffeehouse, did a double-take when she saw him, came skidding to a stop, and reversed course and came into the shop.

"Jake!" She headed straight for him, balancing on heels so skinny and high that he wondered how she didn't turn an ankle on a daily basis.

He was about to make small talk—he had no idea about what—when she grabbed his arm and pulled him out of line and toward a quiet corner of the room.

"What happened last night?" she demanded.

He was a little taken aback, both by the fact that she knew something had happened last night and by the fact that she felt entitled to hear more about it.

"Why?" he asked.

"Because Breanna's upset, and I want to know what you did."

The accusation and the lack of caffeine combined to create a slight, nagging headache between his eyes. "This doesn't have anything to do with you."

"It doesn't," Gen admitted. "But I love Bree and I want to know what's going on."

Jake considered telling her off for her nosiness, or maybe just walking out of the place entirely and driving away. But he got the feeling that Gen was sincere and that her interest in Breanna's well-being was genuine.

Besides that, Gen might be able to pass along some useful information.

Considering it all, he rubbed his eyes with his fingertips. "Look … this isn't a conversation I can have without caffeine. Have a little mercy."

"Fine," Gen said grudgingly. "Get your coffee. I'll be waiting." She pointed toward a table at the back of the room.

The coffee helped some, and so did the few minutes it took to order it and bring it back to the table. The time had allowed Jake to think about how much he wanted to tell Gen and what he wanted to know from her in return.

What he wasn't going to do was let her berate him for something that was not his fault and that was none of her business in the first place.

By the time he got over to where Gen was sitting, he'd pretty much gotten his head together to the point where it didn't feel like he was being ambushed.

So, that was something.

"Tell me what happened," Gen said as soon as he sat down.

"No."

"Why not?"

He fixed her with a gaze that said he could hold his own in this particular discussion. "Because it's personal, and I'm not going to talk about Breanna's business behind her back."

"Good answer," Gen admitted. "Okay, I don't need to know what happened. I just want to know what she's upset about."

"That makes two of us." Jake sipped his coffee and slumped down in his seat.

The coffeehouse was only partly full, with people waiting at the counter and others gathered around tables. A group of older women a couple of tables away were debating whether they approved or disapproved of the recent relocation of the dog park. The vote was about half and half.

"What's that supposed to mean?" Gen demanded.

"It means I don't know what the hell happened." He weighed the question of how to say enough to make sense—and to possibly get some useful information out of her—while still being the gentleman he imagined himself to be. "We had a good time. A really good time. And then she just kind of … switched it off."

"Switched what off?" Gen looked at him with interest.

"The sparkle. The fun. That thing you girls do when you're on a date and you're having a good time and you think, hey, this guy's not half bad. One minute it was on, and the next …"

"She turned it off."

"Yeah."

That about summed it up. Privately, he congratulated himself for describing it so effectively.

Gen considered that. At least, the way her forehead crinkled between her eyebrows made it seem that way.

"So, what happened right before she switched it off?" she asked.

He didn't say anything, but the look on his face must have given it away.

"Ah," she said. "I see."

"I'm not confirming or denying anything," he said.

"You don't have to. God, don't ever play poker. You'll lose your shirt." Gen sat back in her seat and crossed her arms over her chest. "Well, well."

"Look. I'm not talking about that," he said. "About what might or might not have happened. What I will tell you is that it seemed like everything was good. Really good. And then all of a sudden it wasn't, at least for her. And I don't have a clue why."

"Oh, come on. You must have some—"

"Nope."

"But there must have been—"

"Nada." He raised one eyebrow at her in defiance. "In fact, the only reason I'm talking to you about this is because I thought you might have some idea what the hell's going on. I thought maybe she talked to you."

"No." Gen shook her head slowly. "She didn't. She just said the date was fine, then she changed the subject. But I could tell something was wrong."

"Well, that doesn't shed much light, does it?"

They both thought about that for a while as the buzz and hum of the coffeehouse went on around them.

"I'll tell you what, though," Jake said after a long, heavy silence. "I don't want you thinking she's upset because I acted like an asshole last night. I didn't."

Gen looked skeptical. "Well, maybe you don't *think* you did...."

"No." He pointed a finger at her. "I didn't."

"Okay."

He didn't know if Gen believed him. She probably didn't. Hell, she didn't know him very well, and he didn't know her. He was just a guy claiming that a woman's upset feelings weren't his fault, just as men through the millennia had done before him. But whether she believed him or not, it was the truth.

Still, that left the question of what had happened, and how, and why.

"She didn't say *anything* about what was bothering her?" he tried again.

"Nothing."

"Well ... shit." Jake scratched the stubble on his chin. "Should I call her?"

"Yes." Gen's answer was immediate and definitive.

"Are you sure? If she's upset ..."

"I'm sure. If you two did what I assume you did last night, then you have to call. It's an inviolate rule."

He'd assumed as much, but now that he had an actual woman telling him so, he guessed there was no way around it.

"But what do I say?"

"The exact words don't matter," Gen said. "What's important is that you let her know *she* matters. That it wasn't just a one-time fling."

"She does, and it wasn't."

Now that he considered it, he wondered if that wasn't exactly the problem.

Chapter Twenty-Three

Breanna needed to keep her mind on something other than Jake, so she threw herself into being useful.

She washed another load of laundry, scrubbed the floor in the boys' bathroom, worked in the garden, then cleaned the inside of the oven. With that done, she decided to bake a batch of muffins and take them over to the Whispering Pines, even though she wasn't scheduled to help Mrs. Granfield today.

She was mixing the batter in a big stainless-steel bowl when her mother came into the kitchen and peered at her with that Sandra gaze that had more than once made grown men quake.

"Girl, what's gotten into you today? Why, I haven't seen you sit down more than a minute since you hauled yourself out of bed." Sandra stood just inside the kitchen door with her hands on her thin hips, her favorite bunny slippers on her feet.

"Nothing's gotten into me," she said, attacking the batter with her spoon as though it deserved a severe punishment. She didn't look at her mother. Sandra had a kind of spooky sixth sense about what was going on with her children, and Breanna worried that eye contact would be as good as a confession. Not that what she'd done required a confession—except maybe in church. "I just thought Mrs. Granfield would like some fresh muffins for her guests."

"Well, I figure Dora Granfield can make her own damn muffins, if she's a mind to, even with a bad hip."

"She could," Breanna said, trying to adopt a breezy tone, "but now she won't have to."

"*Mm hmm*," Sandra said. To others, it might have sounded like agreement. But to Breanna, who'd lived in the same house with the woman almost all of her life, it sounded like, *I know there's something up, and I'm going to find out what it is.*

Breanna bent down to pull a couple of muffin tins out of a low cabinet.

"So, how was your dinner with Mr. Handsome?" Sandra asked, a note of suspicion in her voice.

Again, Sandra had zeroed in on the issue with unerring accuracy.

A simple *fine* hadn't worked with Gen, and it would work even less with Sandra. Breanna adjusted her strategy a little. Maybe if she talked about the date without talking about herself or Jake, she could change the subject just enough.

"Jackson's changed the menu a little bit," she said, referring to Jackson Graham, the head chef at Neptune. "You remember the seafood pasta? That's gone now, which was kind of a disappointment until I tried the new calamari steak entree. I swear, Jackson is a genius. Kate's a lucky woman." Kate Bennet, Gen's friend, was Jackson's live-in girlfriend.

"Uh huh," Sandra said, still scrutinizing Breanna.

She wasn't buying it, clearly, but Breanna gamely kept trying. "When was the last time you and Dad went to Neptune? You two deserve a night out."

Sandra let out a very Sandra-like grunt. "What I *deserve* is not to have my leg pulled like it's the damned Thanksgiving wishbone."

"Mom …"

"Don't 'mom' me," Sandra groused. "Something happened with that man, and it didn't have anything to do with the damned calamari steak."

Breanna put down the muffin tins and faced her mother. "I don't want to talk about what did or did not happen. It's private, and I don't want—"

"Do I look like one of your girlfriends?" Sandra said. "I don't need to hear you dishing about your man. In fact, I'd prefer not to, truth be known. All I want to know is, do I have to send one of your brothers to pound some sense into him? Why, Liam would have a right fine time doing it, I suspect."

"No! Of course not." Breanna picked up the spoon and started pounding the crap out of her muffin batter again, even though it was well past being mixed thoroughly. "The date was fine! It was … fine! Why doesn't anybody believe me when I tell them the damned date was fine!?"

Sandra eyed the way Breanna was manhandling the batter, and said wryly, "That's a stumper, all right."

It was a relief getting over to the Whispering Pines, where she wouldn't have to think about her love life. At least, she *thought* she wouldn't have to think about it. Until her cell phone rang and Jake's number popped up.

She stood behind the reception desk looking at her phone, trying to decide what to do.

"I believe you're supposed to tap the little picture of the telephone on the screen to answer the call," Mrs. Granfield said helpfully as she looked over Breanna's shoulder. "At least, that's what my grandson told me when he visited last week."

"What?" Breanna looked up, startled. "Oh. Right. That's … I know. Thanks."

"Personally, I'll stick with my regular telephone," Mrs. Granfield said, pointing to the big landline phone that stood proudly on the reception desk, a relic from the days when push-button dialing had newly replaced the rotary method. "So much simpler."

By the time Mrs. Granfield had moved on, making her way slowly toward one of the downstairs guest rooms, Breanna's phone had stopped ringing.

Could she get away with not calling back? She considered it, then decided that if she were a man and didn't call back the day after sex, she'd be the kind of insufferable jerk she and her friends all complained about.

So, she would have to call back. But that didn't mean she had to do it now.

Breanna made her way around the B&B, looking for absolutely anything that needed to be done. She changed some sheets that didn't need changing, arranged the muffins she'd brought in a basket atop a pretty cloth, cleaned a bathroom that was already perfectly clean, and then, lacking anything else to do, found a bottle of wood polish and a rag and started cleaning the stair banister.

"Dear, you don't need to work so hard," Mrs. Granfield said as she watched Breanna bend down to rub one of the balusters with the cloth. "Why, I didn't even think you were coming in today."

"I just … thought you might need some help," Breanna said.

"It's not that I don't appreciate everything you do, but my goodness, you must have your own things to attend to." Mrs. Granfield wrung her wrinkled hands in concern.

"Well … yes. I guess I do," Breanna admitted.

If even Mrs. Granfield was noticing that she was inventing work to avoid dealing with her issues, then it was probably time to suck it up and take care of things.

She finished what she was doing, said goodbye to Mrs. Granfield, gathered up her purse and her jacket, and went out to her car. She climbed into the driver's seat but didn't start the engine. Instead, she sat there, parked on Main Street, and fished her cell phone out of her purse.

What was she going to say to him?

She still didn't have a plan for that when he answered on the second ring.

"Breanna." He sounded as though he hadn't expected her to call but had hoped she would. A hint of surprise, a warmth, a low rumble in the timbre of his voice that made her feel hot and maybe a little lightheaded.

"I was just … I thought I should … You called." Just seconds into the call, and she was already fumbling it.

"Yeah. I didn't need anything in particular, I just wanted to hear your voice."

It was exactly the right thing to say, and she found herself melting just a little. Some of the tension she'd been feeling drained out of her, and she opted for honesty.

"Jake … I'm sorry for the way I left last night. What happened between us freaked me out a little, I guess."

"That's not usually the reaction I hope for from women."

"It wasn't you. You didn't do anything wrong. I just felt … I don't know what I felt. I should try to explain it."

"Not on the phone, though. I want to see you." His voice, low and intimate, made her remember things from last night— things that stirred up reactions she wasn't ready to feel in a car on Main Street.

God, she wanted to see him, too—despite the confusion, and the conflicted feelings, and all of the complications he was sure to bring into her life. And then there were the boys. She needed to be there when they got out of school.

"I can't today."

"Can I see you this weekend? Saturday?"

Breanna hesitated. "I promised Lucas I'd take him to the zoo."

"I love a good zoo," he said.

The thought that he wanted to come along—to be a part of a family outing—was jarring and alarming, and also sweet. As appealing as the thought was, she wasn't ready to take that kind of step.

"I can meet you afterward," she told him.

The Charles Paddock Zoo in Templeton was tiny, with only a small array of animals, but Lucas loved it for reasons that were unaccountable to Breanna.

He especially liked the alpacas, with their wooly coats and their faces that looked like they belonged on a particularly goofy stuffed animal. When Breanna, Lucas, and Michael arrived at the zoo, Lucas ran directly for the alpaca enclosure, grabbing the railing with his hands and bouncing up and down on the toes of his sneakers in excitement.

"Aren't they cool, Mom?"

They went through some variation of this routine every time they visited the zoo—Lucas exclaiming in amazement and Breanna reassuring him that she shared his opinions.

Michael's part in the routine was to look bored and put out, and he flawlessly kept up his end of the deal, standing apart from the group with his arms crossed over his chest and a scowl on his face.

"Why did I have to come?" he asked. "You could have just brought Lucas. I have stuff to do at home."

"What kind of stuff?" Breanna asked pleasantly.

"Just stuff."

She went to stand behind him, wrapped her arms around him, and nuzzled her cheek against his. "You had to come because it's no fun without you."

She felt him relax a little, and she knew that her sweet boy, the one who'd loved to cuddle with her before he hit adolescence, was still in there somewhere beneath the exterior of teen ennui.

"Let's go see the porcupines," she suggested.

"I don't even like the porcupines," he said.

"Yes, you do," Breanna said. "They're your favorite. Don't deny it."

"Mom ..."

"All right," Breanna said patiently. "If you don't like them, we can just skip them this time."

Michael squirmed slightly. "I guess we could see them for just a little bit."

Seeing the whole zoo—including the less-favored animals, the aviary, and the amphibian area—took barely a half hour. When they were done, Breanna suggested that they stop on the way back for ice cream.

Even Michael had a hard time being blasé about ice cream, so they went to a shop in Paso Robles that had both indoor and outdoor seating.

Breanna got the boys settled at a patio table with their cones while she sipped from a cup of coffee.

Throughout the outing, she tried to stay focused on the boys, but it was hard not to think about her impending talk with

Jake. Twice during the ice cream stop, she got out her phone to text him, then put it away, not knowing what to say.

She'd have to figure it out soon enough.

After the zoo and the ice cream, Breanna dropped the boys off at home and met Jake at the Moonstone Beach boardwalk, no more than twenty yards from her house. She'd picked the location carefully. It seemed to her that difficult conversations were easier when you had something to do to. Walking on the boardwalk would, at the very least, allow them to avoid eye contact should the conversation go sour.

Things started on a light note.

"How was the zoo trip?" Jake asked.

"It was okay," she told him. "Lucas had a good time."

"What about Michael?"

Breanna shrugged. "He made a big show of being put out, but by the end, he was having fun, too."

"Huh. So the angsty thing is an act, then?" Jake asked.

"I'm not sure," she said. "I think some of it is and some of it's not. It comes and goes. Like weather."

"And you're afraid he can't handle the thought of his mom dating, I gather."

Breanna looked down at the path in front of her. A fat, fluffy squirrel scurried through the brush to one side. "He's going through a rough time."

"I figured." He shoved his hands into his pockets as he walked.

"I shouldn't have left your house that way. I'm sorry if I made you think … well, that I regretted what happened between us."

They squeezed to one side of the boardwalk to make room for a couple coming the other way. "So you don't regret it, then?" Jake asked.

"No. I don't. It was just maybe a little soon, that's all."

It seemed to him that she was making this more complicated than it had to be, but he was open to the idea that he might be wrong. "I won't pretend to know what it's like to deal with dating somebody new—and everything that comes with that—when you're raising kids," he said. He'd never had kids. You could imagine what it might be like to be responsible for two other lives, but that probably didn't come close to the reality of it.

Her head tilted downward, she shot a quick, tentative look at him that made his heart speed up a little.

"So ... you and your ex never wanted kids?"

"She didn't. I did." Just four words, and in those four words lay a world of hurt, of misunderstanding, of conflict and unresolved longing. He could have said so much more, but he figured that was better saved for another time.

"I'm sorry."

"Yeah, well ... I figure it's good we didn't, considering how things worked out." If his divorce had felt like surgery without anesthetic, then going through it with kids would have been like trying to remove his own spleen with a mirror and a butter knife.

No thanks.

There was no point in hashing out every nuance, so he said what most needed to be said—the thing he'd really come here to tell her.

"Listen, this thing between us—I don't want it to end just because you feel like we rushed things. We can slow down if you want. Hell, we can go back to the beginning and start over. This has the potential to be something really good. Let's try not to screw it up."

He knew he hadn't been as eloquent as he'd wanted to be, but that was okay. He got the gist of it out there. He'd said what he thought, and now the rest was up to her.

Jake knew he was on the right track when her expression, which had been serious or even grave before, turned to amusement, her lips quirking up into a half grin.

" 'Let's try not to screw it up?' Nice speech, Travis."

"Well, you know, I write my own material," he said. "But I try to be modest."

She was smiling, and he felt the warmth of it deep in his chest. He wanted to pull her to him and kiss her, but instead, he reached out for her hand and held it in his.

"So, dating, then?" He wiggled his eyebrows at her. "The movies, the malt shop, that kind of thing? Maybe at the end I can try for a kiss?"

"I don't think there's such a thing as a malt shop anymore. And I don't know that I want to go back *all* the way back to the beginning."

"All right. Maybe I'll try to feel you up, then. Under the sweater but over the bra. That kind of thing." The banter—the ease and fun of it—felt good. He didn't want it to end.

"Something like that," Breanna agreed, grinning.

He couldn't wait to get started.

Chapter Twenty-Four

Now that they had the ground rules established, Breanna and Jake settled into a regular routine of dating. They went out a couple of times per week, usually on Friday or Saturday night and again once or twice during the week.

There was a good amount of kissing and a little bit of groping, but they'd tabled the matter of sex for now—though neither of them was entirely satisfied with that situation.

Still, for Jake, the whole thing was not at all disagreeable. He liked spending time with her. He liked talking about her day, or his, over a long dinner. He liked holding her hand during a walk on one of Cambria's forest trails. And he sure as hell liked the kissing and groping. He figured they'd get around to the sex again sometime soon, and when they did, it was going to be better for the wait.

Sure, he was experiencing a certain amount of frustration. But he was tough. He could take it.

In the meantime, he kept working on the Moonstone Beach house, and Breanna kept bringing Michael—and now Lucas, too—over to help.

At first Jake had worried that the construction zone might not be safe for Lucas, who was only eleven. But he figured out safe things the kid could do, stuff he couldn't mess up but that would make him feel like he was working on his new home.

On a Wednesday afternoon a couple of months into the slowed-down dating, Jake had Lucas sand part of the deck of the main house while he and Michael worked to tear out some old linoleum in an upstairs bathroom.

Downstairs, some of his guys were working on the kitchen, rerouting plumbing so the sink could be put in a different location. Jake wasn't a plumber, so it was just as well that he wasn't involved in that.

Jake showed Michael how to score the old linoleum, scrape beneath it to pull it up from the floor, then use a heat gun to remove the adhesive underneath. Because the job involved sharp objects, heat, and, underneath the linoleum, an original wood floor that he was trying to preserve, Jake kept a close eye on the boy for the sake of safety—and so he didn't gouge the wood with the scraper.

"Look at that," Jake said with admiration as they pulled up a square of the old flooring to reveal a layer of oak the color of caramel. "Your mom's gonna love this."

Michael squinted at the wood in skepticism. "It's all scuffed up."

"That's now," Jake said. "Before I do my magic."

"You have floor magic?" The kid's voice might have sounded a little bit mocking, and Jake thought he saw him roll his eyes.

"Well, not me. But I have guys, and they have magic. Trust me, it's gonna be great."

Michael had started this whole thing grumpy and defiant, but he'd been at this a while now, and Jake caught flashes of enthusiasm here and there, when Michael accidentally dropped his act.

SEARCHING FOR SUNSHINE 183

"What kind of floor am I going to have in my room?" he asked. It was the first time Michael had inquired about the details of his room.

"Just like this." Jake pointed to the oak they'd uncovered. "If it's not too damaged. The crappy old carpet that's in there now is going to go, obviously. There's oak underneath, we just have to see what condition it's in."

"Could I maybe help you pull up the carpet in there so we can see?"

Jake felt unaccountably pleased that Michael not only cared about his room, but that he also wanted to be a part of working on it. He clapped Michael on the back companionably. "I guess this bathroom can wait. Let's go take a look. But first, let's see how your brother's doing."

They went outside and checked on the progress of the sanding, and Jake pronounced it superior—which he would have done whether it was or not. In fact, the kid was actually doing a pretty good job. Maybe the boy was up to more real work than Jake had realized.

"Hey, kid. You up for ripping out some crappy carpet?"

Lucas looked up, his face alight as though Jake had offered him a trip to Disneyland. "Really? Can I?"

"Grab a scraper and let's have at it," Jake said.

The floor underneath the carpeting in Michael's room was pretty much the way Jake had said it would be. Oak the color of brown sugar, showing a good bit of age and wear but still very much salvageable.

He and the boys pulled up a corner, and Jake stood with his hands on his hips, looking at it with satisfaction.

"That's good quality oak. Boys, it will forever be a mystery to me why someone would cover premium flooring like this with cheap-ass nylon bullshit carpeting."

It occurred to him, too late, that Breanna might object to him using the words *ass* and *bullshit* in front of her impressionable young offspring. But the boys seemed to be looking at him with fresh admiration, so he decided not to backpedal.

"So, why do they?" Michael wanted to know.

Jake shrugged. "Comfort on their feet, I guess. Sound dampening, especially for upstairs rooms. Carpet was probably in fashion at the time."

"But it's not now?" Michael was looking at him attentively, and Jake wondered if this irritable teenager could be interested in interior decorating. Anything was possible, he supposed.

"Now, most home buyers would cut off their left arm for original oak floors. Well, probably not an arm. Maybe a finger. Here, let's get this up the rest of the way."

They worked for another hour or so, and Jake was surprised when Breanna showed up at five to pick them up. He'd been so absorbed in the work, and so pleasantly engaged with the boys, that time had passed without him noticing.

By the time she got there, both of the boys were dirty and sweaty, but they were also alight with enthusiasm, talking over each other to tell her what they'd done on the house that day.

"Mom! I helped sand the deck and then I pulled up some crappy carpeting," Lucas announced.

Jake wondered if Breanna would raise an eyebrow at the use of the word *crappy,* but she just looked at her son with love and amusement.

"Check out the floor in my room, Mom," Michael said. "Jake says it's original oak. It's gonna be cool."

"Maybe we can start thinking about how we're going to decorate the room when it's done," Breanna suggested.

"Yeah," Michael agreed. "I've had the same stuff in my room since I was a kid. We haven't changed, like, anything."

Jake wondered if Michael didn't realize that he was still a kid—and then decided that he probably didn't. That was the problem with adolescence, wasn't it? The world saw you one way, and you saw yourself another way. The dissonance could be a lot to take.

He was still pondering the rough waters of the teen years when Breanna told the boys to go out and say goodbye to Sam so they could get going.

Once they'd left the room, she lingered behind, looking at him in a way that made the blood redistribute in his body.

She reached up on her tiptoes and pressed a kiss to his lips.

"Thank you."

"For what? Not that I'm arguing."

"For getting them excited about the house. I really want them to love it here. But Michael ... I wasn't sure he was going to come around." Her eyes were shining with emotion, and he felt the swell of pride that came with pleasing the woman in his life. He wanted to do more of it.

And soon.

"Hey, I've got an idea," he said. "Let's all go out on Friday night. I mean the boys, too. All four of us."

Something in her eyes dimmed, and she took a step back from him. What had he said wrong? Where was this sudden chill coming from?

"That's really a nice idea, but ..."

"But what? I get the feeling that I said something wrong, but hell if I know what it is." He ran a hand down her arm to smooth over whatever it was that was bothering her.

"I just … I think it's best if we keep things between us for a while."

He shoved his hands into his jeans pockets and rocked back on his heels. "The kids already know me. It's not like I'm some stranger. I like them. And it seems like they don't completely hate me, so …"

Breanna took another step back, putting more space between them. "I have to do this in my own time."

"Do what? Breanna …"

"Mom! Come on!" Michael called to her from out in the yard, where Lucas was wrestling companionably with Sam.

"I'd better go." She headed toward the door.

"Breanna, hey. Don't you think—"

"I'd really better go." She left him standing there feeling like an idiot, like he'd committed some kind of crime by trying to be a part of her life.

Chapter Twenty-Five

Breanna broached the subject with her mother that evening while they were cleaning up after dinner. The boys had helped to clear the table, and now they were upstairs doing their homework while Breanna and Sandra loaded the dishwasher, put away leftovers, and scrubbed pots and pans.

"Jake wants to bring the boys on one of our dates," she said tentatively. She was sure her mother would lecture her about the dangers of bringing children into a new relationship prematurely—and she'd be right to do it.

"About time, I'd say." Sandra attacked a stainless steel pot with a scrub brush as Breanna gaped at her.

"What? But …"

"Man's going to get involved with a woman, he ought to figure out whether he wants a part in her family," Sandra said. "Otherwise, what the hell's the point?"

"The point?" Breanna said incredulously. "The *point?* The point is that I'm trying to make sure that whatever's happening between me and Jake is real before I bring my children into it."

"You been dating the man awhile now," Sandra observed. "You don't have some kind of inkling yet about whether it's real, well, I'd say it's time to move on, stop wasting everybody's time."

Breanna was used to her mother's directness. Still, she found herself feeling hurt and surprised.

"I'm not wasting anyone's time. And … I have an inkling."

"Do you, now?" Sandra looked at her daughter appraisingly. "Well, that's interesting. I figure that inkling of yours has to be a positive one, or you'd be done already. So, what's the holdup in him getting to know your boys?"

"He knows the boys. They're working with him at the house. They know each other."

Sandra grunted. "They know him as the guy who's fixing up the house, I guess. But they don't know him as their mama's boyfriend."

"He's not my boyfriend."

Sandra faced her daughter with a withering look. "Does the man himself know that? If he doesn't, I guess you ought to tell him so he's not throwing away good time and effort on something that's not going anywhere."

The conversation was beginning to make Breanna's head hurt, and she waved her hands, covered in bright yellow rubber gloves, in front of her face in a futile effort to clear away her confusion.

"Let's take this one point at a time. Yes, it might be going somewhere. No, I'm not wasting anybody's time. And, okay, he's probably my boyfriend. But I'm not ready to bring the kids into it."

Sandra seemed satisfied with the item-by-item rundown. "I guess that's fair enough. What did the man say when you told him no?"

"He … he looked surprised. And kind of hurt."

"*Hmph.*" Sandra's expression softened, and she looked at her daughter with concern. "Seems to me one of you is moving a little faster'n the other one. You might want to ask yourself why that is."

Breanna wasn't sure what her mother was getting at, but she was pretty sure she wouldn't like it.

"Mom. What are you talking about?"

Sandra shrugged her thin shoulders and went back to scrubbing the pot in her hands. "Maybe he's rushing things because he's on the rebound from his divorce."

"I don't think that's—"

"Or." Sandra interrupted Breanna pointedly. "You're dragging your feet because you feel guilty as hell for moving on, like maybe you're cheating on Brian."

Breanna didn't say anything, but the way she stood frozen, her jaw a little slack, told Sandra she'd hit the center of the bull's eye.

"It's something to think about," Sandra said. "*Hmph*. Your uncle Redmond kept his distance from the love of his life because he wanted to be careful, make sure he wasn't hurting anybody. Look how it worked out for him."

Jake asked himself, not for the first time, whether he was putting all of his eggs in a basket that had a giant hole in the bottom of it. Or maybe the basket was hurtling over the edge of a cliff.

He could deal with the lack of sex. He could deal with going slowly, and with waiting to make their relationship clear to her kids. He didn't have to get there today. But he had to know that they would get there eventually.

He had to know whether she even wanted that.

On top of all of it, he'd had an offer of a date with an attractive woman who wasn't Breanna, and he was starting to wonder whether he was an idiot for turning it down.

The woman in question was Mark's housemate—a dark-eyed hipster chick in her twenties who'd given Jake the eye when he'd picked up Mark for a run to Ted's a few days before. When Mark had gotten home that night, Kye had asked him to fix her up with Jake—a prospect that had pissed Mark off a little, because he'd had designs on her himself.

Jake had said he wasn't interested, but now he wondered why the hell he shouldn't be. Breanna didn't want to sleep with him, she didn't want to take their relationship further, and she didn't want her kids to know they were a couple.

Which, he guessed, they weren't—not considering all of that.

The night after Breanna had nixed his idea to go out with the boys, he got home, walked Sam, took a shower, and then, in a pair of sweatpants and a T-shirt, a sweating beer in his hand, he plopped down into a chair in his living room and called Mark.

"Tell Kye I'm up for going out if she is," he said without preamble. "That is, if you're cool with it."

"I'm not," Mark said. "But, hell. She's not gonna go out with me, so she might as well go out with somebody. And you're an okay guy, I guess."

"Well, thanks," Jake said. "I think."

"But what about Breanna?" Mark asked. "Is that over?"

Was it over? Had it ever really started?

Jake scrubbed his hand over his face. "Ah, jeez. I don't know. Just … tell Kye what I said, okay?"

They went to Ted's, which should have been a tipoff to Kye that Jake had issues. What kind of guy took a woman to Ted's on a first date? The place was a dive with sticky floors, a bad smell, and bathrooms that were usually out of order.

But Jake wasn't interested in impressing her—he was only interested in soothing the sore spot inside him that Breanna had put there when she'd held him at arm's length for so long.

They met at the bar on a Friday night, with the jukebox pumping out rock over the chaotic noise of a bigger-than-average crowd.

Kye came in about ten minutes after Jake, wearing what looked like some kind of short schoolgirl dress with a pair of socks that reached halfway up her thighs. The outfit drew so much attention to the three inches of exposed flesh between the tops of the socks and the bottom of the dress that Jake could barely take his eyes off of it. She was wearing a bright red bow in her hair that he supposed was intended to be ironic.

They found seats at the bar and ordered their drinks—a beer for Jake and a white zinfandel for Kye. It seemed like an unlikely choice for her—with her self-conscious coolness, shouldn't she be drinking some kind of local craft beer? He wondered if the selection, like the bow, was intended to project coolness through its very lack of the same.

She turned to him, her fingers brushing the stem of her wineglass, her lipstick the red of strawberries, or maybe Dorothy's ruby slippers.

"I'm glad you decided to do this," she said. "I didn't think you would."

"I didn't think I would, either," he said honestly.

"Because of Breanna Delaney?" she asked.

Jake rubbed the back of his neck with his hand, chagrined. "Yeah, well ... I am seeing her. But we're not exclusive, so ..."

She gave him a slow, seductive grin. "I'm seeing someone, too, but we're not exclusive, so ..."

"You wanna play some darts?" he asked.

She scooted down off her barstool in a way that was blatantly sexual, though he wasn't sure what made him think so.

"Lead the way," she said.

Jake wasn't sure when Breanna's brother came into the bar. All he knew was that he was drinking beer and playing darts, flirting with Kye, having an okay but not excellent time, when he looked up and saw Liam Delaney glaring at him from a table in the center of the room, where he was sitting with his fiancée.

His first reaction was, *oh shit.* His second reaction was to remind himself that he wasn't doing anything wrong. He and Breanna *weren't* exclusive, as he'd told Kye, and anyway, he didn't answer to Liam Delaney.

And it wasn't like he was screwing Kye in the middle of the dance floor. They were playing darts, that was all.

Until that night, Jake wouldn't have called himself childish. He wouldn't have considered himself someone who would play games to make someone else jealous. He would have thought himself above using an available woman in a drama that had nothing to do with her.

But that night, he found out he was wrong about all of that.

With Liam's eyes still on him, Jake turned back to the dartboard, put his arm around Kye, and then slid his hand slowly down to rest on the small of her back. Kye shot him a look that was both surprised and pleased, and she leaned into him, shaping herself to the side of his body with the sinewy grace of a cat.

Her move made Jake's nether regions spring to attention— a reaction that flooded him with an irrational and yet powerful guilt.

A few minutes later, when he looked back toward where Liam had been, the table was empty.

We'll see what happens now, he thought.

Chapter Twenty-Six

Breanna was upstairs in the laundry room, moving a load of clothes from the washer to the dryer, trying not to think about the fact that she was doing such a thing on a Friday night.

She could have been out with Jake and the boys, eating pizza and bonding as a potentially happy foursome, but she'd turned him down, and so here she was, taking the last sheet of fabric softener out of the box and contemplating how to get her whites whiter.

She heard a commotion in the house and had just started to contemplate the nature of it when Liam came charging up the stairs, Aria at his heels.

"Breanna? The goddamned laundry can wait. We need to talk." His face was all outrage and thunderstorms—not an unusual state of affairs for Liam—and he took her arm and started to pull her toward her room.

"Liam, stop. Just calm down. Think about what you're doing." Aria had hold of his other arm and was trying to calm him down. Usually she was good at that sort of thing, but right now, her efforts seemed to be having no effect.

"I've thought about it all I need to. She's my sister, and she needs to know." Liam's jaw was tight and his eyes were narrowed in an expression that more than once had made the ranch hands wonder who'd fucked up and was about to get fired.

"What's going on? What is this about?" Breanna disengaged her arm from Liam's grasp and faced him with indignation.

"If you need to tell her, then tell her," Aria said to Liam. "But for God's sake, calm down first."

"Yeah. All right." Liam ran a hand through his hair, his face red, his eyes shooting rage.

"Aria? What's this about?" Breanna asked again.

"That asshole Jake Travis—"

"Wait." Breanna interrupted Liam before he could say another word. The boys were home, in the next room. She didn't want them to hear whatever Liam had to say. "Let's do this outside."

It was dark out, and the big wrap-around porch was illuminated only by the light beside the front door and the warm yellow glow filtering through the living room windows. Liam was pacing angrily with his hands on his hips, Aria watching him with concern.

"All right," Breanna said, her hands clasped in front of her, unsure about what was to come. "Just tell me."

"Did you know he was seeing somebody else?" Liam demanded. "Did he tell you? Because if he's screwing somebody behind your back, I'm going over there to kick his ass."

"You're not going to kick anybody's ass," Aria said soothingly, her hand on Liam's arm. She turned to Breanna. "But, did you know? Oh, Breanna …"

Breanna's brain was having a hard time processing what she was hearing. None of it made sense. "Wait. Just wait. What are you talking about?"

"Maybe you should sit down," Aria suggested.

"I don't want to sit down. Just tell me what's going on."

Aria looked like she didn't want to say what she was about to say. "We were over at Ted's. Liam and I. Jake was there. And … he wasn't alone."

Was that all? That didn't mean anything. He might have been with a friend. He might have run into someone he knew. The fact that he was at the bar with another woman didn't mean he was seeing her. Even as she thought it, she knew it was a steaming load of horse shit. But she clung to the idea anyway.

She deliberately made her voice sound casual, unconcerned. "Oh, well, that's not—"

"He had his hands on her," Liam interrupted.

Stunned, Breanna looked from Liam to Aria.

"He did," Aria confirmed. "Oh, Breanna, I'm so sorry."

Breanna felt as though the ground were crumbling out from beneath her feet stone by stone. Soon she would go tumbling into the deep beyond, lost, unmoored.

"What?" Her voice was barely a whisper.

"That asshole," Liam ranted. "That fuckin' … I'm telling you, I'm going to rearrange his goddamned teeth. And Kye goddamned Ferris? Not enough that he's cheating on you, he's gotta do it with a damned teenager?"

Breanna blinked a few times in shock. "Kye Ferris?" Breanna knew the girl, if only to wave hello to at the supermarket. Kye Ferris was at least ten years younger than Breanna—maybe as much as fifteen. She was legal to drink, surely, but not by much.

Was there anything more certain to make a woman feel old, used-up, and past her prime than hearing that her boyfriend was cheating with someone barely out of adolescence?

Not cheating, Breanna reminded herself. Not that. Because hadn't she insisted to Jake that they keep things casual? Hadn't she refused every effort he'd made to take their relationship to another level?

"Breanna? Are you okay?" Aria peered at her with concern.

"Of course I am." She wasn't, but she was determined not to show it. "And he's not cheating."

"I don't know," Aria said. "The way he touched her …"

"I didn't mean that," Breanna said. "I meant, he's free to see anyone he wants. So am I. He can do whatever he wants with Kye Ferris."

The thought of what he might be doing with her made Breanna feel ill, but she had to be an adult about it. She had to be mature. She had to put her heart's tender feelings aside to look at it rationally.

For the first time since he'd arrived, Liam stopped looking pissed-off and looked surprised instead.

"You two are"—he made a vague gesture with his fingers that suggested dancing, but that Breanna was sure meant sex—"but you're still seeing other people?"

"We're not"—she motioned toward his hand gesture—"whatever that's supposed to be."

"You're *not?*" Aria gaped at her.

"No," Breanna said. "We're not. I mean, there was the one … But we're … Jake and I have decided to take things slowly." Of course, Jake hadn't decided any such thing. Breanna had decided for both of them. But still.

"Are you bullshitting me?" Liam demanded.

Breanna composed herself, smoothed the front of her T-shirt with her hands, and said, "Thank you both for worrying about me. And thank you for coming here to tell me. Really. But it's fine. Jake's free to do what he wants. And you don't need to worry about me. It's good. I'm good."

She wasn't good—not at all—and she had an intense need to do violence to Kye Ferris. But Breanna, unlike Kye, was a mature woman. She would handle this. Hadn't she kept her distance from Jake to protect herself from exactly this? To keep herself safe?

She didn't feel safe at the moment. She felt gutted. But it would have been so much worse if they'd taken things further.

Wouldn't it?

Chapter Twenty-Seven

Jake got home that night feeling like shit. Breanna probably knew by now that he'd been out with Kye, and she was probably hurt and angry. Kye had probably figured out that Jake had been using her, and she probably didn't feel too good about it, either.

Basically, he'd fucked up on more than one front, and he was starting to wonder why any of these women wanted anything to do with him in the first place.

"Come on, Sam."

He snapped on the dog's leash, went outside, and walked the huge beast in the darkness of the rural night. A couple of porch lights here and there allowed him to see his way, and a brilliant blanket of stars overhead reminded him of his relative insignificance in the greater universe.

He'd thought going out with Kye would make him feel better—make him feel like he was moving forward instead of being stuck in one place—but it hadn't. It had only made things worse, and now he felt as though he'd dug himself a hole that he didn't know how to climb out of.

He didn't want Kye Ferris. He wanted Breanna, and he'd had some childish notion that sending her a message through her brother would make her jealous and send her running into his arms.

But he knew Breanna well enough to know that her mind didn't work that way. She rarely acted on impulse, and she wouldn't suddenly want to commit to him just because he'd gotten handsy with a cute younger woman at Ted's.

She'd be hurt, but she'd be quiet about it, feeling the hurt deep inside in a place other people couldn't get to. He hadn't thought about that—the hurt—when he'd put on his little show for Liam. But now that he was fully considering how Breanna was going to feel, the bitter burn of regret settled into his stomach, making him wonder if he even deserved her.

"You should try to find a better person for yourself," he told Sam. "Somebody who's not a dick."

Sam looked at him briefly, then went back to sniffing a clump of weeds by the side of the road.

Breanna tried to put it aside.

What she'd told Liam was true: She and Jake didn't have a commitment. They weren't exclusive—or, at least, they'd never said they were. Jake could see whomever he wanted, even a preteen like Kye Ferris.

She went through her normal routine, finishing the laundry, making sure the boys turned off their phones at bedtime, answering her e-mails—there was one from Julia, her sister-in-law in Montana, and another from the PTA president about next week's fund-raiser—and then tucking herself into bed at a reasonable hour.

She lay there looking at the ceiling, telling herself not to call Jake and not to text him, no matter how much she might want to tell him everything she was feeling. Yes, it would be satisfying to tear into him and pour out all of her disappointment and jealousy. But what purpose would it serve? What would it change?

If he was really dating Kye Ferris, he was unlikely to stop just because Breanna was mad. And even if he did, where would that leave them? You couldn't build a relationship on *I'm faithful to my girlfriend because I don't want her to get pissed.*

And what did those words even mean? What was *faithful,* when they didn't have a commitment? What was *girlfriend,* when she'd told him she wanted to keep things light?

She'd known getting involved with Jake was a bad idea. And yet she'd done it anyway. If she was lying here feeling like crap, she only had herself to blame.

She picked up her phone from the bedside table, opened her texting app, and then forced herself to put the phone back down. She was *not* going to text him. Even if he was with Kye right now. Even if every molecule in her body was screaming out for her to stop him from sleeping with her.

What if she was too late? What if Jake and Kye had already slept together?

What if they were at it right now?

Be an adult, she told herself. *Act like a damned grownup.*

Breanna closed her eyes and tried to sleep. It didn't work. Every time she began to drift off, she imagined Jake with that girl.

Finally, she threw off her covers, got out of bed, and changed out of her pajamas and into a pair of jeans and a sweatshirt.

Screw it. I've got to know.

The thing about driving across town on a Friday night to find out whether your man was screwing someone else was that it was so full of contradictions. You wanted to know, but you didn't want to know. You wanted to catch them and feel that triumphant, indignant rage, but what you really wanted was to find out it was all some big mistake.

Add a heaping dollop of self-recrimination for being sad and desperate enough to do it in the first place, and you had a perfect storm of shame, anger, and betrayal.

All of that was surging through Breanna as she drove up to Jake's place and parked her car at the side of the road. He was here; his truck was in the driveway, and the porch light was on. *She* was probably here, too. What were they doing? Were they talking, laughing, making out?

Were they in bed?

"Shit. Shit." Breanna wiped a couple of hot tears from her cheeks as she sat in her car and pondered what to do.

She realized that she needed some excuse for going to the door. She couldn't just say that she suspected he was with someone else and had shown up to catch him in the act. She needed a cover story.

A few possibilities came to mind:

1) She was here to tell him she was sorry for nixing the idea of going out for an evening with the kids.

2) She wanted to talk about something regarding the house. A new idea for the kitchen countertops, maybe, or a thought about window coverings.

3) She wanted to apologize for Liam's rudeness. She wasn't sure if Liam had even said anything to Jake that evening, but he was Liam—it was a safe bet that he'd been rude.

The last one had some appeal because it allowed her to position herself as the better person—she wasn't here to break up impending sex. No, she was simply here to maturely observe that Liam had no right to interfere in anyone's life.

Gathering her courage, she got out of the car, went up the front walk, and knocked on the door. She didn't bang—banging suggested an urgency she was trying to pretend she didn't feel. Instead, she knocked politely but firmly, in a way that suggested she had all evening to wait for a response.

She steeled herself for the possibility that he would come to the front door mussed and half-dressed, smelling of guilt and young woman.

When she got no answer, it was both a relief and a conundrum. He was here, clearly. Was he hiding out on the chance that it might be her?

She knocked again, louder this time.

"Jake?" She called his name through the door.

"Breanna?" The voice came from behind her, and she jumped a little, startled. She spun around to find him coming up the front walk with Sam. They were alone.

"Oh … Jake." She'd forgotten all of her scenarios for what to say to him and just stood there lamely, relieved that he wasn't naked and in the arms of another woman.

But that didn't mean he hadn't been.

"What are you doing here?" Jake asked. "I mean, I'm glad to see you, but …"

Breanna grasped mentally for one of her three excuses, then decided it was pointless. Jake was going to see through her no matter what she said.

"Where is she?" she asked instead.

To his credit, Jake didn't pretend not to know who she meant. "She went home. At least, I assume she did. We said goodbye at Ted's."

"Oh." Breanna felt embarrassed, maybe even humiliated, and she drew herself up to her full height to combat the feeling. "Are you sleeping with her?"

"No. Come inside so we can talk about it." He started past her with Sam, headed for the front door.

"There's nothing to talk about. You don't owe me anything."

"Stop it. Just come inside." Jake unlocked the door, snapped off Sam's leash, and went inside, looking back at Breanna to see if she was going to follow.

At first she just stood there, not knowing what to do. If they went inside to talk, it was likely going to end with Jake breaking up with her, explaining that he was with Kye now. They'd still be friends, maintain their professional relationship, blah blah blah.

She didn't want to be friends, and if he really was with Kye now, she didn't know if she could bear to hear it.

Still, she'd come here to find out what was going on. The only way to do that was to follow him inside.

Jake had expected that his little show with Kye would yield some kind of result with Breanna. He just hadn't expected it to happen so fast. Liam must have shattered the speed limit rushing home to tell her what he'd seen.

She looked so hurt, so sad. He felt like an ass for playing her.

Great job, genius.

At first he thought she wasn't going to come in the house, but then she did. She crossed the threshold hesitantly, but he could see her straightening, arranging her features, trying to be brave.

God, he was an asshole.

He got Sam settled in the bedroom with a chew toy so he wouldn't try to crush Breanna by climbing into her lap. Then he sat down on the sofa and gestured for her to sit beside him. She perched on the edge of the cushion on the far side of the sofa, putting as much space between them as she could.

"So. You're dating Kye Ferris." Her back was straight, but her voice was a little wobbly.

"Dated—one time. That's all."

"I see." Breanna folded her hands in her lap primly. "It's none of my business, of course. We're not exclusive. You're free to see whomever you like. I just thought that if you were having a ... a sexual relationship with someone else, I have a right to know. And now I do. So." She grabbed her purse and stood up.

"Breanna, sit down. Stop acting like that."

"Like what?"

"Like you're consulting with your doctor about a bad diagnosis. This is me. Sit down and let me talk to you." He reached out and caught her hand in his. She pulled it away, but she did sit down. At least that was something.

He took a deep breath and opted for the truth.

"Look. I went out with Kye because I was mad. I wanted to hurt you, but now you're hurt and I feel like shit about it. So, I'm sorry. There's nothing going on with her. Just the one date. We met at Ted's, we said goodnight at Ted's. No sex—no kissing, even. Just a couple of games of darts and a beer or two. And me putting on an act so Liam would tell you about it."

Breanna looked stricken, her eyes wide. "You did it to *hurt* me?"

"Well ... to make you jealous. But, yeah. And that makes me an asshole. But the Kye thing—it was nothing. It was theater. I've already apologized to her for that, by the way."

After Liam had left Ted's, Jake had confessed his real motivations to Kye, who should have been pissed off but who had, instead, called him sweet and kissed him on the cheek. Her reaction had made him feel not only pathetic but old as well.

Now, he waited to see what Breanna would do. If she walked out, he couldn't fault her for it. He'd probably have done the same.

"Jealous? But why?" She looked genuinely baffled, as though the words he'd said didn't make any objective sense.

He rubbed his face with his hands, his elbows propped on his knees.

He needed to make her understand.

"You wanted to take things slow. I get that. I do. But ... we're not sleeping together. We don't have any kind of commitment. You don't want to include your kids, or to even let them know we're seeing each other. We've been together awhile now ..."

"Not so long," she protested. "Just a few months ..."

"Yeah. A few months." He ran his hand through his hair. "But it seems like forever when I knew the first day ..."

"You knew what the first day?" she whispered, her face pale.

In for a penny, Jake thought.

"I knew I wanted you. I knew I wanted to be with you. I knew you were the one. I won't say I knew I was in love with you—not that soon—but ... I know it now. I love you, Breanna. And every day, every time we see each other, you just push me away. You want me around, sure, but at a distance. At arm's length. I don't want to hold back anymore. I don't want to be patient. I want *you*. All of you. And everything that comes with that."

She looked stunned. She opened her mouth, then closed it again.

"Jake ..."

"Don't say anything." He put up a hand to stop her. "Because it's either gonna be that you don't feel the same way, or you'll say something you're not ready for just to smooth things over. But you came over wanting to know what tonight was about, and now you know."

His heart was pounding, and he could feel beads of sweat between his shoulder blades. Honesty had been his only real option, but now that he'd been honest—dead honest—he was terrified about where that would lead.

It was just as well that Jake had told her not to say anything. Breanna was so stunned by his pronouncement that she had no words left in her head anyway.

She sat on the sofa, a good two feet of space between them, and stared at him. She reached a hand toward him, but he stood and stepped away so she couldn't reach him.

"Don't. Not yet, I mean. If you touch me, then I'll touch you, and ... next thing we know we'll be in bed, and I don't want to do that until we know where we are." He stuffed his hands into the pockets of his jeans.

"Jake." She found her voice, finally, and considered what she wanted to say. "I didn't mean to hurt you. I just don't want to make a mistake."

He nodded and tucked his hands into his armpits in a gesture of self-defense. "I get that, but you've got to risk it at some point if you want us to be together. Or maybe you *don't* want us to be together. Maybe that's what you've been trying to say all this time."

She didn't say anything.

"Look, go home. Think about it. Think about what you want. If you want me, let me know. If you don't ... Well, it's gonna hurt like hell, but I guess I'll survive."

Breanna blinked a few times, processing the fact that he was asking her to leave. She got up slowly, but she didn't yet move for the door.

"So, this is an ultimatum?"

"An ultimatum? No. I wouldn't say that." A muscle flexed in his jaw, and she could see that he was nervous. "It's more a statement of purpose. I want to move forward. If you can't do that, if you need to stand still for whatever reason, that's okay. But I can't stand still with you."

He was right that if she answered him now, she was going to say the wrong thing. Either she would rush into his arms and tell him that she wanted him—which she did, so much—or she would break it off in a desperate bid to protect herself.

She couldn't do either of those things, not now. She needed time. She needed to think.

She realized with a sudden, jarring dread that either way, they still had to work together.

"The house …"

"It's almost done. Nothing left but details and cleanup. If this doesn't go the way I want it to, I'll be done and out of your hair in another week." He gave her a wry smile. "But I really hope it'll go the way I want it to."

There was nothing left to say for the moment. Nothing left to do but take time by herself to think.

Chapter Twenty-Eight

Breanna had so many reasons not to be with Jake.

She didn't want to put her heart at risk. She didn't want to be irresponsible. She didn't want to involve her boys in a relationship that might end badly.

But in the end, the one that weighed most heavily on her mind was the thought that she was cheating on Brian.

She'd lost him a long time ago, so long that she sometimes had to look at his picture to remind herself about the details and the contours of his face. It had been so long that she'd forgotten what it was like to be part of a couple, to belong to someone every bit as much as you belonged to yourself.

But there wasn't a time limit on grief, she figured. There wasn't a moment when you were just done being lonely and sad. You couldn't simply cross the finish line and congratulate yourself on having survived.

She had the option of being with someone new, but Brian didn't. Where was his happiness? Where was his second chance?

If the Delaneys knew nothing else, they knew loyalty. The Delaneys were loyal down to their bones, down to the very marrow of their souls. Who would she even be if she could just walk away from Brian's memory to love someone else, to move on with her life?

She thought about all of that alone in bed after she left Jake. She'd hurt him, she knew. She'd had no business getting involved with him if she couldn't move forward, couldn't give him what he deserved from a woman.

Since Brian had died, Breanna had her role. She was a loving mother, a dutiful daughter, a steadfast sister and friend. She helped others. She volunteered, donated, and made herself useful every day in a thousand ways.

She'd wanted to have a house of her own because she'd felt ready to claim something that was just hers. And maybe those feelings had spread, leading her to believe she could have something with Jake.

But she'd be foolish to think that her actions wouldn't have consequences for the other people in her life. And she'd been kidding herself if she'd thought she could set aside the commitment she'd made to Brian.

She couldn't sleep, but she had to try. She had so many things to do the next day, mostly for other people—she had to help Mrs. Granfield, prepare for the move to the new house, help organize an event for the Historical Society, put in some time for the PTA.

People expected her to be there, both mentally as well as physically. She couldn't let them down.

She'd let Jake down, and she'd let herself down. She could at least show up for everyone else.

In the morning, Sandra peered at Breanna with an appraising eye.

"What's the matter with you, girl? You look like you've run a marathon in tight shoes. *Hmph*." She let out a sound that might have been a laugh, amused at her own humor.

"I'm fine."

She didn't feel fine—didn't feel anything vaguely similar to fine. But she didn't want to discuss it. And even if she had wanted to discuss it, Sandra would be the last person she'd want to talk to, considering the woman's near supernatural ability to divine her children's thoughts. She needed to keep some things, some feelings, to herself, and that would be impossible if she opened up to her mother.

"Well, that's a hot, steaming pile of fresh manure, and I guess we both know it," Sandra said. "I suppose it's got something to do with that contractor of yours being out with that Ferris girl last night." Breanna must have looked surprised, because Sandra scoffed. "Your brother talks to me, you know. At least *somebody* does."

"Jake can see whomever he wants." The line hadn't been very effective last night with Liam, and Breanna didn't expect it to be any more helpful now. But it was what she had.

"Oh, for God's sake, girl," Sandra said. "Just admit it threw you for a damned loop. There's no shame in it. Why, I guess anyone would have been upset under the circumstances."

When Sandra put it that way, Breanna had to admit that maybe the stoic act was a little stupid. She slumped a little, her shoulders dropping from where they'd been somewhere up around her ears.

"Oh, God." Breanna rubbed her tired eyes and ran a hand through her hair. "Okay, maybe I'm a little … thrown. And maybe I had a rough night. But that doesn't mean it's anything I can't handle."

Sandra had been making a pot of coffee, and she held a bag of French roast in her hand, waving it around a little for emphasis. "I don't believe I accused you of being near collapse," she pointed out.

Breanna thought that maybe if she kept her head down and focused on the job at hand—making breakfast for Ryan and Liam so they could get to work on the ranch at dawn—her mother might let the subject drop.

She should have known better.

"Either you two had an understanding that you wouldn't be going around with other people—"

"We didn't."

"—or you didn't, but either way, it doesn't mean you want to hear about him hittin' the town with a woman half your age."

That last bit jolted Breanna, and she turned to gape at her mother.

"Half my age?! She's not sixteen!"

Sandra let out a grunt. "Heh. Kinda looks like it, though. You have to wonder about a man, wants to go out with someone who looks like she oughta be hanging streamers for the damned junior prom."

For the first time since Liam had burst into the house with the news the night before, Breanna smiled, just a little. Sandra didn't have to offer words of wisdom, or an embrace, or heart-warming platitudes to make Breanna feel better. She just had to be Sandra.

"I love you, Mom." Breanna pulled her mother into a quick, businesslike hug.

"*Hmph.* Well." Sandra squeezed back for just a second, then went to put some bread into the toaster.

Gen heard about the Kye incident early, before Breanna had even showered and dressed for the day. Ryan heard it from Liam out on the ranch that morning, and Gen heard it from Ryan when she called him to tell him that J.R., at less than a year and a half, had said his first sentence.

Naturally, Gen led with the thing about the sentence when she burst into the main house that morning with J.R. on her hip. Once everybody had indicated that they were duly impressed, Gen pulled Breanna aside and hissed in an angry whisper, "Bree, I am so sorry about Jake. The asshole. I'd thought he was better than that."

Of course, Breanna explained that they hadn't been exclusive.

"Well, that's crap," Gen said, putting the baby down to let him toddle around on the kitchen floor. "Just because you weren't wearing his letterman's sweater doesn't mean he can parade around town with another woman."

At this point, Breanna was sick of trying to act nonchalant. Putting up a front was just too damned much work. She sank into one of the chairs at the big kitchen table and sighed.

"He said he did it to make me jealous."

"What!?" Gen's sudden exclamation upset J.R., who started to cry. She sat down next to Breanna, picked the boy up, balanced him on her knee, then began to bounce the knee and the boy up and down in the classic pony ride style used by mothers for generations.

"Oh … it's not his fault, really," Breanna said, feeling every bit of the weariness brought on by her sleepless night. "I mean, it is. It was a stupid thing to do. But I get why he did it. He's tired of being put off. And I don't blame him."

"But—"

Breanna put up a hand to stall Gen's argument. "He told me he loves me."

If the idea had been to prevent a potential rant by Gen, this had done it.

"Oh," she said. "Wow."

"Yeah." Gen propped her chin on her hand, her elbow resting on the table. "He wanted things to move faster between us, but I stalled. He wanted the boys to know we were a couple, but I wasn't ready."

Gen jiggled her son and looked at Breanna with concern. "But you're sleeping together, right? So that's—"

Breanna shook her head.

"You're *not*?" Gen gaped at her.

"We did, once. And then I said I wanted to slow things down, and since then …"

"Oh, jeez. I can see why he tried something desperate."

Breanna could see it, too—though that didn't make things any clearer. "I don't know what to do," she moaned.

"Well, do you love him back?"

Gen asked the question so matter-of-factly that it seemed like it should be simple. But it wasn't simple at all—not to Breanna.

"That's not the point."

Gen raised her eyebrows. "How is it not the point?"

"I have other things to consider!" Breanna threw her hands into the air in frustration. "Other *people* to consider! The boys—"

"The boys will handle it if you decide you want a relationship. They're not little kids anymore. They'll be fine."

Gen was gazing at Breanna with kindness and concern, but Breanna didn't want either of those things. She didn't want the kindness because she wasn't sure she deserved it. And she didn't want the concern because it implied that she was in a position to *need* concern, and that was the whole point of this, wasn't it? Hadn't all of this drama happened precisely because Breanna knew how to protect herself without anyone else's help?

"I notice you never answered the question," Gen pointed out.

"What question?"

"The one about whether you love him."

"I don't know what I feel."

Gen reached out and put a hand on Breanna's arm. "Yes, you do. You just don't want to admit it. But you'd better get over that soon, because if last night was any indication, he's tired of waiting."

Chapter Twenty-Nine

It was true, Jake was tired of waiting. But that didn't mean he'd had to act like an ass.

The morning after his confrontation with Breanna, he poured himself a cup of coffee in his kitchen and took inventory of the many and varied ways in which he'd been a total fool.

Telling her the truth about what he wanted and how he felt wasn't one of them; that part he'd gotten right. Going out with someone he wasn't interested in just to prove something to himself made the list, though. So did putting on a show with her to force Breanna into some kind of action.

He wished he could undo it, but he couldn't.

"Asshole," he muttered to himself under his breath as he sat at his kitchen table and swallowed those first, bitter sips.

Sam was whining to go outside, so Jake got up, opened the front door, and stood just inside the threshold while the dog went out, found a promising clump of grass, and peed. Both relieved and grateful, Sam came back in, and Jake got back to his wallowing.

He probably didn't deserve for Breanna to commit to him after the way he'd acted. She'd be well within reason to congratulate herself on avoiding a relationship with a man who had the maturity of a middle-schooler.

He hoped like hell she wouldn't do that, though. Eight hours since he'd made his pronouncement and he already missed her with an ache that felt like his heart was being pulled from his chest.

He hadn't been entirely sure that he loved Breanna until he'd heard the words coming out of his own mouth the night before. But as he'd said it, he'd known that it was true. He knew it even more surely this morning, with the possibility that he'd ruined everything hanging over his head.

Sam came over to where Jake was sitting and laid his enormous head on Jake's thigh. The dog let out a huge, wet sigh, his eyes sad.

Did he miss her, too, or was this just Sam feeling sympathetic and trying to comfort him? Either way, Jake appreciated the solidarity. He rubbed Sam's head with his hand.

"I know, boy. I know."

Feeling sorry for himself wasn't going to help anything, but it was the weekend, and Jake didn't have anything else planned.

"Ah … fuck," he said to the dog.

Breanna decided that the best thing to do was to avoid the whole thing.

Actually, it would be wrong to say she decided it. Because her lack of action was about *not* deciding. Not committing. Not taking a stand one way or another on her relationship with Jake and where she did or did not want it to go.

She knew what her heart wanted. But when you were a single mother, you had to think of what was practical and what was right. You couldn't just think about your own selfish yearnings. You couldn't just think about your heart.

Hadn't her heart wanted her to die along with Brian back when she'd gotten the news? Hadn't everything inside her screamed for her to crawl under her covers and weep, shutting out the world until the very planets stopped spinning?

But she hadn't done that then, and she couldn't follow something as capricious as her feelings now. If widowhood had taught her anything, it was that sometimes you had to put your feelings aside and do what was best for those around you.

And what was best for her sons was stability. Yes, she was moving them to a new home, and that was proving to be rough on Michael in particular. How could she add to that upheaval by bringing a man into their lives? It was enough that they would be adjusting to new rooms and new routines. How could she also ask them to adjust to what they would surely see as her trying to replace their father?

She couldn't do it. But she also couldn't imagine saying goodbye to Jake.

Someone on the outside looking in would have said Breanna used work as an avoidance tactic. She would have said she was just getting on with her life. Either way, she'd somehow agreed to prepare twelve pies for the community's Memorial Day picnic at Shamel Park.

It had seemed like a simple enough thing at the time: just a little cooking to help her neighbors celebrate the beginning of summer.

But now, a few days before the picnic, surrounded in the kitchen by the ingredients for pound upon pound of pie filling, she began to question her own sanity. Surely only a psychotic break would have prompted her to sign up for this.

Today was Friday, and she hadn't talked to Jake since their confrontation a week before. She'd filled the days since then packing for the move, preparing for the pie extravaganza, and generally obsessing over any domestic task she could invent rather than obsessing about Jake.

There was still a little work to do on the house, but Breanna hadn't been taking the boys over there. They'd been asking why, and she hadn't known what to tell them.

Now, as she stood at the kitchen cleaning and cutting strawberries for the pies, Michael, who had just gotten home from school, was badgering her for answers.

"But *why* can't I go? Jake's going to be finished with the whole house before we even get to do anything else." Michael's face held the petulant expression he used when he felt he was being treated unfairly. Which was most of the time.

"There will be plenty for you to do," Breanna said mildly. "We'll have to haul our things over there and unpack, and there's all of the new furniture to choose."

"Oh, boy. Unpacking. I can hardly wait," Michael said dryly.

"Well, good," Breanna said, intentionally ignoring the sarcasm. "Then you'll have something to look forward to."

"And you won't even tell me why I can't go," Michael persisted. "That's not fair. If you're punishing me for something, I should at least know what it is."

"I'm not punishing you."

"Then why can't I go?"

Breanna, exhausted from lying awake at night and from her son's relentless arguing, set down her knife, let her shoulders fall, and sighed.

"Michael, you can't go because I said so."

"That's not a reason."

"Well, it's all the reason you're going to get. Now, if you keep standing here, I'm going to make you cut strawberries. So either grab a knife or go find something to do." Breanna rarely lost her temper with her kids, but an edge was creeping into her voice that said she was about to. Michael must have recognized that, because he gave her one last glare and then left the kitchen. If the room hadn't had a swinging door, he'd have slammed it.

As Michael went out, Sandra came in. She gave the boy a curious glance and then focused on Breanna.

"Well, what burr's gotten under that boy's saddle this time?"

Breanna let out a very Sandra-like grunt. "He wants to go to the Moonstone Beach house to work with Jake, and I said no."

"And I'll bet he wants an explanation, and you aren't giving one," Sandra said.

"Exactly."

"*Hmph*. If it was me, I'd let him go on over there and hammer some nails for a while, work out some of that attitude of his."

"Well, it's not you," Breanna said shortly.

Sandra considered her daughter. "Thank the good lord for small favors."

There wasn't much left to do on the Moonstone Beach house. It had been four long months of renovations, but Jake was almost ready to put the finishing touches on this job and call it done.

And not a minute too soon.

Since things had gone to hell with Breanna, it was more than a little awkward to continue working with her. But she'd kept her distance since things had imploded, and that helped him to focus on the task he'd been hired to do.

It wasn't just her that he would miss. He was also going to miss the house.

Jake walked through each room surveying all that he'd accomplished. The kitchen, which had been cramped and dark before, was now big, bright, and efficient. The front room had more windows, fresh drywall, and a new fireplace. The bathrooms had been gutted and redesigned, with shiny new fixtures and gleaming tile. The guesthouse had been expanded and modernized while keeping the house's historic feel. Everywhere, hardwood floors gleamed and natural light streamed in, creating a warm and welcoming feel.

Jake was pretty damned pleased with himself.

He'd sent his crew home yesterday, since they'd finished everything he couldn't easily do himself. Now, with the morning sun streaming in through the windows—many of which Jake had installed—he walked through each room with satisfaction.

Outside, the house maintained the same classic farmhouse look it had been built with back in the 1920s. It was big and solid, sky blue with white trim. Inside, it was all sunshine and warm wood, with walls the color of fresh butter.

He imagined Breanna and the boys living here, going about their lives in this space that Jake had made for them. And thinking about it made a hard ache pull at his chest.

He'd begun to hope that maybe he might have a part in that life. Now, the idea that he wouldn't stung almost as badly as his divorce had. When had Breanna come to mean more to him than his ex had? How had she gotten that kind of power over him? How had he let that happen without even noticing?

No point obsessing over it. No point worrying it like a loose tooth. He still had work to do.

There was nothing left but a few details. He was attending to one of them—screwing in the wall plates for the electric switches and outlets—when he heard footsteps coming in the front door, which was standing open.

On his knees in front of a low outlet, he turned and saw Michael standing just inside the front door, looking somewhere between pissed-off and sheepish.

"Michael. I didn't expect you today." He got up, walked over, and moved to shake the boy's hand. Jake had always thought that a good handshake went a long way toward making a boy feel like a man.

Michael kept his hands stuffed in his jeans pockets, ignoring Jake's, which was still extended to him.

Okay, pissed-off, then.

"Something on your mind?" Jake said.

"What did you do to my mom?"

Jake had to admire the kid's spunk, putting it right out there like that. Coming to him like this took guts. He deserved a straight answer, but Jake didn't know how much Breanna had told him—or intended to.

Jake retrieved his hand, which had still been awkwardly extended.

"What exactly do you think I did?" he asked.

"That's not an answer."

"No, it's not." Jake had a couple of choices here. He could decide that his erstwhile romance with Breanna was none of Michael's business and send him on his way with some happy bullshit about protecting Breanna's privacy. Or he could be straight with the kid and show him the respect Jake had come to feel for him over the past months.

He opted for the latter.

"Come and sit down," he said, leading Michael out to the front porch. Jake sat on the top step and motioned for the kid to sit next to him. When they were settled, he laid it out as simply as he could.

"I don't know whether your mother told you we were seeing each other."

"She didn't tell me, but I knew. Everybody knew." His eyes were guarded, maybe hostile. Probably just hurt.

"Yeah, well ... She doesn't want the same things I do. So, it looks like it's not going to work out between us." He hated like hell just saying the words. Part of him felt that if he didn't say it, it might not be true.

"Like what?" Michael said. "What do you want that she doesn't?"

Jake rubbed the back of his neck with his hand. "Hell, kid. Just ... everything. A relationship. Maybe even marriage eventually. More kids. The whole bit."

"And she doesn't want that? Why not?"

"You'd have to ask her."

"Jake ..."

"Look. I'm not sure I understand it myself," Jake said. "She says she's not ready. But I don't know what that means. Maybe it just means she doesn't love me."

"But you love her." It wasn't a question.

"I do, yeah. But it's gotta go both ways, or it's not gonna work." Jake shot a glance at the kid out of the corner of his eye. "Are you even supposed to be here?"

"No. She wouldn't bring me, so I rode my bike."

"Does she know you're here?"

The boy's silence was all the answer Jake needed.

"Michael, you're going to get me in trouble with your mom." Though, now that he thought about it, what difference did it make at this point? "You got a cell phone?"

Michael nodded.

"Call her and tell you where you are so she won't worry. Then you can help me with these wall plates."

Jake and Michael worked side by side, fitting the plates over the outlets and wall switches and screwing them in place. As they worked, they talked about life, divorce, death, and the struggles of adolescence.

"My mom always acts like she doesn't need anything. Like she doesn't need to meet anybody new, or get married again, or anything like that. But she's always sad. She doesn't think we know she's sad, but, God, we're not stupid."

"No, I can see that you're not," Jake agreed.

"And what about us?" he said. "She thinks we'll curl up and die or something if she gets married again. I know I'm supposed to hate the idea of having a stepdad, but sometimes I think it might be kind of cool."

"You do?" Jake stopped what he was doing and looked at Michael, who was intently screwing a plate into the wall.

The kid shrugged. "I mean, I don't know. Maybe. But how will any of us know if we don't try it?"

"Getting married again isn't something your mom can just try. Once it's done, it's done. Mostly." He thought of his own divorce, and how nothing was ever as simple as being done. Not really.

"Yeah, I know." The shrug again. "But you've got to take chances sometimes, right? You can't always do what's safe. What does she want, to be stuck taking care of us kids and my grandpa and my uncles for the rest of her life?"

"I don't think she thinks of it that way," Jake said. "As being stuck, I mean."

Michael finished with the wall plate, grabbed another one out of a bag Jake had left on the floor, and went to work on the next one. "It's like she doesn't want to be happy."

"Or maybe she just doesn't know how to be," Jake said.

"I guess."

Jake thought about how it must feel to be raised by a perpetually unhappy mother—and what a difference it would make if she were truly happy for once in her boys' lives.

"You should tell her what you think," Jake said. "What you told me. I mean, why not? What do you have to lose?"

Michael shrugged, but Jake could tell he was thinking about it.

They were in the kitchen working on the plates above the countertops when Jake heard a knock on the front doorframe. Sam rushed past them to investigate, a massive black blur.

"Michael? Are you here?" Breanna called into the big, empty house.

"Tell her," Jake said.

Chapter Thirty

When Breanna realized that Michael had left without telling her, she'd been furious. At first she'd assumed that he was out on the ranch. While it was uncharacteristic of him to volunteer to work with his uncles, he sometimes liked to walk to the creek and sit in the grass amid the buzzing insects, throwing rocks into the water and thinking his unknowable thoughts.

But then he'd called to tell her he had gone to the Moonstone Beach house on his own, despite her having told him clearly that she didn't want him to go. She'd started running through a list of possible punishments in her head before she'd even left the house to go get him.

No phone, she thought. *No computer. No TV or video games.* And if that wasn't enough, he could be at the mercy of his uncles for a week, mucking out stables and shoveling cow shit from the barn.

Jake must have read her expression accurately, because as soon as he saw her, he started trying to placate her on Michael's behalf.

"Look, don't be too hard on him," Jake said. "He was just—"

"Michael, get in the car," Breanna said, cutting Jake off.

"Mom, we just got done with the—"

"Get in the car."

However difficult Michael had been of late, he clearly knew when not to push his luck. Sulking, he went out the front door and headed toward the car, which was parked on Moonstone Beach Drive.

"You might want to cut him some slack," Jake said when Michael was out of earshot. "I think he came over here to try to kick my ass."

Whatever Breanna had expected to hear, it hadn't been that. "He ... what?"

"The kid came storming in here asking what I did to his mom. He was trying to defend you, which took balls, if you ask me. It was him trying to be a man, trying to protect someone he loves. If you try to lecture or punish or badger that out of him, then you're not only doing him a disservice, you're disrespecting your own accomplishments as a parent. And that would be a damned shame."

Breanna let that sink in a little.

"That was quite a speech," she said after a while.

"Yeah, well." He rubbed the stubble on his chin. "I'd been planning it since ten minutes after he got here."

Breanna told herself to take a breath and consider what Jake was telling her. While she was doing that, it occurred to her that the house was done—or very nearly so.

"Oh, my God," she said, looking around in wonder. "The house ..."

"I was gonna call you later today and let you know. It's move-in ready. What do you think?"

"You weren't even scheduled to finish until next week."

"Yeah, well … sexual frustration can really boost a guy's productivity." He grinned ruefully. "Not that I'd write a self-help book recommending it."

Breanna had seen the house during the various phases of the renovation. She'd seen it as recently as a week before. But then, dozens of little details—a missing molding, a door with a round hole where the knob would be—had told her the place wasn't ready for her yet, that it was still in its final stages of becoming.

She'd told herself to be patient, to think about other things. And she had. She'd been so preoccupied with everything that had happened with Jake that she'd almost forgotten that her new home was waiting for her.

But now, here it was, warm and gleaming, clean and made whole.

"Oh, Jake."

She almost forgot. She almost threw herself into his arms with joy and gratitude. She could see that he'd almost forgotten, too. His eyes had been sparkling with pleasure, but then, suddenly, they hardened.

She had taken a step toward him, but then, with the aborted hug, she retreated again.

"Thank you. It's beautiful," she said.

"It's my job. I'll have the final invoice over to you later today."

She shouldn't have been stung by the tone of his voice—she knew that—but she was anyway.

"When can we move in?" she said.

"Whenever you want. It's your house." He dug a set of keys out of his jeans pocket and handed them to her. "I've just got a little cleanup to do, and I'm out of here."

He walked out of the room, his boots clomping on the hardwood floors. Sam hurried after him, his tail swishing.

She was desperate to walk through the house taking in every nuance, caressing every surface. But she was just as desperate not to be in the same space as Jake any longer than necessary.

If she stayed here with him, in this house where he was breathing the same air, one of two things would happen. Either she would have to endure the pain of his distance, or she would lose her last ounce of self-discipline and kiss him so long and hard that the sun would rise and set and age and eventually die without her ever letting him go.

Her son was waiting for her out in the car, and they had a lot to talk about.

She tucked the keys into her purse and went outside to deal with her boy.

"Michael, what were you thinking?"

She'd waited until they'd gotten back to the ranch before she'd started in on him. Now she couldn't put it off any longer, but she was trying to be reasonable and clear-headed. She tried to keep the mom-scold out of her voice.

"I wanted to know what happened. Why you two broke up." Michael was sitting on his bed, looking down at his sneakers.

She stared at him. Had he really said that? How did he know what had happened between them? She'd tried so hard to keep the boys out of it, to keep them untouched should some-thing go wrong between herself and Jake.

Which it had.

Had she let something slip? Had she been that obvious?

"What do you mean?" She was stalling for time, and she hoped she wasn't being transparent about that, too.

"I mean, you were Jake's girlfriend, but then something happened, and you were upset and wouldn't let me go over there anymore. That's what I mean, Mom. Obviously."

She ignored the snotty tone with which he'd delivered that last word.

"I wasn't his girlfriend."

"Mom, jeez. You don't have to lie about it. I'm not a little kid."

Suddenly, a flare of anger shot through her. "Did he tell you that? Is that what Jake said? Because—"

"Nobody had to tell me." He rolled his eyes at her in the time-honored way of teens everywhere, since the first adolescent boy had crawled out of the cave to go mastodon hunting against his parents' wishes. "I have eyes. I have ears. I notice things. God."

"But he talked to you about it."

"A little." Michael shrugged.

"What did he say?" she asked, exasperated. Sometimes, talking to Michael was like trying to push a rock up a mountain while wearing roller skates.

Suddenly, the words that had been so hard to coax out of him began to come. "He said he loves you and wants to marry you and have kids and everything, but you don't love him. Why not, Mom? Jake's cool. He talks to me and shows me how to do stuff. And he doesn't treat me like a kid, the way you do."

Breanna could have argued the last part, but there was so much to deal with here that defending her own treatment of Michael was low on the priority list.

"He said I don't love him?"

"Well, you don't, right?" Michael gave her a skeptical look. "You must not or you wouldn't have broken up with him. And, you know, I guess that's fine if that's how you feel. But I don't get why I can't still go over there and work with Jake and hang out and stuff."

"It's done," she said. "The house. It's finished. There's nothing more to do."

So many thoughts were running through her head that she had to pick them out and address them one by one.

"He said he wants to marry me?"

"Well, not right now, obviously. But someday. And he said you didn't want that. Even though it would be awesome."

Her head was spinning with all of this new information. Jake wanted to marry her? When had he decided that? She'd been telling herself that she was protecting her boys by slowing things down with Jake. Now Michael was telling her that he *wanted* them to be together. Had he been hoping for her to re-marry all this time? Or had he only started having these thoughts since he'd met Jake?

She raked her hands through her hair, trying to get her thoughts together. "Michael … you shouldn't have gone over there when I told you not to."

"Mom, that's not the point. That's …"

"It *is* the point. I told you not to go, and you did. Without even telling anyone where you'd gone." Focusing on this—the thing he'd done wrong—put her on steadier ground, so she decided to stick with it.

"Fine. I suppose you're going to punish me."

Everything Jake had said about Michael came back to her—that he had shown courage going to Jake, that he'd just been trying to protect his mother, and that she would be doing her son a disservice if she didn't recognize what it had cost him to do it.

"No. I'm not."

"You're not?" His eyebrows rose in surprise, and in that moment he looked so much like his father that Breanna almost burst into tears.

"Not this time."

"Why not?"

She ruffled his hair—something she used to do when he was small but that he'd objected to for some time now. Somehow, she couldn't seem to help herself.

"Just don't do it again," she told him. "Don't run off without telling me where you're going. Okay?"

"Okay." He didn't mention the much-hated hair-ruffling, but he self-consciously straightened his hair again the moment she released him.

"Michael? I love you."

"I love you, too." Even at thirteen, even with his need to be adult and cool and independent, he could still say the words. She hoped he would never stop.

She started to walk out of the room, and he stopped her.

"Mom?"

"Yeah?"

"I'm sorry. For leaving like that, I mean."

"All right." She gave him a reassuring smile. She headed back toward the door, then hesitated. "You really like Jake?"

"Yeah, Mom. I really do."

It was something to think about.

Chapter Thirty-One

Breanna approached Lucas later that day while he was out at the stables grooming one of the horses. Lucas had been riding since he was small—both of the boys had—but he'd just gotten to the age where Liam had insisted that he learn how to do a proper grooming. Lucas hadn't hit his growth spurt yet, so he had to stand on a step stool to reach the mare's back with his curry comb.

Breanna hadn't been out to the stables much lately. She used to ride a lot when she was younger, but somehow, that had fallen away along with so much else over the past several years.

The place smelled like hay, manure, and above that, the gentle ocean breeze drifting in from the west. A fat black fly buzzed in front of her, and Breanna swatted it away.

"How's it coming?" she asked Lucas companionably.

"Pretty good," he said, stretching to comb the far reaches of the big animal. "I think Daisy likes it."

"I'm sure she does." The mare snuffed out a breath as if to confirm it.

"Did you have a good ride?" Breanna asked.

"Yeah. Uncle Liam took me out to the southeast pasture. He said I didn't really need him, but you told him I couldn't go alone." He shot her a tentative look, and her heart broke a little.

If even her sweet, good-natured, go-along-with-anything boy was questioning her parenting, then maybe she really should consider whether she was being overprotective.

Thinking back, she tried to remember when she'd been eleven. Had she been required to stay with her parents or her uncle on a ride? No, she remembered, she hadn't. She'd spent most of her childhood on a horse, exploring every recess of their property and beyond. When had she decided that the freedom she'd enjoyed as a kid wasn't good enough for her own boys?

When she'd lost Brian—that was when. The world had shown her that pain and grief and even death were as close as a knock on her front door, and that lesson had pervaded her every action since then. How much had that cost her? How much had it cost her sons?

"Lucas?"

"*Hmm?*" He was focusing on the task in front of him, and the tip of his tongue poked out the side of his mouth in his concentration. He'd always done that—whether he was four years old and coloring, or five and learning to ride, or eleven and mastering the art of grooming. The sight of it caused a fresh wave of love to swell into her chest.

"What do you think of Jake?" she asked him.

"He's cool. He let me hammer stuff and sand the deck, and I really like his dog."

Lucas climbed down off of the step stool and exchanged his curry comb for a dandy brush. He went back onto the stool and started brushing out the mare's coat.

She caught her lower lip lightly between her teeth as she considered her next conversational gambit. "Did you know that he and I … that we weren't just friends?"

Lucas threw her a disdainful glance. "Of course, Mom. Duh."

Just another way in which she'd underestimated her boys. Had she really thought they were so unobservant?

"Why didn't you say anything?" she asked.

Lucas shrugged. "I dunno. I guess I just figured there wasn't anything to say about it. Jake's nice and you need a boyfriend, so …"

This last bit caused Breanna to let out an unladylike guffaw. "Who says I need a boyfriend?"

"Gramma Sandra. And Aunt Gen. And Aria. Lots of people."

Breanna wanted to be angry, but she found herself laughing incredulously instead. "Pretty much everybody, then. And they talked to you about it?"

"No, they talk to each other. I don't think they even notice I'm listening." He stepped down off of the stool and began working on the horse's flank with the brush.

Breanna realized that what Lucas said was true—people just talked, and when a kid was in the room doing something else, they tended to assume that he didn't have ears, or that those ears somehow didn't work. But they did work—very well, indeed.

"And you agree with them? That I need a boyfriend?"

Lucas shrugged again—it seemed that had been the preamble to every thought he'd had today. "I guess. Why not? Uncle Ryan got married, and Uncle Colin, and Uncle Liam's going to. If everybody else has a girlfriend or a wife or somebody, why shouldn't you have a boyfriend?"

He'd laid out his argument with such simple logic, it was difficult to disagree with it.

"Unless you don't like Jake," he said.

That thought was jarring to her, and she was a little taken aback. "I like him. But … what about your dad? I wouldn't want you to ever think I was trying to replace your father." Tears shimmered in her eyes at the thought.

Lucas, who surely didn't remember his father, stopped his work and looked at her thoughtfully. "If you love somebody, and then they're gone and you love somebody else, that seems like a thing you should be allowed to do. At least, it would be if I were making the rules." He applied his brush to the horse's shoulder, having finished making his case.

Jake e-mailed Breanna the final invoice for the renovations, and she paid him electronically. The money had just plunked into his bank account silently and stealthily, without any words having been exchanged between them.

That had to mean something, he thought. If she'd wanted to see him, bringing a check would have been a good excuse. But she hadn't done that. She'd asked for wiring instructions via e-mail, and she'd finished the whole transaction without ever having to see his face.

The whole thing seemed so final.

He'd worked for her, and now the job was done. He'd loved her, and now it seemed like that was done, too.

Jake was uncertain of what he'd done wrong, but it was surely something. You didn't tend to feel this much like shit unless you'd epically screwed something up somewhere.

Yeah, there'd been the thing with Kye—not his proudest moment—but that wasn't what had ended things with Breanna. The problem had been his insistence on them moving the relationship farther and faster than she'd wanted to go.

That was what people did, wasn't it? They moved forward. They found something good and then they went with it. They didn't just stand in one place, motionless while the world spun beneath them.

Except, he realized, standing in one place was exactly what Breanna had been doing for nine years, ever since her husband's death. At first, it had been understandable—smart, even. When you took a blow like that, you had to take time to regroup. But now, it seemed to him that Breanna's failure to move on had become a bad habit that she would need to break if she ever wanted real happiness.

But, hell, maybe he was kidding himself. Maybe she wasn't stuck—maybe she just didn't want to move forward with him. He couldn't fool himself that a guy like him was a good match for a woman like her—a woman whose net worth rivaled that of third world dictators or titans of industry. Who was he, anyway? He was a blue-collar guy with credit card debt, a meager bank account, and only a vague sense of how he might change either of those things.

She could do better than him. He knew it—and it was likely she did, too.

Jake pushed himself off his sofa, determined not to sit and feel sorry for himself. Sam, sensing the possibility of a walk, got up from where he'd been sitting on the rug and looked at Jake hopefully, his tail wagging.

"Not right now, big guy," Jake told him. It seemed like Sam understood him, because the dog's eyes took on a look of disappointment and sadness that had Jake feeling pangs of dog-owner guilt. He was probably projecting.

He gave Sam a new rawhide chew toy out of a package on the counter and rubbed the dog's head. "I've gotta get some work done. Can't sit on my ass forever. Dog park later, okay?"

The dog was too absorbed with the toy to respond.

They were heading into the high season for construction in Cambria. Out-of-towners had a tendency to visit the town during the spring, fall in love with it, and buy houses that needed renovation. This wasn't the time to lie on the couch drinking beer and counting his problems. He had a meeting with a potential client in a half hour, and he needed to be ready for it.

He went upstairs to shower, trying to put Breanna Delaney out of his mind.

Fat chance of that.

Breanna had a lot to think about other than Jake Travis.

She had to move herself and her boys into the new house, and that would, thankfully, take all of her time and mental energy in the coming days.

She'd been packing for a while now in anticipation of the house being finished, and she was almost done. Foolishly, she'd thought it would be easy because they weren't taking any furniture with them from the ranch. She hadn't wanted to leave her parents with the depressing sight of empty rooms, so she was only taking their personal items. Beds, dressers, side tables—all of that would stay.

So why were there so many boxes, so many things?

There was nothing like a move to make a person realize how many useless items they'd accumulated over the years. Books, clothes, photo albums, the kids' artwork from when they were small, the Christmas and birthday and Mother's Day presents received over a period of years, the random tchotchkes picked up at this shop or that one on a vacation or at a local boutique.

There was no way Breanna could sort through everything right now, no way she could make all of the necessary decisions about what to donate or throw away and what to keep. Plus, she was moving into a much larger space, so it didn't seem essential to pare down her belongings. Wanting to get into the new house sooner instead of later, she opted to pack everything and deal with issues of storage later.

She'd given each of the boys a stack of cardboard boxes and had instructed them to pack everything, leaving nothing in their rooms except the furniture. Michael had complained, but after a certain amount of motherly wheedling, Breanna had finally succeeded in getting him on task. Lucas was excited about the move and had needed no prodding.

They would be ready to pile everything into Liam's truck for the move to Moonstone Beach soon. But first, Breanna needed to deal with the issue of furniture delivery.

Breanna rarely took advantage of her wealth, except for indulging in the pleasure of donating to the charities of her choice extravagantly and at will. She had always tended to live so simply that spending money just wasn't a priority.

But now, she had to admit that it was nice to be able to furnish a new home and guest house with the things she wanted without having to worry about the damage it was going to do to her bank account.

Her mother had taught her to seek a good value, and she'd done that. Everything she'd chosen was reasonably priced and of good quality. It wasn't like she'd walked into a furniture showroom and had begun throwing hundred-dollar bills at the salespeople.

Still, it had been fun choosing the contents of her new home: sofas, beds, dressers, and a big, butcher block kitchen table that reminded her of the one she'd gathered around at the ranch for three meals a day since the time she'd been big enough to sit in a chair on her own.

The appliances were already in place—that had been part of the renovation—but the rest of the house was a series of open spaces waiting to be filled.

"I'd better get over there," she told her mother after breakfast a few days after Jake had announced the house's completion. "The beds are coming at ten. Or, during a window of time that begins at ten. I really hope I'm not over there all day waiting for the guy to show up."

"Well, I don't imagine it's going to be much of a hardship spending time in that house," Sandra observed. "She's a beauty, all right."

"She really is."

Sandra and Orin had gone to see the house the same day it had been finished. Orin had looked pinched and had made a lot of fussy noises and complaints. The content varied, but it amounted to him not understanding why Breanna and the kids needed to leave a perfectly good house where they'd been happy enough for quite some time. But Sandra, to Breanna's gratitude and relief, had understood.

"Now, Orin, a woman's got to have a place of her own. A place where she can be the queen bee without having to defer to her mama." She grunted with the satisfaction of having made an airtight argument. "Why, your daughter's been a help to me, all right, but I suspect she wants to start making her own decisions on how to do things instead of always having me tell her what to do."

Breanna appreciated her mother's validation, but she also felt the need to reassure both of her parents about her reasons for moving out.

"It's not that I haven't loved staying with you," she said as the three of them stood in the empty living room of the Moonstone Beach house, sunlight streaming through the windows. "If I hadn't had you two after Brian died, if I hadn't had our house to come home to …" She hesitated, because emotion was choking her voice. "I'm just ready, that's all. I'm ready to be on my own. I'm ready to move on."

"Just not with Jake Travis, is that it?" Sandra inquired.

"Mom …"

"I'm just saying, if you were all that ready to get on with your life, you might not have tossed that man to the curb, where someone else might pick him up and take him home."

"What's Breanna's contractor got to do with this?" Orin asked, looking uncomfortable and rubbing the back of his neck as though ants might have gathered there. "How'd she toss him to the curb? He finished the work, didn't he? Did a good job, too, far as I can see."

It seemed that Breanna's attempts to keep her relationship with Jake low key had worked on only one person in her household—her father.

"Now, you never mind about it, Orin," Sandra said.

Orin, looking relieved to have been let off the hook on this particular subject, went into the kitchen to inspect the appliances.

"I didn't kick him to the curb," Breanna protested when her father had left the room. "I just don't like ultimatums."

"Issued an ultimatum, did he?" Sandra asked.

"Well … yes. Sort of."

"Well, that's clear as mud," Sandra quipped.

Breanna turned to her mother, exasperated. "He was talking about … about making commitments. Going out with the kids. And marriage!"

"Horrors. That's some kind of monster you've got there."

"Mom, you're not helping." Breanna fixed her mother with the kind of withering look she used on the boys.

Sandra propped her hands on her narrow hips. "Well, I'd apologize, but I guess I don't see what's so wrong about a man wanting to take you and your boys out on the damned town. Though I'll admit the marriage thing is a little fast."

"He didn't actually mention marriage to me. He mentioned it to Michael. Which is another thing I'm unhappy about." She explained that Jake had told Michael he wanted marriage and children eventually, presumably with Breanna. The fact that he had told all of that to Michael had gone against Breanna's clear and specific wishes to keep the children out of her dating life.

"It wasn't his business to talk to Michael about those things," Breanna said. "I wanted the kids to be protected from this. I wanted them to be kept out of it."

Sandra looked appraisingly at Breanna for a long while.

"You've got opinions," Breanna concluded.

"Well, I'd say so."

"You might as well just say them. You know you're going to anyway."

"All right." Sandra counted out her arguments on her fingers. "One: It makes no damned sense that you want to protect your boys from something that ought to be their business. If a man stands half a chance of being involved in your life long term, I'd think the boys deserve their say. Two: I'd say it speaks well of Jake that he talks to Michael like a man. You ought to consider trying it yourself. Three: You ask me, Jake ought to be taking things to the next level at this point. I'd be suspicious of him if he didn't. Yet you seem to consider it some kind of crime. And four: It hurts a man's pride to told that his woman wants to keep her options open. I'm not surprised he cut his losses."

Breanna didn't know which argument to refute first, so she simply sputtered, "I ... I'm not his woman!"

"*Hmph*," Sandra grumbled. "I don't expect that's going to change anytime soon with that attitude of yours."

Chapter Thirty-Two

If Sandra didn't approve of the breakup with Jake, then neither did Breanna's own heart.

Here she was moving into her own gorgeous, beachfront, freshly renovated house, and all she could think about was how lonely the place felt without Jake inside it.

He was too intricately involved in the creation of this place, that was the problem. He'd built much of the interior with his own hands. How could she ever separate the house from the man who'd put his own heart and soul into it?

These were some of the things going through her head as she, the boys, Liam, and Ryan all worked to transfer box after box from Liam's truck into the new house.

The morning sky was clear, and the air was warm. The crash of the waves served as background music, and the scent of saltwater permeated the air. Insects buzzed in the high grass of the yard. She had plans for the landscaping, but that would come later.

"Seems like you ought to be happier than this, Bree," Ryan remarked over the box he was holding in his arms. "You've been waiting for this for a while."

"I'm happy," she protested. "I'm just … busy, that's all."

"Uh huh." He said it in that skeptical way that suggested he was agreeing with her just to humor her.

"I have a lot to think about, that's all!" she insisted. "The move, and the boys, and the living room sofa hasn't even been delivered yet, and … and I don't know what I'm going to do with the guest house!"

"That's a lot, I guess," Ryan agreed mildly. His deep brown eyes were filled with concern for his sister, and that infuriated Breanna. How was it that he could read her so well? She didn't want to be read, didn't want to be transparent. All she wanted was to get on with her life.

"Are you going to stand there, or are you going to take that inside?" she said irritably.

"Well, all right." Ryan walked past her to climb the front porch steps.

"What's gotten into you?" Liam was coming back the other way, leaving the house empty-handed to get another box from the truck. "Yelling at Ryan's like kicking a damned puppy. One of those cute little cocker spaniel ones with the ears and the big eyes."

"Don't you start," Breanna warned him.

"You break up with that Travis guy, and now you're acting like you've got sand in your underpants." Liam shook his head sadly. "If you're this miserable without the guy, there's a reason. Something to think about." He moved toward the truck before she could lay into him.

Breanna hadn't asked for relationship advice or personal counseling. All she'd asked for was some help moving boxes. What made her brothers think they had a right to butt in? What made them think this was any of their business?

Of course, if Breanna were being honest, she would have to admit that she'd offered unsolicited relationship advice to her brothers on more than one occasion. And she'd done it out of love.

Hefting a box from the back of the truck, Breanna resolved to get her mood in order. She had a beautiful new home. She had her healthy, wonderful sons. She had brothers who cared about her.

The least she could do was try to ignore the metaphorical sand in her underpants.

"Ryan?" she said the next time he passed her. "I appreciate your help with the move. Really."

He raised his eyebrows in surprise. "What else would I be doing?" he asked.

It was that simple, really. When she needed something, there was nowhere else he would even consider being than right here, helping her.

Which made it that much more puzzling that she felt so alone.

Jake filled his days with work and other things that he thought might get his mind off Breanna.

He started a new job across town, a tear-down of a nineteenth-century log cabin to make way for new construction. He walked Sam and took him to the dog park. He did handyman jobs around his own house, which had been needing a little TLC, having been neglected in favor of all the other things he had to do. He called his mom, who was still down in Los Angeles. And he hung out with Mark, who'd originally just been a guy to spend time with, but who was quickly becoming a real friend.

The two of them were jogging on the Harmony Headlands trail south of Cambria on a warm morning. Up ahead, a lizard scurried across the trail in front of them. Red-winged blackbirds perched in the trees, and nameless creatures rustled in the under-brush to the side of the path.

They'd gone a couple of miles, and they were both working hard and sweating a little, muscles warm as their shoes crunched on the dirt trail.

"I don't know, man," Jake said as they crested a low hill. "I should be over it by now."

"This is Breanna again, right?" Mark asked, reminding Jake that he might be talking about this issue a little too much.

"Breanna, yeah." As he ran, he thought about how to artic-ulate his feelings—which wasn't easy, being a guy. Growing up, he'd never learned to talk about his feelings. He'd learned to suppress them. He liked to think he'd evolved above that, though. "She's probably moved into the house by now."

"It's a great house," Mark said.

"Yeah."

"And you thought you were going to be living in it with her," Mark prompted him.

"Well …" To say that he had presumed such a thing would be going too far. But the thought had occurred to him. Of course he'd imagined that their relationship might progress, and if it did, that they might eventually live together in the house she'd chosen and that he'd revived from the dead. It had made perfect sense. There'd been a symmetry to the idea, a certain fat-ed, it-was-meant-to-be kind of quality. "Is that such a crazy idea?" he asked.

"Well, no," Mark admitted. "But it kind of only works if the woman's on board."

Jake scowled and focused on the trail, his breathing, the strain of his muscles. But Breanna kept nudging her way back into his head.

"I don't give a crap about the house," he said. "I mean, it's a great house. But it's just a house."

"It's what the house represented," Mark said, sounding a lot more enlightened than he should have, given his bear-like stature and his fashion choices—the man was wearing a SpongeBob T-shirt. "You wanted the family, the kids ... the home. The whole bit. I get it."

Somehow, being fully understood irritated Jake when it should have soothed him. "It's not like I thought it was going to happen right away," he said in his own defense. "I just thought ... eventually."

"Sure."

"It's not like I wanted to drag her back to my cave by the hair."

"You didn't exactly want to let her come to the cave under her own power, though," Mark pointed out.

At that observation, Jake stopped jogging and stood with his hands on his hips, breathing hard. "What the hell is that supposed to mean?"

Mark stopped and leaned forward to catch his breath, his hands on his knees. His face was red and sweaty. "Don't lose your shit, man. I'm just saying that you rushed her. You stand here telling me, *It's all good, there was no hurry, I thought it would happen eventually*"—he did a high-pitched imitation of Jake's voice, if Jake were a little girl—"but in reality, when it didn't happen on your timeline, you cut bait and ran." He gave Jake a pointed look, eyebrows raised and mouth pursed in righteousness, and then started to run again, leaving Jake standing there.

"That's ... I didn't cut bait!" Jake had to sprint to catch up with him. By the time he got there, he was sputtering with indignation.

"You cut bait," Mark said.

"That's bullshit. There's only so many times you can get told that she's not ready before you decide that hey, maybe she's never going to be ready. Or maybe she's ready for something, just not for you."

They followed the trail up a hill until it broke into a wide-open view of the rugged coastline.

"You dated what, a few months?" Mark pointed out.

"Yeah, but that's long enough for things to go somewhere. Not marriage, maybe—if I even want that—but somewhere. But all I ever heard was no. No taking me home to dinner with her family. No spending time with her kids as a couple. No … well … *anything*."

Mark did a little double-take as they ran. "Does that *anything* mean what I think it means?"

Jake realized that he'd given away more information than he'd intended. He waved Mark away. "Nah, that's … Shut up."

"Dude," Mark said, shaking his head sadly as he ran, "if no anything means no *anything*, then I totally get why you cut bait."

"I didn't cut bait."

"Yeah? Well, you're sure as hell not fishing."

Chapter Thirty-Three

Breanna had been in the new house for three days when she found the journal.

Things were coming together; most of the new furniture had arrived and had been placed, and she was slowly making her way through the boxes she'd brought from the ranch.

Early on a Saturday morning while the boys were still in bed, she was going through the contents of one of the boxes when she found an unfamiliar item: a book with an old, worn, leather-bound cover.

She'd never seen it before, so she opened it. She found page after page of her uncle's familiar scrawl, black ink on white paper.

It was her uncle Redmond's journal from the year he'd died.

Breanna sank down onto the cushions of her new sofa, the journal in her hand.

How had the book gotten into her box? There was no telling how these things happened. There had been so many things to deal with, so many random belongings. Breanna must have picked up the book and packed it without noticing that it wasn't hers.

She wondered for a moment about the moral and ethical implications of reading it. The book wasn't hers, and the words inside weren't meant for her. But Redmond was gone. Surely there would be no harm in it now.

Part of her said she should close the book and return it to the ranch—give it to Orin, or maybe to Redmond's son, Drew.

But she missed Redmond—had missed him so much since his passing. The allure of the book pulled at her. If she could read his words, know his thoughts, it might make her feel close to him again, just for a while.

She told herself that she would read just a page, just an entry. But one entry led to another, and before she'd consciously made a decision to do so, she was devouring page after page of the book, the unpacking forgotten.

Redmond, in life, had been stoic and reticent. He'd tended toward one- or two-word sentences: "Yep." "Nope." "I suppose." His presence every day at the ranch, and every day in Breanna's life, had been solid and comforting, but his thoughts had been his own.

At first, the journal entries mirrored that stoicism, that stolid silence.

Rain today. We need it. The herd looks good. Two calves born this morning.

It was about what Breanna had expected from Redmond: clear, fact-based observations about the workings of the ranch and the world around him.

Breakfast at the vet's hall. Pancakes and bacon. Spoke to Earl Walters about his new grandson.

Occasionally, a longer entry appeared, with Redmond's thoughts about the various members of the Delaney family. In clear, economical script, he offered his thoughts on Liam's tendency to get into bar fights; Ryan's marriage, which he considered to be a positive development; Colin's decision to live away from the rest of the family at their ranch in Montana.

There were entries about his own life and how much he regretted having decided not to pursue his true love, Drew's mother. He'd walked away from that relationship decades before because the woman was married. Mostly, he knew that had been the right thing, he wrote. But there wasn't a day when he didn't miss her, when he didn't feel the loneliness of a life in which he'd never loved again, had never found another partner.

And, of course, there were observations about Breanna. She'd known there would be. With a mix of fascination and trepidation, she tucked her legs up under her on the sofa and began to read.

Shame about Bree. Losing a husband and having to raise two boys on her own is something a woman should never have to bear. When you love somebody, you want to take away their pain, but there's nothing for it. She tries to be strong, that one. Always helping everybody else, always there when you need her. Her mother taught her that. All that work, all that helping, is supposed to cover up the fact that she's stuck in one place, stuck in grief. She can't move on. I guess I know something about that.

Was that really what Redmond had thought of her? That she kept herself occupied with busy work to hide the fact that she had never gotten past her grief? And was he right?

After Redmond's death, when the family had learned about his long-ago affair, they'd all pitied him. The way he'd been alone for thirty years pining away for the woman he'd loved had made everyone shake their heads in sadness and incomprehension.

She'd judged him right along with everyone else, hadn't she? Breanna had been right there bemoaning Redmond's insistence on remaining lonely and stagnant until the day he'd died.

Now, here in black and white, was the evidence that he'd thought the same of her. He'd considered their situations to be similar. Both of them mourning a lost love, both of them alone, both of them rooted to the ground, unable to make new lives for themselves with new loves.

He had pitied her. Did everyone?

Breanna was still reading when Lucas came downstairs, sleepy-eyed, his hair sticking up in a comical case of bedhead.

She barely noticed him until he was standing right in front of her.

"Good morning, sweetheart." She reached out and pulled him into her arms.

"Morning." He yawned.

Breanna breathed him in, his warm, early morning scent, the smell of shampoo in his hair.

"How'd you sleep?" she asked.

"Okay. Mom? Could we hang out with Jake again sometime? I guess you don't like him anymore, but maybe just me and Michael, then. Do you think we could?"

The idea that she didn't like Jake anymore—that Lucas could believe such a thing—gave her a little jolt, a slight realignment of her reality. She'd made so many people believe so many things that weren't true. That she was strong. That she was selfless. That she didn't need Jake, or anyone.

She was a fraud.

"We'll see, sweetie."

"*We'll see* usually means no," Lucas observed glumly.

"Not this time. This time it means ... we'll see."

Jake had protested Mark's line of thinking about the fishing and the bait. He'd made all of the appropriate noises about taking offense. But the truth was, he'd been thinking about it. Possibly, the guy had a point.

Jake had a suspicion that maybe he hadn't been as patient as he'd made himself out to be. Maybe he really had rushed Breanna. And maybe it had something to do with his divorce.

He'd gone into his marriage with plans. He'd planned to have a happy home, a family, kids. He'd planned to be at a certain place in his life by a certain time. When his marriage had imploded, it had blown his timeline all to hell. He'd told himself that was okay, that he would adjust. But had he adjusted? Or had he attempted to hurry Breanna along so he could get back on track toward his goals as soon as possible?

Jake thought about all of that as he drove down Highway 1 toward Cayucos, where he was scheduled to meet with a potential client. The drive wasn't long, but it gave him time to think. More time than he wanted, really.

It wasn't Breanna's fault that his life goals had been delayed, or that his ex had abandoned him, or that he felt the desperate need to redeem himself in terms of women, love, and family.

It wasn't her fault that he'd had a bad experience with a woman.

So why was he making her pay for it?

There was a certain irony to the fact that he thought he might want to spend the rest of his life with Breanna, but he wasn't willing to wait a few months—or however long it might take—for her to decide she felt the same.

Sam, sitting in the back seat of the extended cab of Jake's truck, whined at him, as though the dog had divined his friend's feelings.

"I'm being an ass, aren't I?" Jake asked the dog.

Sam let out a low, throaty sound that Jake took to be in the affirmative. Either that, or Sam was laughing at him.

He got to Cayucos and parked at the curb next to the job site. Then, before he could talk himself out of it, he dug his cell phone out of his pocket and called her.

She picked up on the second ring.

"I'd like to talk," he said without introduction. "Could I come over and pick you up for lunch later?"

Breanna told herself to say no, that her heart would be safer if she let him pass her by. But Redmond's words echoed in her mind: *She's stuck in one place, stuck in grief. She can't move on.*

So, almost against her own will, she'd found herself with a lunch date with Jake.

Her head said it didn't mean anything, that she was just trying to prove something to herself—and maybe to Redmond. But her heart knew better. Her heart ached to see his face, to hear his voice, just to be with him.

Damn it.

She was nervous as the morning wore on, but she tried not to think about it. He'd told her he would be coming up from Cayucos at about noon, and they were set to meet at Robin's on Burton Drive at twelve thirty.

Until then, there was a lot to do. Breanna was in the midst of unpacking, and the chaos of boxes, packing materials, and their various belongings littered the living room.

Sandra had bought a new set of dishes a couple of years ago—a rare indulgence for her—and she'd given Breanna the old set, which was in various stages of being unpacked and put away.

None of the windows had curtains or blinds, and that was a task she had to attend to—she needed to go to the Lowe's in Paso Robles, buy the materials, and install whichever window coverings she chose. It was a big house with a lot of windows.

For now, she would focus on the bedrooms. The rest she would get to a little at a time.

All of the work helped to distract her from the looming lunch date, the prospect of which filled her with such conflicting emotions—excitement and fear, eager anticipation and dread—that she thought she might need a decoder ring to sort it all out.

She didn't have a decoder ring, but she had the next best thing: a sister-in-law who was also a close friend.

She called Gen at the gallery, which opened at nine-thirty on Saturdays. Gen would be unlocking the place, turning on the lights, and setting out tea service and cookies for her customers right about now.

"Hey, Bree. What's up?" she said in a chirpy voice when she answered the phone.

"Oh, you know … just unpacking. The boys are upstairs getting their rooms together—or at least, they're supposed to be. Last time I checked, Michael was texting on his phone, and Lucas was reading Harry Potter. Again."

She was stalling about the real purpose of her call, and she told herself to just come out with it.

"You must be really excited about the house," Gen said. "Having a fresh new place that's all your own is so great. When Ryan and I built our house—"

"I have a date with Jake." There. It was out there.

"You … Oh. Really."

Breanna could practically hear Gen's brain changing gears.

"But it's not really a date, because he called and said he wanted to talk. That's usually bad, right? When a guy says he wants to talk? Doesn't that usually mean they want to tell you they're moving on and forgetting about you and they want closure?"

That was the *fear* and *dread* part of what was going on in Breanna's head—the idea that she might be getting her hopes up about seeing him again just so he could finalize their breakup.

"No," Gen said.

"No?"

"Men don't talk about moving on and closure. That's a girl thing. When a guy doesn't want to see you again, he just never calls."

Breanna considered that bit of wisdom. "Really? Are you sure?"

"Believe me. I had a certain amount of experience with this before I met Ryan. To men, *closure* means losing your phone number."

"Okay." Breanna took a few deep breaths to calm herself. "Okay."

"What I really want to talk about is the fact that you're worried about it," Gen said. "You want to get back together with him. When did this happen?"

"I don't know," Breanna moaned, not even bothering to deny it. Because that thought had been going through her mind endlessly since he'd called. "It's just … I miss him."

"Oh, Bree." Gen breathed out the words on a sigh, as though she were immeasurably relieved that Breanna had finally discovered a truth that everyone else had always known. "I really hope it works out. I hope you'll give him another try. He seems good for you."

"I don't know. The boys—"

"The boys like him," Gen said, interrupting her.

"I know they do. But liking him is one thing. Coping with a new man in their mother's life is something else. What if—"

"Don't get ahead of yourself," Gen said, jumping in before Breanna could let the *what ifs* run away with her. "Don't worry about what might happen if this, or if that. Just go on your date and see what happens."

"Right," Breanna said. "Okay. Right."

"And if the date goes well, you might consider … you know … sex."

"Gen!"

"I'm just saying. There's nothing like an orgasm to clarify your thinking."

Breanna, in her experience, had found exactly the opposite to be true. Still, it was something to think about.

Chapter Thirty-Four

Jake wrapped up his meeting on time, and he and Sam got into his truck to head up to Robin's at just after noon. Plenty of time to get to Cambria to meet Breanna.

He put his phone in the center console, then remembered that he'd left his clipboard with his notes on it inside the house at the job site. The impending date with Breanna was messing with his brain. It was lucky he'd gotten through the meeting at all.

"Be right back, Sam." He left the dog in the truck while he went inside to retrieve his paperwork.

When he came back to the truck, the phone was missing and the dog had a mischievous look on his hairy face.

"Okay, Sam. What did you do with my phone?"

Sam just panted softly and drooled.

"Seriously. Where is it?"

He could call the phone to make it ring—if he had a phone to call with. Which he didn't.

Jake did a quick search of the car, then considered his options. He could search more thoroughly, but then he'd likely be late for Breanna. Which really wouldn't help him in his quest to get back together with her.

The phone was in the car somewhere, obviously. He just hoped it wasn't in the dog's gastrointestinal tract.

"All right, let's just go," he said. "But I'm going to hire a trainer for you. Don't think you can just get away with this shit."

The dog thumped his tail on the car upholstery happily.

Breanna arrived at Robin's promptly at twelve thirty, and she considered whether to get a table or wait for him outside. When he wasn't there by twelve thirty-five, she decided to get the table—it would make her more comfortable while she waited.

Her nerves were making her jittery and maybe even a little sick, so she ordered a glass of wine to calm her down. Breanna wasn't a wine-at-lunch kind of person usually, but one had to make adjustments for extreme circumstances.

She was seated in an alcove in the front room of the restaurant, a cozy spot with hardwood floors and a stained glass window. The restaurant was filling up with tourists and locals drawn by the quaint atmosphere and the well-regarded menu.

She sipped her Chardonnay and rehearsed what she was going to say when Jake arrived. What if he wanted to get back together? Did she want that, too? What if he insisted on taking things further than she wanted, faster than she wanted? Was she willing to do it if it meant she'd have another chance to be with him? And what if Gen was wrong? What if he was the odd man who did talk about things like closure? What if he'd asked to meet her so he could say goodbye?

She was so wrapped up in her thoughts that she barely noticed when he was twenty minutes late, then thirty. Then she did notice, and she became alarmed. Had he changed his mind? Had he decided on the version of closure Gen said most men preferred? Was he just going to leave her here and forget they'd ever met?

Breanna pulled out her phone, contemplated calling Jake, then called Michael instead.

"How are you guys doing?" she asked.

"Fine, Mom." She could almost hear his eyes rolling.

"Did you eat lunch?"

"Yes."

"Did Lucas?"

"Yes, Mom. God. You don't have to check on us. We're not babies."

She knew that, but she couldn't explain to him that she was checking on him to avoid calling Jake.

When she'd hung up with Michael, she decided that she couldn't avoid it any longer. She dialed Jake's number and felt large butterflies hammering her gut with their wings as the phone rang and then went to voice mail.

Shit.

She'd been stood up, and he wasn't even showing the courtesy of calling to let her know. He didn't even have the good manners to take her phone call.

She paid for her wine, told the server she wouldn't be eating lunch after all, and went home to her boys.

This, right here, was a Murphy's Law–level fuckup.

Jake was late and getting later. His phone was lost somewhere in the car. Traffic on Highway 1 was at a standstill, and there was no way to get off the road to find an alternative phone so he could call Breanna.

He tried searching the car from his spot in the driver's seat, but he hadn't found the phone the first five times he'd done that, and he wasn't likely to get a better result now.

"Shit," he muttered to the dog, the car, and the greater world around him. "Shit."

He'd never stood up a woman in his life—even the ones he hadn't been all that excited about seeing. To stand up Breanna—with whom he was already on shaky ground—was both horrifying and embarrassing.

An ambulance and then, later, a police car passed him on the shoulder of the road, lights flashing. An accident, then. He took a moment to wish the best for the poor bastards involved. Whatever had happened, it had blocked the entire highway, both ways, so it must have been a hell of a wreck.

Much like his love life.

Anger and dejection turned to worry soon after Breanna got home from Robin's. She was trying not to think about Jake and about why he'd abandoned her at the restaurant. She considered doing something worthwhile—more work on the house, maybe—but she couldn't focus, so she decided to waste time on Facebook instead, a surefire way to turn off her busy brain. A quiz on what kind of cheese she was seemed preferable to worrying about why she wasn't worthy of love.

The locals of Cambria might have been geographically isolated from the rest of the world, but they were as plugged in technologically as anyone else. There was always news of local happenings on Facebook, which Breanna found to be useful. She was able to keep up with who was doing what, which local organizations were holding events, who needed volunteers for what purpose, and who felt which way about the latest increase in water rates.

Now, the locals were passing information back and forth about an accident on Highway 1 south of town.

Phrases jumped out at her as she read.

Both lanes blocked. Multiple vehicles. Serious injuries.
Oh, God.

There'd been an accident—a bad one, on the same highway Jake would have used to get here. And Jake hadn't shown up. He hadn't called, and he wasn't answering his phone.

She heard a sound—a low, wounded-animal sound—come out of her own throat.

Oh God, oh God, oh God.
Jake.

It hadn't occurred to Jake that Breanna might think he'd been hurt—or worse. It had occurred to him, however, that she might be pissed.

Here he was trying to patch things up with her, and he'd left her waiting more than an hour at a restaurant without so much as a phone call.

That is, if she was at the restaurant at all anymore. Which she probably wasn't.

When he found his damned phone, it would be too late— she likely would have blocked his number.

By the time the road was cleared enough for cars to pass through, Jake was rehearsing in his head how he might persuade Breanna that he hadn't intended to leave her sitting at Robin's nursing a glass of wine and planning his demise.

Traffic started moving slowly, and as Jake inched his truck past the accident, he could see why the blockage had been so long and so complete. A big rig lay on its side across the center median. At least three other cars had been involved—it was hard to tell which belonged to accident victims and which to good Samaritans—and the roadway was a mess of smashed vehicles, broken glass, random car parts, and emergency vehicles.

People were standing under their own power and talking to the cops—so that was good—but someone else had been loaded onto a gurney and was being put into the back of the ambulance.

Jake took a moment to reflect—there but for the grace of God—and then hauled ass toward Cambria to talk to Breanna. At least he could provide evidence of the reason for his delay, if it came to that.

He'd have taken pictures, if only he'd had his damned phone.

Chapter Thirty-Five

Breanna wanted to be at the ranch, because she needed her family. She didn't want to leave the boys alone again, so she piled them into the car and then went to the ranch, where she could fall apart amid people who loved her.

She *shouldn't* fall apart. Not yet, anyway. She didn't know that Jake had been involved in the accident. It was possible he had merely changed his mind about wanting to see her and had opted out of the lunch date.

Except that Jake wouldn't do that. He *hadn't* done that. She knew that as surely as she knew the sun would rise and fall and the cattle on the ranch would moo and graze and her own mother would cook and fuss and love everyone. She knew Jake hadn't stood her up intentionally the way she knew the most basic truths of her life: that Brian had loved her and then died, and that you never could take life for granted.

She needed her family. They would know what to do.

By the time she got to the ranch, her heart was pounding and her face was lined with stress. The boys knew something was wrong, but it was her role to protect them, not to further worry them. She brushed off their questions, much to her oldest son's irritation.

"I'm just tired from the move, that's all," she told Michael, who was sitting beside her in the passenger seat, just recently grown tall enough to sit in the front and brave the hazards of airbags. Had Jake's truck had airbags? Surely it did. Breanna's thoughts spun to wreckage, to injury, to things worse than hospitalization and surgery and pain.

"You're lying. Something happened," Michael said flatly.

Lucas, in the back seat, was absorbed by a game on his phone. She hoped he hadn't heard.

"Girl, what in the world?" Sandra asked when she saw Breanna. Immediately, the older woman's face registered alarm.

"Boys, go on upstairs," Breanna told them.

"I'm not a child," Michael said.

It was true, he wasn't. It was time she stopped treating him like he was.

"You're right," she said. She whispered to him, "Could you maybe take Lucas upstairs and get him settled in watching TV or something? Then come down, and we all can talk."

He nodded somberly, then said, "Come on, Luke. Let's see if Uncle Liam's here."

A few minutes later, he was back. Lucas had found Liam, and the two of them had gone to the stables to visit the horses. Michael waited silently, looking with concern at his mother.

"It's Jake," Breanna told him and Sandra when Lucas was safely gone. "He was supposed to meet me for lunch at twelve thirty. He never came. He didn't call, and he's not answering his phone."

"Well, I'm sure there's a good reason," Sandra said. "The man wouldn't just—"

"There was an accident on the highway north of Cayucos. A big one. Jake was coming from Cayucos."

Sandra's face registered several things—alarm and concern among them—before settling back into her usual stoic expression. "You sit on down and we'll talk about what to do," she said.

Once he was past the accident, Jake pulled over to the side of the road and searched for the phone. He found it wedged under the back seat, tooth marks in the case, the screen cracked. He pushed the button in an attempt to bring it to life, but the thing was dead.

He muttered a few choice curses to the dog, repeated his threat to get a trainer, and then drove to Robin's.

Of course, as he'd predicted, Breanna was no longer there. The hostess said she'd waited more than a half hour and then had left, looking pissed-off and sad. The hostess was judging him, clearly, but he didn't have time to deal with that. He thanked her and left.

Next, he drove to the house on Moonstone Beach. He knocked on the front door, but no one came. He even tried the guesthouse, but no luck. The place had the feel of being empty.

After that, he weighed his options. Knowing Breanna, she was probably at the ranch if she wasn't at her own house. He could drive straight there, or he could find another phone and call her.

He judged that showing up in person would increase his chances with her, but on the other hand, what if she'd gone somewhere else? If he showed up at the ranch and she wasn't there, it would only delay him being able to explain what had happened.

Jake made a quick stop at home and locked Sam inside the house. He took a moment to berate himself for not getting a landline. But nobody had landlines anymore, did they?

He got into his truck, planning to head toward the ranch.

Breanna's thoughts were too scattered for her to be able to form a coherent plan. That was one of the reasons she'd needed to be here with Sandra. The Delaney matriarch was nothing if not cool under pressure.

Sandra knew a lot of people on the Central Coast, having spent decades attending community events, potlucks, fundraisers, parades, and various other get-togethers that attracted people from all walks of life.

She couldn't think of anyone she might know in the emergency rooms of either of the local hospitals, which were not very local, actually—each of them was around thirty miles away.

She did know one of the 911 dispatchers for the sheriff's department in San Luis Obispo. Sort of. She knew the woman's aunt Shirley, and that was enough.

Sandra called Shirley, who called her niece, who wasn't working that day but who knew the man who was. He couldn't come to the phone for obvious reasons, but through a phone relay that involved several people, Sandra eventually ended up talking to a guy who was working the reception desk at the sheriff's office and who agreed to poke around and find out what was going on.

Sandra was able to glean various pieces of useful information, none of which included names, but some of which included the makes and models of the vehicles involved in the crash.

When Sandra told Breanna that a black Toyota Tundra had been demolished and that its driver had been extracted with the Jaws of Life, Breanna paled and sank into one of the kitchen chairs.

Jake drove a black Toyota Tundra.

"Oh, God. I have to get to the hospital. I have to—"

"We don't even know which one they took him to. We don't even know—"

"Well, *find out!*" Breanna never yelled at her mother. But she was yelling now.

"We don't know if it's him, Mom," Michael said softly, his hand on Breanna's shoulder.

But Breanna knew. In her heart, she knew. You always thought tragedy wouldn't affect you, that it would pass you by and leave you unscathed in favor of other, less fortunate people. But then you got the knock on the door and you realized you were that less fortunate person.

Tragedy didn't spare anyone, and Breanna had no reason to believe that fate would be kind to her now, when it had never shown kindness or mercy before.

"It's him," she said. "It's him. I know it's him."

"I'll call the hospitals," said Sandra, who shared her daughter's pragmatic outlook on life and all of the things it might bring. "We'll find out where they took him."

Sandra seemed to agree with Breanna that, yes, Jake was likely the person whose body had been mangled in the crash, and that made Breanna lose whatever composure she'd had. A sob rose from deep inside her and tore loose. She realized that Michael was beside her, holding her. She clung to him.

A few minutes later, Sandra returned from the kitchen, where she'd gone to make her phone calls without the distraction of Breanna's emotional breakdown.

"They took the Tundra driver down to San Luis Obispo," she said grimly. "Don't know the name. They wouldn't say. Gave me some crap about confidentiality."

"All right." Breanna took a deep, shuddering breath and wiped her eyes. "Let's go. Lucas can stay here with Liam. Michael, you should, too."

"No. I want to come."

She looked into her son's eyes and saw something mature, something adult, looking back at her. She nodded. "All right."

"We'll take my car," Sandra said. "I don't want you driving like this. We'd better hurry."

Sandra didn't have to say what Breanna was thinking: They had to hurry because if they didn't, they might be too late.

If Jake had fully understood Breanna, he would have rushed directly to the ranch. But he didn't—not yet—so he wasted precious time stopping to buy her a bouquet of flowers. In his experience, women expected flowers when you'd done something to make them mad.

By the time he got on the road to the ranch, he was feeling pretty good about his chances. He was sure Breanna would be angry when he saw her, but no matter how pissed she might be, he knew he had a rock-solid explanation for everything.

She had to forgive him, because none of it had been his fault.

He was standing on pretty solid ground, he figured. All he had to do was show up and make his case.

As he drove, he mentally rehearsed what he would say. *I'm so sorry.* He would have to lead with that, even though he hadn't been to blame. It was never wrong to apologize to a pissed-off woman. Phrases like *beyond my control* and *never happen again* seemed like they might be useful.

But the problem wasn't just that he hadn't shown up today. She hadn't wanted him even before this. He would overcome that, too. He would reassure her that he wasn't going to rush

her. No more ultimatums. No more insisting that things progress on his terms instead of hers.

He had to make her give him another chance. He had to.

He pulled up to the main house at the ranch, gathered up
the flowers and his courage, and got out of the truck. He walked
up the front porch steps, raised his hand to knock on the door—
and was surprised when the door flew open before he even
made contact.

Breanna, Sandra, and Michael were in the doorway, apparently on their way out. All of them had looked tense and upset when the door opened, and all of them had identical stunned
looks on their faces when they saw him standing there.

Breanna burst into tears, then threw herself forward and
into his arms, crushing the bouquet of roses he'd brought.

He didn't know what was going on, but whatever it was, it
looked like Breanna wasn't mad anymore. So, that had to be a
point in his favor.

Chapter Thirty-Six

There was more hugging, and some crying, and not just from Breanna. As soon as Breanna let go of him, Sandra grabbed Jake in a hug so fierce he thought she might crack a rib. Michael's eyes were red, but he wasn't quite on hugging level with Jake yet, so he gave him a manly clap on the back and turned away.

Everybody was talking at once, but eventually everything came out: the way Jake had been stuck behind a complete traffic blockage with a broken phone, and the way the Delaneys had been certain that he was either dead or grievously injured.

That was when Jake began, for the first time, to truly understand Breanna. After what she'd been through with her husband, she didn't worry about potential tragedy in the vague way that other people did. She waited for it, certain that it would come. She didn't just know intellectually that bad things happened, that lives changed or ended in an instant. She lived it in her core.

Jake had never lost a close loved one, so death was an abstract concept to him. But it wasn't that way for Breanna. For her, death was real and certain. It was a constant companion that shadowed everything she did and everything she might do. It haunted all of her attempts to love and be loved.

All this time he'd thought that Brian was the other man standing between them. But he'd been wrong. The other man was Death.

After a little while, Sandra hustled Michael out of the room so Jake and Breanna could be alone. He told her everything he'd wanted to say: how he'd been wrong to rush her and that he wanted to be with her, no matter what. If she needed to wait before they took their relationship to the next level, then he would wait. He would wait for sex, he would wait for commitment, he would wait for her to let him into her kids' lives.

However long it took, he would wait.

"You're worth it, even if I have to wait forever," he told her. "I can't imagine why I ever thought you weren't. I'm an idiot, basically. I don't want anyone else, and if I'm still waiting when we're old and eating early bird specials and riding in those mobility scooters, then I'll just wait."

"No," she said.

He raised his eyebrows in alarm. "No?"

"No. I don't want to wait until we're old and using mobility scooters."

"You don't?"

"No." She took his face in her hands and kissed him deeply. Then she pulled back and smiled at him just a little, her eyes still red. "Take me to the house on Moonstone Beach, Jake. Right now. Take me home."

It wasn't until she was convinced that Jake was hurt or dead that Breanna realized how stupid she'd been. She'd told herself she was keeping her distance from him to protect her children from the upheaval of a new man in their lives. She'd told herself she was being smart. She'd told herself it was about mature behavior and responsible parenting.

She'd told herself so many lies.

The biggest lie of all was that if she could keep him at arm's length, then she could protect herself from complete devastation if she should lose him.

She'd thought she could keep herself from loving him so much that those feelings might break her.

When she'd thought he was in the accident, she'd known she was too late. She already loved him that much. She already was that vulnerable. She already ran the risk of the same kind of pain she'd endured with Brian.

Now, she had two choices: risk losing him to some nameless tragedy, or lose him for certain by forcing him away.

Only one of those options offered her any hope for happiness.

She couldn't stop herself from loving Jake any more than she could stop herself from loving her boys. Any more than she could have stopped herself from loving Brian. If pain one day came, then she would endure the pain.

She had no choice.

She would tell him all of this later. There would be time to talk, time to sort it all out and tell him everything he needed to know about her. Today, she would show him what he needed to know.

Breanna had asked Sandra to keep the boys for a while so she could work things out with Jake. Sandra had turned Breanna toward the front door and had given her shoulders a push.

"You go on, now," she said, her voice gruff. "Don't you worry about those boys. They're with family. You take care of things with that man of yours."

Breanna hadn't even objected to the phrase *that man of yours*. It was simply the truth.

Now, Jake and Breanna arrived at the house on Moonstone Beach and she led him inside, with the sound of the surf humming and pounding behind them. He'd barely closed the door when she turned and stepped into his arms.

"Are you sure you want this?" he said. She was so close to him that she could feel the vibration of his words through the hard wall of his chest.

"I'm sure."

"Because I shouldn't have rushed you before. If you're not ready …"

"Jake. I'm ready."

And she was. The thought that she might have lost him had made it clear to her, finally, that being with him was worth any potential pain, any risk. She wanted to be close to him, and she didn't want to be afraid any longer.

"Come upstairs," she said.

She led him up by the hand, and as she did, it seemed to her that this was right in so many ways. Him being here, in this house he'd helped to create, felt like it was meant to be.

In her room, her sunny, fresh room that he'd revived for her out of hard work and pure will, she turned to him and pulled his shirt off over his head. He tangled his hands in her hair and brought his mouth to hers, devouring her with his kiss.

After that, she stopped thinking about love and risk and potential reward. She stopped thinking entirely. Instead, she simply felt. Felt the warmth of his skin, the feel of his hands undressing her and then gliding across her body, the sensation of being exactly where she was meant to be, with exactly the person she was meant to be there with.

She unbuttoned his jeans and slid them down over his hips, and then took him in her hand. His eyes closed and his lips parted, and he moaned the sound of her name.

Making love with Jake this time was different than before. Then, she'd been with him despite the nagging voice in her head that said he meant danger. Her body had reveled in the sensations, but her mind had been issuing urgent warnings. Now, all of her was eager, all of her was ready. She couldn't wait to be wrapped around him and to have the delicious feeling of him inside her.

When they were both fully undressed, she took his hand and drew him to the bed. They fell back on it, and his weight on top of her made her feel safe and loved and protected.

She wanted him to hurry; wanted him now. But Jake had been waiting for this, and he seemed determined to take his time. He touched and kissed her face, then moved down her body, to her throat, over her breasts, down to her belly and beyond, to the part of her that was becoming the center of her existence.

He explored her with his tongue and she squirmed on the bed, bringing her body ever closer to him, to his mouth.

Breanna was older than Kye Ferris. She was a mother. Her body bore the signs of childbirth and of the slow but inexorable decline that had begun when she'd hit her thirties. But he made her feel beautiful. He made her feel perfect. His attention to her, his fascination with her, his total absorption in learning the curves and planes of her made her believe there was nowhere he would rather be, and no one he would rather be with.

She wanted him inside her, but this had been so impulsive that she hadn't planned for it.

"Jake," she said.

"*Mmm.*"

"I didn't know this was going to happen. I don't have anything."

He rose up to look at her, and comprehension dawned. He got up, found his jeans, fished around in the pocket, and brought out a square foil packet.

"I was going to try to get back together with you today, and a man can always hope," he said.

She sat up and smiled. "Optimism can pay off sometimes. Here, give me that." She reached for the condom, and when he gave it to her, she helped him put it on. He groaned as she rolled it onto him. He trembled with need.

Breanna pushed Jake down onto his back and straddled him. She eased him into her, loving the sensation of his body merging with hers.

She moved on top of him, taking the lead, and that felt right, too. It was right that after all this time, after all of this waiting, she should help herself to this moment, to this man. That she should relish every moment and every sensation.

Because she was no longer afraid, she told him the truth.

"I love you," she said, her mouth inches from his.

He gathered her to him, kissed her with a raw, ferocious need, and then rolled her onto her back, their bodies still joined.

There were no more words, no more thoughts. Just the glory of their bodies moving together and Breanna rising, rising, and then crashing on wave after wave of pleasure.

He followed her down into the abyss, into that place from which neither of them would ever want to return.

Afterward, when she was lying in his arms and they were warm and sated, he answered her.

"I love you, too."

"You don't have to say that just because I did," she said.

"I have to say it because it's true."

And she knew it was. She knew.

Chapter Thirty-Seven

The next step, after that, was the thing he'd wanted in the first place. They got cleaned up, went back to the ranch, and then went out for pizza with the boys.

At the kids' request, they drove down to Morro Bay to a place that had arcade games and big-screen TVs blaring whatever sports events happened to be available.

Jake figured that, under the circumstances, his job was to spoil the crap out of the kids, plying them with quarters for the games and then coming through with ice cream later on.

He expected some resistance from Breanna on the spoiling, but he didn't get any. Instead, she looked relaxed and happy, laughing at Lucas's jokes and holding Jake's hand under the table.

"I didn't think it would go like this," Jake said when the boys were busy in the game room exclaiming over someone's score.

"Like what?"

"When I realized what was going on—what you thought had happened to me—I thought you'd be too scared to give me another chance."

"This is better," she said, and kissed him.

After the pizza and the ice cream, they went to the movie theater down the street to watch the latest Star Wars movie. Breanna wasn't particularly into Star Wars, but Jake and the kids exchanged opinions and commentary on the best and worst movies of the series, the relative purity of the early movies, and the affront that was Jar Jar Binks.

Afterward, they went back to Breanna's house and Jake hung around while she sent the boys up to bed.

"You can stay," she told him, running a hand up his arm.

It was tempting, but he had to play this right.

"I'd better not," he said. "I don't want to push it with the boys. Plus, I have to walk Sam."

"All right."

They kissed for a long time before he headed out the door, whistling a happy tune, certain that he would be back tomorrow, and the next day, and the day after that.

The morning after pizza night, Michael came to Breanna while she was in the kitchen making waffles.

"Is Jake going to move in?" he asked.

Michael tended to be blunt by nature, but even so, Breanna was surprised by the directness of the question.

"Why would you ask that?" It was, of course, not an answer.

"I just want to know."

"Well ... no. Not yet. But he might, someday." She was nervous, waiting for his answer.

Michael nodded somberly. "That would be okay."

Breanna blinked. "It would?"

"Yeah. I like him. And you seem really happy since we found out he wasn't in the accident. Like, really happy. I like it

when you're happy." He shrugged and studiously avoided looking at her.

Breanna pulled him into a hug. "I like it when I'm happy,
too."

Lucas came downstairs rubbing his eyes, still groggy from
sleep. "Are you making waffles?"

"Yes. Do you want some?"

"Yeah." He sat at the table, still looking unfocused.

She put a fresh, hot waffle in front of him.

"If Jake moves in here, can Sam sleep in my room?" Lucas
wanted to know.

Clearly the boys had been talking about the possibility between themselves. Breanna felt a little bit ganged-up on, but she
didn't really mind.

"We'll have to see what Sam wants," she said.

Privately, she thought he would probably like it just fine.

The subject came up again a couple of weeks later, after
dinner at the ranch. Jake and Breanna had been visiting the
ranch a lot lately, having dinner around the big kitchen table with
the boys, Sandra and Orin, Ryan and Gen, and Liam and Aria.
Delaney dinners were big, messy affairs, with noise and chaos
and a seemingly endless supply of food emerging from Sandra's
stove and oven.

Jake had been blending in with the family seamlessly, trad-
ing good-natured gibes with Ryan and Liam, teasing the boys
about this or that, and bonding with Sandra in a way that was
common for people who were good at judging character.

After dinner, Jake jumped in to help Sandra and Breanna
with the cleanup, which prompted Liam to ask him if he wanted
a ruffled apron that said KISS THE COOK. Jake suggested that

Liam bite him, and with the male bonding properly attended to, they all settled into their roles, comfortable with the world.

"So, when are you moving in with my daughter and my grandsons?" Sandra asked, handing Jake a wet dish to dry.

"Mom," Breanna began.

"Now, don't *mom* me. I've got eyes, haven't I? I guess I can see where things are going without a damned road map."

Breanna didn't deny that things were, in fact, going in exactly the direction Sandra thought they were.

"Breanna hasn't asked me yet," Jake said. "And that's fine. I can wait. I'm a patient man. At least, I've learned to be."

"The boys say it's all right with them," Breanna said. "Just FYI."

"They do?"

"They do," she said.

"*Hmph,*" Sandra said with satisfaction.

Jake carefully dried the dish in his hand and then placed it in the cupboard. "Only one other party we need to check with," he said.

"Who might that be?" Sandra wanted to know. "You got another live-in family member I don't know about?"

"Oh, you've met him," Jake said.

Sandra let out a cackling laugh, understanding. "Those boys have always wanted a dog of their own. Though I think that one of yours is more dog than they can handle."

"They're ranch kids," Breanna protested. "There's no such thing as more dog than they can handle."

Breanna began to doubt the wisdom of her words the next day, when Jake brought Sam to Breanna's place for a test run.

"We've got a new dog bed, his favorite food, some treats, and a couple of new bowls with his name on them," Breanna said.

"That's a pretty sweet welcome," Jake said. "I hope he appreciates it."

Jake brought Sam in the front door, let him off the leash, and watched as he bounded into the arms of the boys, who were waiting with tummy rubs and Milk-Bones.

"Come on, Sam. Come see the upstairs," Lucas said. He ran up with the dog hurrying after him.

Seconds after the dog vanished from view, they heard a large crash from upstairs, followed by Lucas yelling, "No, Sam!"

"Did I mention he needs some training?" Jake asked Breanna.

"I kind of gathered that when he knocked me flat on my back the day we met."

"Well ... what he lacks in self-control, he makes up for in enthusiasm," Jake said.

There would be a mess upstairs, one of many to come. But messes could be cleaned up. Having control and avoiding crises was overrated.

Breanna was going to take it all as it came: the mess, the chaos, the risk.

And the love.

Made in the USA
San Bernardino, CA
18 September 2018